FORBIDDEN *Heat*

FORBIDDEN BOOK TWO

R.L. KENDERSON

ALSO BY R.L. KENDERSON

NOVELS IN THE FORBIDDEN SERIES
Paranormal Romance

Forbidden Blood

Forbidden Heat

Forbidden Temptation

Forbidden Addiction

Forbidden Claim

Forbidden Seduction

Forbidden Mate

BOOKS IN THE DIRTY LOVE SERIES
Contemporary Romance

Rumor Has It

Friends with Benefits

One-Night Stand

Meant to Be

It's Complicated

BOOKS IN THE TAKE ME SERIES
Contemporary Erotic Romance

Take Me in the Night

Take Me in the Dark

STANDALONE NOVELS
Contemporary Romance

Wicked Chemistry

Object of My Desire

Five Dates Only

Wrong number

STANDALONE NOVELLETES & SHORT STORIES

Summer Heat

The Hottest Player

French Kiss

Moon Craving

FORBIDDEN

Heat

Forbidden Heat
A Forbidden Series Novel
by
R.L. Kenderson

PUBLISHED BY:
R.L. Kenderson
(Renae Anderson Au & Lara Kennedy)

ISBN-13 978-0-9904144-5-2

Editor: Jovana Shirley, Unforeseen Editing, www.unforeseenediting.com
Cover Designer: EmCat Desings, www.facebook.com/EmCatDesigns

DEDICATION

For our moms.
Thank you both for being so supportive and for telling everyone you
know that we wrote a book even though a part of you both might be
horrified by the "love scenes" your daughters wrote.
I love you, Mom!

Chapter One

*T*his was it. She was about to lose the fight to stay conscious.

Payton Llewelyn knew she was wounded. Her hip burned, her head throbbed, her ears rang, and all she wanted to do was sleep for the next five days.

What happened?

Even thinking hurt.

The last thing she remembered was leaving the restaurant after having dinner and drinks with friends. Concentrating hard, she willed her brain to recall what had followed. She'd been on the phone as she walked to her car when—

Shit.

Out of nowhere, three human men had emerged from the darkness and tried to grab her. Just behind them, a fourth man had appeared, but he'd left her in a state of shock and confusion. She'd been stunned because rather than going after her, he had attacked the first three men. Confusion had set in because her nose told her he wasn't of the Homo sapiens variety.

She'd fought the man who'd grabbed her while her rescuer wrestled the other two. Her bulky winter coat had hindered her movements, but she'd still thought she might win the struggle with her captor until she heard a loud noise and then felt a sudden piercing sting in her side. She had been unprepared for the sharp pain, and it had knocked her off balance, causing her to crack her skull on the pavement. That was why she had lost consciousness in the middle of the parking lot.

So, now, she lay motionless, using all her strength to will her eyes open and her body to move. Fainting again wasn't an option. She needed to get out of there and find help. She didn't know what had happened to the humans, and she knew the fourth man was a shifter, but he hadn't smelled like—

Before she could finish her thought and attempt to force herself up, someone lifted her from the ground and carried her. It was the shifter.

Have I been saved? Or am I in more danger?

She tried to get a better read on who held her, but she was in a fireman's hold, moving fast. All the bouncing made the pain in her side and head sharper, and she had to concentrate on not passing out.

They stopped, and she heard a vehicle door open, stuff being moved around, and then something hit the ground. She was laid down on the seat. The upholstery carried the aroma of the male shifter, and her alertness increased. At that moment, she knew why his scent was off.

He wasn't a cat-shifter like her.

He was a wolf-shifter.

Cat-shifters and wolf-shifters weren't friends—not in Minnesota, not anymore. The Minnesota Pride hadn't been on good terms with the Minnesota Pack for almost ten years.

Shit.

She should really try to leave. If only she wasn't hurt and so damn tired…

She heard one door close before the opposite side opened, and then she was pulled until her head was placed in the wolf-shifter's lap. Her left hip ached, and she rolled over to ease some of the pain, curling into the stranger.

He gently stroked his hand over her hair, moving it out of her face as he spoke, but the buzzing in her ears prevented her from making out the words.

Is he my rescuer or my captor?

Despite the unknown situation, his actions soothed her. Her adrenaline crashed, and as her fatigue settled over her like a heavy blanket, she wasn't sure if she even cared anymore.

She should have been wary, but she was so tired. Instead, she felt surprisingly safe and protected, not afraid at all. Maybe tomorrow she'd feel differently, but she could worry about that tomorrow.

She buried her nose in his waist—breathing in the scent of wolf, rich cedar, and pure male—before she relaxed and let the blackness consume her.

Fuck. Fuck. Fuck.

Damien Lowell slammed his fist against the steering wheel. What the hell had he been thinking? He was either a dumbass or crazy—or a crazy dumbass. He looked down at his lap. Only a fool would take an injured she-cat to his property, his wolf-shifter property. Oh, and he couldn't forget, she needed medical attention.

But what else could he have done? He'd needed to get her out of there, and he didn't know how to contact her family. Maybe that was just an excuse. He had people he could call to figure out how to get a hold of her parents.

No.

He didn't want anybody else taking care of her, nor would he trust anyone else to keep her safe until he found her family. The smart thing was protect her himself. He snorted. If he thought that was the only reason, he was fooling himself. Thankfully, he had bigger problems than his need to have her close to him.

Damien glanced down again. Payton was passed out with her face buried in his crotch. His only intent had been to cushion her injured head. He hadn't realized she would burrow herself in his lap. Now, he had to tell his dick that this was not the time or the place to make itself noticed. She'd been shot, for Christ's sake, her lavender scent almost completely covered by the smell of blood. Not to mention, he should be worrying about his own injuries—after he took care of Payton.

He blindly reached behind the truck's seat, searching for the extra clothes he kept back there, to find something to press against her wound. Something brushed against his fingertips, but he couldn't quite reach it, so he carefully raised himself to grab it. Just as he snagged the sweatshirt, he felt Payton's fingernails dig into his back, causing him to drop it as he swerved into the lane next to him. He quickly straightened the truck because the last thing they needed was to be picked up by the cops.

This time, prepared for her reaction and expecting the pain from her nails, he snagged the garment and lowered them both back onto the seat. Payton immediately relaxed her hold on him, and he pressed the cloth over her hip to help stop the bleeding. Putting pressure on her wound brought awareness of his own. His shoulder ached from the gunshot wound as he used his muscles to stanch her blood flow. The movement also pulled on his back muscles where one of Payton's potential kidnappers had cut him from neck to waist. He was better off than her but not by much.

Instead of focusing on his injuries, he told himself to be grateful he'd been at the restaurant to save her. They both might be wounded, but she was safe, and he'd get her patched up soon. Then, he'd move on to his next problem. What was he going to do with her after she was stable?

He'd been born and raised in Minneapolis—until about ten years ago. Before then, the shifters—both wolf and cat—had lived in harmony on the Minneapolis side of the Twin Cities area. The two subspecies of shifters had always gotten along. They'd each had their identifiable parts of the cities they called their own, respecting each other's territories yet often commingling.

Before Damien was even born, his grand-pap and Payton's grandfather had started a business together—L & L Construction. Things had gone well for years until his paternal grandfather passed away and his father, Dwyer, inherited the role of alpha and half the construction business. His father, until recently, had had good intentions, but he was somewhat of a screw-up, and everyone knew what the road to hell was paved with.

Ten years ago, when Damien was twenty, the Minnesota Pride had kicked the Minnesota Pack out of the Twin Cities, forcing them to scatter around the rest of the state. Damien had been working on his college degree at the time, and he hadn't noticed what his father was doing to the pack and L & L Construction, not that he could have done anything to stop his father. He was the second son, and no one had wanted his opinion, but he could have tried.

The biggest blow had been losing their half of the business and a major source of income. They had survived, and life had been acceptable for the last ten years until about twenty months ago when Damien's older brother, Donovan, died. Dwyer had blamed Vance Llewelyn, Payton's father, for everything.

Things had gotten worse since then, and now, Dwyer wanted revenge. His father had discovered a secret ally—a mysterious cat-shifter who had contacted his father, asking for help. In exchange for Dwyer's and the pack's help, the cat-shifter had promised his father that he could reclaim his half of the business, and they could come back to the area. Of course, his father had jumped at the chance, but Damien thought it was too good to be true.

His father hadn't listened when Damien confronted him, and with the cat-shifter's identity a secret, he hadn't had many options. He was lucky his father had even told him of the plan to get rid of the Llewelyns, which included kidnapping Vance's children.

Vaughn, two years older than Damien, was one of Vance sentinels, ensuring Vaughn could take care of himself. Plus, his new mate was a vampire with her own exceptional strength. But Payton was small, alone, and without a mate to help protect her. Damien had known he had to do everything he could to prevent her from being kidnapped.

Damien understood what drove his father. Damien wanted, more than anything, to return home, to his place of birth, to the place he grew up. But he also knew this was not the way.

He vowed to himself they would return someday when he was an alpha—and he would be alpha. His father and he both knew that Damien was stronger and smarter. Damien knew his father's plans would only end in failure even if his father was too blind to see it.

Until then, he planned to do everything he could, in an honest and trustworthy way, to salvage what was left of the pack's chances to make their way back to the place where they belonged.

He looked at his lap and sighed. He only hoped he was doing the right thing.

The cat-shifter sat back in his favorite chair, put his feet up, and sipped his drink.

Tonight was the night, the night his whole life was about to change.

The famous proclamation, *The King is dead! Long live the King!,* rang through his head

Technically, his king was an alpha, but that was just semantics. And he wasn't exactly dead yet, but he would be soon.

The cat-shifter glanced at his watch. By now, the first step in his plan—getting rid of the alpha's children—was already taking place. He laughed out loud to the empty room. He had manipulated that stupid Dwyer Lowell into helping him. When he'd found out that Dwyer's oldest son and successor had died, he'd known Dwyer would be vulnerable, and he was right.

He'd told Dwyer if he helped execute the Minnesota Pride's alpha and helped him replace Vance, he would let Dwyer and the Minnesota Pack come back to Minneapolis. *Stupid wolf.* He had Dwyer right where he wanted him.

He'd paid Dwyer to kidnap and kill Vance's son, Vaughn, his new daughter-in-law, and his daughter, Payton. Vance's heirs had to be out of the way before he stood any chance of becoming the next alpha of the cat-shifters. He was smart, and he'd made sure the money trail led straight to Dwyer. The wolf wouldn't know what had hit him.

He'd handled Dwyer pretty easily, and the only part they'd argued on was killing Vance. They both wanted the privilege. Dwyer held a strong grudge because of his pack's exile, but the cat-shifter held a stronger grudge. His went way back before any feuding between the Pride and the Pack, and the right to take out Vance belonged to him. Dwyer could go fuck himself.

He took a sip of his drink and smiled. Once Vance found out about his children, the alpha would be vulnerable. That was when he would strike. Not only would he be rid of Vance, but Vance's mate, Lilith, would also be his—as she should have been from the beginning. It was just another reason for him to send Vance to hell.

The cat-shifter went over all the steps in his head. After Vance was gone, his sentinels would have to go, too. They were too loyal to Vance. Yes, there would be a lot of changes in the Pride before long. Soon, he would be alpha with Lilith at his side, and her belly would be full with his child. No one would dare question his authority.

The cat-shifter finished his drink with a gulp, glanced one last time at his phone, and relaxed. *Yes, life is going to be good.*

Chapter Two

"An attempt has been made to kidnap my son and daughter-in-law, and my daughter is missing."

When alpha of the Minnesota Pride, Vance Llewelyn, called the emergency meeting at ten o'clock at night, Saxon Einar never thought it would concern something so serious.

"Also, we are one sentinel down because whoever is behind these attacks mistook Sawyer for Vaughn."

Vance explained how someone had broken into Vaughn and Naya's new home while they were gone, but Sawyer, one of his fellow sentinels, and Naya's friend Kenzie had been getting it ready for the new couple to move in. The intruders had mistaken Sawyer and Kenzie for Vaughn and Naya.

Also, Payton had been on the phone with her mother when she was taken. Their distraught alphena had heard her daughter's abduction through the phone.

The news was sudden and shocking. They had lived in relative peace for many years, and the last thing Saxon had expected was to hear of attempts on the lives of the alpha's family.

"Correction," Vance continued, his blue eyes filled with many emotions, "we are down two. Until we know what is going on, Vaughn has taken Naya to stay with the Guardians, and she refuses to stay there without him." Vance looked at his mate. "Honestly, it is probably for the best," he said to Lilith more than anyone else.

He turned back to the group. "Because someone has decided to come after my family, we will go to an undisclosed location. We can't be sure that Lilith and I won't be next. However, I am still your alpha, and I am still in charge. Just because you can't see me doesn't me I'm not running the show.

"Right now, we know that Sawyer and Kenzie were kidnapped by humans. Before the line went dead, Sawyer managed to tell me he detected a faint trace of wolf odor on them. It's not much, but it's a start, and we will get to the bottom of this.

"Tegan, Camden, Reid, and Saxon will be coming with me, and they will be the only ones to know where we are going. First, Saxon and Tegan, check out the scene at the restaurant where Payton had dinner and see if you can find anything. Zane, you will stay here and monitor the bunkhouse, looking for anything unusual. Make sure you have your cell on you at all times. Phoenix, you will join Vaughn."

There was a distinct huff in the crowd.

"Boss, are you sure that's necessary?" Phoenix asked.

Zane chuckled.

She was really asking why she had to go babysit. Everyone knew Phoenix liked being close to the action. She punched Zane in the shoulder while her emerald green eyes shot fire. It only made him laugh harder, and Saxon shook his head at the sentinels' insensitivity to the situation. Phoenix was pretty easy to piss off, and sometimes, it could be fun to rile her up, but this was not the time to joke around. When Vance gave Zane a look, he wiped the smile off his face.

Their alpha turned his attention to Phoenix. "Yes, I'm sure. While I'm certain the Guardians will do an excellent job at protecting Naya, she is carrying my future grandchildren. I want a sentinel there who is not her mate. Understood?" His tone was firm and told Phoenix there should be no further questions on the matter.

Phoenix swallowed. "Yes, sir."

"Good. Vaughn will call you in half an hour with directions." He addressed the whole group again, "Also, we will not tell anyone that Sawyer and Kenzie have been abducted in Vaughn and Naya's place. This is another reason we are sending them to the Guardians. I know Sawyer smelled wolves, but my gut tells me someone closer is behind this. The kidnappers had too much information. Not many knew Vaughn was moving, much less where. So, if anyone asks, say Sawyer is out questioning others. There is a chance the kidnappers will dispose of Sawyer and Kenzie if their real identities are discovered." Vance glanced around the room. "Any questions?"

A round of, "No, sir," echoed throughout the room.

"Everyone, go pack. We'll meet back here in twenty."

Everybody hurried to the bunkhouse. There were eight sentinels, and now that Vaughn had moved, seven lived in the bunkhouse to be close to the alpha and his family.

Saxon walked into the room he shared with Reid and began packing. Always prepared for anything, Saxon already had a bag ready to go, so he was finished in no time.

Next, he headed to Zane and Camden's room. Camden was still new, and Saxon wanted to make sure he didn't need help. When he entered, Zane was leaning back with his elbows on his bed while Camden grabbed a bag from the closet.

Saxon parked next to Zane and watched Camden scrub his hands through his blond hair. His lean build was filled with tension as he stuffed supplies into his bag.

"Can you believe this? Who would hurt Payton? Or Vaughn and Naya?" Because Camden wasn't from the Minneapolis-St. Paul area, he hadn't grown up with their history.

"Well, it's been ten years, but the only one I can think of is Dwyer Lowell," Saxon said.

"It's possible. But why would he wait all this time?" Zane asked.

"Do you think he's the one behind this?" Camden asked.

Zane sat up. "I don't know, but I know the boss isn't going to give up until he finds out. I'm sure you guys will track him down by the end of the week." He hit Saxon on the arm. "Right?"

"Without a doubt," Saxon said. Whoever was behind this was going to regret crossing them.

"Fuck," Zane said under his breath.

They both knew someone had to stay behind to watch the property, but it didn't mean Zane was happy about it.

Camden finished and swung his bag over his shoulder. "Who knows? Maybe they'll show up here, and you can take them out, Zane."

As Saxon stood, Zane grunted and replied, "Maybe," but they all knew he didn't mean it.

Whoever was behind this had to know their alpha was smart enough to go to a secondary location, considering everything that had happened.

"Sorry," Camden said with sincerity before he left the room.

Zane shot him the finger behind his back. He hated being pitied.

Saxon followed but paused in the doorway. "You never know. Maybe you'll get lucky, and something exciting will happen," he offered Zane.

He snorted in response and flopped back on the bed. "Yeah, right, and maybe an angel will fall from heaven and screw my brains out."

Dante Leonidas looked around at each of the Guardians—the protectors of the Vampire species—from his position in front of his desk. The nine of them—himself, Ram, Hunter, Tempest, Declan, Sterling, Morgan, and the siblings, Lennox and Lexine—sat in his office at the manor where they lived and worked. With a group their size and news this big, a lot of strong feelings were in the room.

"To reiterate, Princess Anaya will arrive here soon with her shifter mate along with one of his sentinels."

Dante had called the meeting right after he'd gotten the phone call, and they had spent the last ten minutes discussing the princess and how they would help.

"We will accommodate them and do whatever we can to assist them." Dante pointed around the room. "And everyone will keep their opinions to themselves." He dropped his hand and asked, "Does anyone have any questions?"

"So, we're allies with them now?" Lexine asked.

Her twin brother, Lennox, snorted. Even though they were fraternal twins, they both had the same blond hair and green eyes. They were an uncommon sight as one didn't see twins often among vampires.

"Yes," Dante answered. "They have threatened the princess's life and her future offspring. If they need our help at taking down whoever is behind this, we are going to help them."

There were murmurs all around.

Dante held up his hands, and everyone quieted. "Have any of you personally had problems with the shifters?"

Ram scoffed. "They seem to have more problems among themselves."

"They *are* half animal," Tempest said with a raised brow.

Dante slammed his palm on the desk. "This is going to stop." His patience was wearing thin as these weren't the first comments made toward the shifters. "Even the king and queen are trying to get along with them. Most of what you believe is what your parents told you. Now, I'll ask again, have any of you personally had a problem with a shifter?" Dante didn't wait for their answers because he already knew what they would say. "No. You are judging them on biased information and stereotypes."

He paused and took a calming breath. "Look. We are going to work together whether you want it to happen or not. Princess Anaya is mated to a shifter. She is having his children. An alliance is inevitable, and you're all going to have to accept it—the sooner, the better."

Grumbles sounded throughout the room.

Dante grunted. "I thought we were more cultured than this." He ran his hand down his face. "I'm older than every one of you. I should be the most unwilling to change."

Morgan spoke up, "You're right. If the princess can mate with a shifter, we should try to get along with them, especially if the king and queen are trying."

Everyone knew they were the most prejudiced vampires.

Dante breathed a sigh of relief but didn't let it show. He was truly trying to keep an open mind, but centuries of prejudice didn't disappear in a week. He had plenty to work on with himself. He didn't need to babysit eight others. "Thank you."

The first thing Sawyer Lennar noticed upon waking was the movement underneath him. Next were the pungent odors of oil and grease saturating the area, followed by the pounding in his head. The last and most alarming thing was that he was tied up and gagged.

He struggled to orient himself, and steadily, bits and pieces of what had happened came to him. He had been upstairs at Vaughn and Naya's house, helping to get the place ready for them to move in. Kenzie, Naya's best friend, had been downstairs, painting the bathroom, when he heard her scream. He'd run to help, but two humans had met him.

His last memories before now were the smell of wolf-shifters, a loud bang, and a pain in his chest.

Have I been shot?

He concentrated on his upper body, and nothing more than a small ache remained. Also, the clothes against his skin were dry, which meant he'd been shot with a dart, not a bullet. It was no wonder that he was still groggy.

He peeked under his eyelids, not wanting to alert anyone that he was awake in case he was being watched. He assessed his surroundings. He was in a van, empty of any backseats, with an unconscious Kenzie lying across from him, but no one else was in the rear. He slowly turned his head toward the front and saw two men.

Sawyer tuned in to their conversation. After a few seconds, he realized they were talking about Kenzie and him.

Correction—they were talking about Vaughn and Naya.

He closed his eyes. *Shit.*

They thought they had kidnapped Vaughn and Naya. They didn't know they had snatched the wrong people.

Sawyer needed to get Kenzie's attention and somehow let her know they had to pretend to be people they weren't. He also needed to get rid of whatever drug they had put in his system. Until the effects wore off, he would only have the strength and reflexes of a human, probably less. Their captors had known what they were doing, and they had come prepared.

"Kenzie," he said. At least, that was what he'd tried to say anyway. With the gag in his mouth, it'd come out as a muffled groan.

He grunted, and the sound of the engine drowned most of it out, but she gradually started to come around. When he was sure she was conscious, he grunted once more. Her lids shot up, and her brown eyes filled with fear.

She looked toward the front of the van. Her eyes went wide when she heard the two men mention Naya and Vaughn as the intended victims.

When she looked back at him, Sawyer tried to show her with his eyes that he was going to get them out of this mess and that everything would be okay. Most importantly, he wanted her to know that he'd die before he let anyone hurt her—ever.

Chapter Three

$\mathcal{D}$amien pulled up to his cabin. He was relieved that they'd made it—until he looked down at the injured she-cat. He had a lot of work left to do. He opened the truck door, and a blast of cold winter blew in, so he quickly moved Payton from his lap with only a whimper from her and got out of the truck. Leaving the engine running so that she would be warm until he was ready to bring her in, he hustled to the door, skipped up the only two steps, and landed on the porch in his rush.

Inside, the first thing he did was swiftly get the wood stove running to heat the cabin before heading through the single bedroom to start a bath in the bathroom. Next, he changed the sheets on the queen-sized bed, and he got the first-aid kit out while the tub filled. After he made sure everything was ready, he headed for his truck to fetch Payton.

He carried her into the bathroom and lowered her to the floor. Her usual golden skin tone was pale from shock and blood loss, and he knew he had to take care of her wounds ASAP.

Taking note of her injuries, he had trouble determining the severity of the damage to the back of her head with her dark hair covering it. She probably wouldn't be happy with his solution, but her well-being came first.

He moved on to her clothes. He removed her shoes and big winter coat first, and then with scissors from the first-aid kit, he cut off her shirt and bra. They were soaked with blood, so there was no chance of saving them anyway.

He paused before he tackled her jeans and underwear. She didn't appear to be bleeding from the gunshot wound on her hip—or at least, bleeding as much as earlier—and he didn't want to reopen the wound when he removed them. He unsnapped her jeans, and he slowly pulled down the uninjured side and then gradually lowered the other side until her jeans were completely off. They were also soaked with blood, so he threw them on top of her shirt in the corner to dispose of later.

He moved back to pull off her socks, and he was momentarily paralyzed. The view in front of him made it difficult to remain impassive. She was stunning. She was about five inches under his six-two, and she was perfectly shaped. She was slender but still had some curves. Her breasts were a little more than a handful—not too big, not too small—and topped with dusky red nipples, which stood out against the pallor of her skin. The hardest part was ignoring the dark curls at the top of her legs.

He closed his eyes, took a deep breath, and told himself to stop being a pussy. So, she was naked and fucking gorgeous. She was also hurt and unconscious, and his job was to clean and dress her wounds, not think about having sex with her. Now, he only needed to communicate that to his dick. He felt like a goddamn perv.

He took another big breath, opened his eyes, picked her up, and set her in the water. It soon ran red with the blood from Payton's wounds, helping him focus on the matter at hand and not on the erection in his pants, which had luckily slowly subsided.

With the matted blood gone from her hair, he inspected her head. Like he'd thought, the only way to get a good look would be to shave some of her thick, long hair. He sighed. He wasn't a master at women, but he knew she'd probably be pissed. Oh well, it couldn't be helped.

He shaved the smallest possible area and threw the long hairs in the garbage next to the sink. The patch was about an inch wide and two inches long, and her hair would cover it, but he still cringed. When the small area was clear, he could see the wound was relatively small and superficial. Thankfully, it wouldn't require any stitches, but the surrounding large bruise was going to hurt like hell when she woke up.

After he did all he could for her head, he moved down to her hip. He flinched when he saw it without the blood covering it. The bullet had more than grazed her skin, but it wasn't a through-and-through gunshot wound at least. It was still going to be incredibly painful, and it would leave a scar after it healed.

The lump in his throat made it difficult to swallow. This was partly his fault. If he had tried to do something sooner or paid more attention, he might have stopped this, and she might not be lying in a bath full of her own blood.

Now was not the time to wallow in guilt. He couldn't change the past, and all he could do was take care of her.

He drained the bathtub to get rid of the bloody water while he washed and conditioned her hair. He filled the bathtub back up and washed the rest of her body. Once cleaned, he let the water out again and wrapped her in a towel.

He stood to carry her to the bed and noticed her hair dripping everywhere. Grabbing another towel for her hair, he moved her onto the bed in his room. He dried her body the best he could without lingering before covering her with one of his flannel shirts from the closet, buttoning it to the top. Lastly, he quickly bandaged her hip while trying his best to keep her covered, and then he tucked the covers around her.

He stood and removed the towel from her hair with a grunt. It was a tangled mess, but he wasn't about to do anything with it and risk accidentally hitting her head wound. He grabbed a comb for when she woke up, and he set it on the nightstand. Then, he observed her for a moment to make sure she was okay. Although she hadn't regained consciousness yet, she had moaned and flinched during the undressing and cleaning process. He decided it was a good sign that she was at least reacting to external stimuli.

Breathing a sigh of relief that she had been cared for, he looked down at himself and saw he was a mess. He had her blood and water from her bath on his clothes. He needed to shower to clean his own wounds.

He grabbed the wet towels off the bed and strode to the bathroom. As he hung up the towels, he heard Payton whimper, causing him to rush to the bed. Worried, he checked her injuries, but they weren't bleeding, and she seemed to be resting comfortably. He paused for a moment, and when she didn't make any more sounds, he shrugged and headed into the bathroom.

She whimpered again.

He went back to the bedroom, and she stopped.

He left, and she whimpered.

When he entered, all was quiet.

He did this a few more times. Every time he was in the room, she would be silent, but when he left, she'd cry.

He shook his head, baffled. She seemed to be okay though, so he headed to the bathroom, knowing it was going be the fastest shower he'd ever taken. He was still worried about her being alone.

Damien ripped off his shirt, and his body screamed with pain. "*Fuck.*"

He had temporarily blocked out the cut across his back, but the dried blood had made his shirt stick to the wound. Damn, it burned. He used the bathroom mirror to inspect it, and he saw the wound ran diagonal from his shoulder to his waist. Swollen and bright red, most of the bleeding had stopped, but removing his shirt had opened up a few spots. From what he could see, it didn't look too deep. Hopefully, it would heal in a few days. It definitely paid to be a shifter.

He finished undressing, entered the shower, and cleaned himself as fast as he could, only spending time on his back. With only a towel around his waist, he headed to the bedroom to grab something to wear. Payton was still out but crying again. He had hoped she would stop while he was in the shower, but at least her cries eased once he was in the room. He began to wonder if it was his proximity that soothed her.

He grabbed a pair of workout shorts and slipped them on. He contemplated putting on a T-shirt, but he didn't want it to stick to his wound again. Plus, now the cabin was quite warm, and Payton was still unconscious. He doubted she would wake up anytime soon to be offended by his bare chest.

After he hung up his towel and returned to the bedroom, he watched Payton for a minute as she lay there. He knew her family had to be worrying about her, and the guilt returned. He had to find a way to let them know that she was okay. Unfortunately, he couldn't trust his packmates to help him.

But there was one person he could trust.

He grabbed his burner phone out of his jeans. The battery light blinked, indicating it was low, and his charger was in the truck. Charging it would have to be taken care of later.

Damien pulled up his phone number list, found the party he wanted, hit Send, and waited for it to ring. When the other line picked up, he explained his situation and what he needed. His contact wasn't exactly willing, and it took some coaxing, but in the end, his friend agreed to do as he'd asked. They promised to be in touch soon, and Damien hung up the phone.

He felt better, knowing that he was doing something to help her family feel at ease, and he hoped he would be able to lie down and get some rest. Sleeping would help his body heal faster, and since he wasn't going anywhere until Payton was better, he knew he should get as much shut-eye as possible.

Payton had slept through his phone call, so figuring it was safe, he headed to the living room to lie on the couch. But, once again, Payton started whimpering when he'd left the room. He returned, and of course, she stopped.

"Shit." What was he supposed to do now?

There was no right answer to this particular problem. Would it be inappropriate to lie next to her while she was in this condition if his presence put her at ease? Or should he go into the other room and hope she eventually stopped?

He concluded the polite thing to do would be to leave her alone, so he went to lie down on the couch, and he covered up with a blanket. He was exhausted after the major adrenaline spike, and he figured he would fall asleep right away.

He was wrong.

After listening to Payton moan for half an hour, he said screw being a gentleman and got up to lie next to her. She stopped whimpering and let out a huge sigh as soon as he entered the room. Then, to his surprise, once he was under the covers, she began to purr. Could she really be affected by his presence? He knew he was by hers.

Her lavender scent invaded his nose, and he wanted to bury his face in her hair, but he made sure to keep some distance between them. Since he felt an obvious attraction, it felt a little wrong to be lying in bed next to her while she was unconscious, but it must not have bothered him too much because that thought was the last thing Damien remembered before he fell into a deep sleep.

Chapter Four

As she slammed her SUV door shut, Isabelle Rand cursed the day she'd met Damien Lowell. She didn't care if the Lowell Pack ever gained permission to return to the Minneapolis area. She didn't like being dragged into the pack's mess. She was perfectly happy with her life, so the last place she should be was on the Llewelyn Pride land without approval.

But since Damien was one of her closest friends, she knew she should do this for him. The fact that he'd called her after midnight last night meant it was important. He wasn't someone to abuse friendships.

Isabelle didn't remember a whole lot about the Llewelyns. She was seventeen when the pack had been kicked out. She had been angrier about the fact that she would have to finish her senior year of high school in a new town than with the pack being exiled. But other than banishing the pack, she remembered the Llewelyns as being nice. She could only hope they wouldn't attack her on sight rather than give her a chance to explain. She preferred to come out of this alive.

As she slowly walked up to the main house, the only sound was the snow crunching under her booted feet. It was around four in the afternoon, and the winter sun was already starting its descent. The curtains were closed in the house, and the faint smell of cat-shifters and the stillness in the air told her they hadn't been here for a while.

When Damien had explained what happened to the Llewelyns' only daughter and her unconscious state, Isabelle understood why he'd wanted someone to talk to them in person, but it seemed her trip might have been a waste. She couldn't help feeling relieved. She felt bad for Damien because he would need to figure something else out, but it looked like she was receiving a reprieve from this possible suicide mission.

Before leaving, she'd walk around the property and make sure she hadn't missed anything. Then, if she didn't find anyone, she would leave a note on the door in hopes that someone would come back and read it.

First, she knocked on the door and rang the doorbell even though she knew there'd be no answer. Isabelle left the front porch, stomping her feet and rubbing her hands for warmth. The temperature was dropping along with the sun, and she was getting cold. She made her way toward the back of the house, noting the lone vehicle parked outside the four-stall garage. The place had definitely been abandoned. Across from the garage was a bunkhouse that she'd glimpsed from the front of the property, and she made her way toward it. This would be her last stop before freedom.

Crossing her fingers just in case fate decided to be cruel, she peeked inside. Unlike the main house where the shades were closed, the bunkhouse's curtains were open but it was dark inside. She approached the front door and knocked, and then she put her freezing hands in her pockets.

She waited for about a minute, and after no answer, she did a silent victory dance in her head. Feeling like a horrible friend for being of no help to Damien while also feeling slightly happy about it, she was just about to turn around and leave when she was slammed into the front door.

"*Ah!*" she yelped with shock and a little pain.

Going by scent, it was a male cat-shifter, and she cursed herself for not noticing him sooner. He was large, towering over her five-six height, and one of his hands was wrapped around the front of her neck while both of hers were trapped in her coat pockets. His grip didn't hurt. It was just a subtle threat to let her know who was in charge. His other hand tilted her head to the side, exposing the rest of her neck to him. The vulnerable position heightened her unease. This was a kill spot for shifters, easily cutting off the air supply, and they wouldn't bare their necks to another unless trust was between them.

She didn't know this cat-shifter, and she certainly didn't trust him. She struggled to get her hands loose, but his big body blocked any attempt she made to free herself.

She didn't know what upset her more—the fact that he'd gotten the jump on her, the fact that she was trapped, or the fact that his rich sandalwood scent had invaded her nose and she wasn't even remotely revolted by it.

"What the hell is a wolf doing on Llewelyn property?" he rumbled the words next to her ear.

His breath, hot on her exposed neck, made her shiver.

"I need to speak with your alpha." Her voice came out sounding breathless, and she was embarrassed.

He pulled her neck a little more to the side. "About what?"

"That's between him and me."

He snickered. "That's what you think."

He leaned down and rubbed his nose and lips from her chin to her winter coat, inhaling her as he went. She was immediately aroused.

Liar, her brain mocked. She had already been halfway there.

It had simply been too long since she lay with a male, and she mentally shook off his laughter toward her. He was a jerk.

He backed away from her and spun her around, keeping his hand around her neck. Of course, he was good-looking with dark blond hair and sea-green eyes. She looked down and swallowed. He was also naked. He must have been in his cat form before he'd found her. It explained why he had been able to sneak up on her, but she was still annoyed with herself for letting her guard down and assuming everyone was gone.

Despite the fact that he had the advantage, she made sure to look him in the eyes. It took all her courage to not look away. Even though he was a cat and she was a wolf, he was still a dominant while she was a submissive, and she had to fight to keep her gaze on his.

His brow raised, and she took the opportunity to slowly remove her hands from her pockets. She moved to grab his shoulders, so she could pull him down and jam her knee into his crotch, but he was quick. He let go of her neck and grabbed both arms before hauling them behind her back. He used one hand to hold her arms and moved the other back to her neck, trapping her again.

"Damn it," she said under her breath.

"I take it, you aren't a sentinel," he said, mocking her.

"Shut up."

He laughed again. "I think I'll be the one giving orders."

Jerk.

He lost his smile and pulled her closer. She gasped when their lower bodies met. He was hard.

"Ignore him. It's nothing personal. He's not picky." She curled her lip at his dig toward her looks, but he continued, "Now, I'm going to ask you again, what is a wolf doing here?"

She was stuck, and deductive reasoning said he was a sentinel and therefore willing to die for his alpha. With a reluctant surrender and a strong hope that he would listen to what she had to tell him, she huffed out a breath. "Fine. Damien Lowell sent me. I'm supposed to let you know that he intercepted Payton's kidnapping, and he has her somewhere safe. She was injured, but he's taking care of her, and she will recover."

The cat-shifter's hand tightened.

"He also wants you to know that he had nothing to do with what happened," she said in a rush.

The cat-shifter released her so fast that she almost fell on him. He reached around her and opened the door. It had been unlocked the whole time, and she gave herself a mental kick for not trying to open it to get away from him when her hands had been freed.

He stepped around her and went inside, but he grabbed her hand and pulled her behind him. They entered the main living area—a large open space that included the kitchen, dining room, and living room—where he pushed her down into a recliner.

"Sit," he commanded.

He turned away, and she gave him the finger as he walked into the kitchen and grabbed his phone off the counter. He hit a few buttons as he walked back toward her. Since he was bare, his erection—*still?*—stood directly in her line of sight. It was difficult to ignore, and she wished he'd put on some pants. Her eyes wandered up to his muscular chest.

Clothes, she amended. She wished he'd put on some clothes.

The cat-shifter turned and pointed a finger at her. "Sit still, and stop fidgeting."

Man, he sure is bossy.

And she wasn't fidgeting.

Isabelle heard someone on the other line say, "Hello?"

The cat-shifter turned his attention to the voice on the phone. "Boss, it's Zane."

Zane—so he has a name. She was beginning to think it was Jerk.

"I have some news. I have a she-wolf here, named…" He looked at her.

"Isabelle Rand," she supplied reluctantly.

"Isabelle. Apparently, Damien Lowell sent her. He has Payton somewhere safe, but he claims he had nothing to do with her being taken. Isabelle says he rescued Payton from her kidnappers." The skepticism was apparent in his voice.

"I'm telling you the truth. Why else would I be here? I certainly wouldn't risk my life if Damien meant to do her harm," she pointed out.

Perhaps *jerk* wasn't a strong enough word for him. Maybe she should upgrade him to *asshole* because she wasn't lying, and neither was Damien.

"She has a point," Zane said into the mouthpiece. He lowered the phone from his mouth to speak to her. "Where is Damien holding her?"

She shrugged. "He didn't tell me that."

Zane narrowed his eyes.

She narrowed hers back. "I swear. The only thing he said was that they were somewhere safe. He didn't want to tell me where because his cell wasn't secure. He said, as soon as she was able to travel with her injuries, he would bring her home."

"Did you get that, Boss?" He nodded a couple of times even though his alpha couldn't see him, and then he moved closer to her. "She smells like she's telling the truth."

"Does she know the extent of Payton's injuries?" his alpha said through the phone.

Isabelle didn't wait for Zane to repeat the question. "No. I just know that they were serious, but she should recover."

Zane stepped away from her, so she wasn't able to hear his alpha's response. The whole time he was on the phone, he stared at her while she tried not to stare at him. She snorted—more like his junk, not *him*.

She really needed to find a male when she returned home. Shifters were pack animals and needed to be close to one another. Part of being close was being intimate with others. If they abstained long enough, they would grow miserable. Besides being aroused, they would be easily agitated, have trouble concentrating, and would be just downright unbearable to be around. They needed to feel the touch of others. It was ingrained in their DNA.

Up until now, she hadn't thought that she was *that* bad. As a shifter, she was used to being naked and having others naked around her, but the fact that she couldn't stop looking at this naked cat-shifter or ignore his scent told her that she was worse off than she'd originally believed.

She supposed it was just the icing on the cake. Damien so owed her.

Lost in thought and her vision unfocused, she didn't notice when Zane had hung up the phone and walked toward her until he was leaning down and directly in her face.

"I'm done. You can stop staring at my dick now."

She wanted to smack the smug look right off his face. *Asshole.* He was definitely an asshole.

She looked straight into his eyes. "Well, it's not my fault you're walking around naked. Plus, I was just thinking about how sorry I felt for you. Must be tough to walk around with something so unimpressive."

She was such a liar. It was very impressive.

Zane stood up and laughed like she'd told him a hilarious joke. He shook his finger at her. "You're funny."

She growled at him. She hadn't meant to be funny. She'd wanted to be insulting. He laughed harder, grabbed her hand, and pulled her behind him as he strode down the hall.

"Where are we going?"

"I'm going to put some clothes on before you eat me up with your eyes."

This time, she held in her growl. She didn't want him to know he was affecting her. Instead, she asked, "Why am I going with you?"

"Because you're not leaving here until Payton comes home or calls us herself."

"*What?*" She tried to yank her hand out of his.

His grip tightened. "Right now, you're our only contact with Payton. If Damien calls you again, we want you here with us. You can either think of yourself as our ally or our hostage, but either way, you're our guarantee that she's coming home."

She'd been wrong before. *This* was the icing on the cake.

She hoped Payton would wake up soon to call her family and confirm her well-being. Isabelle really wanted to get out of this safely.

They reached the doorway of what had to be his bedroom. It had two big beds, each at least queen-sized, sitting against opposite walls yet leaving a fair amount of standing room.

Zane tugged her inside until they were face-to-face, and he wrapped an arm around her. With a smirk, he said, "Looks like we're stuck together, Izzy," before he slapped her butt and released her.

She didn't like her name being shortened. Her parents had named her Isabelle for a reason, and only certain special people called her by a nickname. She certainly didn't like the cat calling her by one. It spoke to an intimacy she didn't share with him.

"My name is *Isabelle*," she said through clenched teeth.

He waved his hand, completely dismissing her request. "Ah, tomato, *tomahto.*"

She wanted to pull out her hair. He was so incredibly frustrating.

It was then she changed her mind about getting out of there unharmed. She wished she had been executed on sight. Hopefully, the cats would kill her soon because she'd rather be dead than stuck with this infuriating cat-shifter.

Yep, Damien sure owed her—if she didn't strangle him first.

Chapter Five

*D*aylight was streaming through the bedroom window when Damien opened his eyes. He woke up, lying on his side and facing Payton, who was still asleep beside him. They were so close that they were practically touching, a lot closer than when he'd gone to sleep. One more inch, and they'd be snuggling. He peeked around her and saw almost half the bed was empty, which meant she'd moved closer to him.

Interesting.

Giving himself a minute before he had to get out of bed, he breathed in Payton's scent, relieved there was no hint of infection. It was still early, so she wasn't in the clear, but it was a good sign that she'd heal well. She looked so peaceful while lying there that he wanted to reach out and touch her. Thankfully, the growling in his stomach and the urge to piss were enough of a distraction.

He glanced at his watch. It was a quarter after one in the afternoon. He was shocked to see he'd slept for about twelve hours. He hadn't expected to be out for that long. As a shifter, he didn't need much sleep, and he usually survived on less than five hours a night. His injury must have been worse than he'd originally assumed.

He gradually rolled onto his back. *Ouch.* His wound still hurt, which wasn't good. After half a day of sleeping, he should be nearly healed by now. It hadn't looked that bad or deep last night in the mirror. He hoped there—

Payton moaned. Startled, he moved to inspect her. He drew the covers down and pulled the bandage away, examining her hip. He was relieved to see it looked good. At least sleep had been good for Payton's body. Just to make sure, he leaned over to inspect her head. He gently lifted her by the back of her neck and moved her hair out of the way to inspect the wound. It also seemed to be better. The swelling had gone down, but it would probably still hurt for a while.

Now that he knew she was okay, it was as if her lavender scent had doubled. He laid her head back on the pillow, still cradling her, not ready to let go yet. He moved her long black hair out of the way. She was incredibly beautiful, and her smell was intoxicating. He wanted to rub his nose along the curve of her neck and shoulder.

He closed his eyes, reprimanding himself for being a dog, only to have them fly open because she ended up doing it to him.

She mumbled in her sleep as she brushed her lips and nose along *his* neck and down to his bare chest. He was instantly hard. Her actions were so completely unexpected that he yanked his hand out from under her head and shot to his feet.

"Shit." He checked to make sure she was okay, but then he spun in the opposite direction and locked himself in the bathroom.

Her head is on the pillow. She's fine.

He, however, was not. His cock throbbed in his shorts, and he rubbed his hand down the length of it to relieve the ache.

It didn't work.

What is wrong with me? He was beginning to feel like a dirty old man.

He took a deep breath and counted to a hundred. He could do this. He could be around her without getting aroused. He just needed to concentrate on her healing.

Right.

He needed to get some nutrients into her and also possibly some medicine. She might wake up soon, and she shouldn't be in pain.

Armed with a mission, he did his morning business, washed his hands, and left the bathroom. Avoiding the bed and blocking out any noise Payton made, he practically sprinted to the kitchen.

My wolf is gone. Gone. Why did he leave me? Come back, wolf. Come back. Come back. Come back...

Payton shook off her dream as she sluggishly came to with that disconnected feeling one gets after a deep sleep. It was the kind where you didn't know where you were, what time it was, what day it was, or hell, even what year. She must have slept really hard.

She rubbed her face and tried to get her bearings. What woke her? Where was she? It was almost like she was missing something, but the feeling was residual, and she couldn't figure out what that something was.

She tried to open her eyes, but she had a headache, and the daylight hurt her pupils. Then, there were the smells. She wasn't at home or any other place that was familiar, and the scent of wolf-shifter was strong.

Wolf-shifter. Payton sat up in bed, jarring her side and sending shooting pains through her head.

"*Oh*," she moaned as the previous night came back to her.

She'd left the restaurant after dinner with friends. Three humans had come out of nowhere and attacked. She had been injured, and then surprisingly, a wolf-shifter had saved her. It was all very strange.

There shouldn't have been any wolf-shifters in the Twin Cities, but she supposed a few would slip past their radar every once in a while. Since this one had rescued her, she was shockingly unconcerned. So, that was not what bothered her the most.

Actually, it was the humans. Something about them and that whole situation disturbed her. She'd been in the lit parking lot of a busy restaurant in a good neighborhood. Why had they picked her to rob? Why there? Unfortunately, thinking only made her head hurt worse. She'd worry about it later. She should be more concerned about the present anyway.

She looked around the room, finally noticing her surroundings. Hardwood floors and walls all around showed that it was a cabin of some sort. From her spot on the bed, she looked through the window and could see the cloudy winter sky and an endless sight of bare trees with a small amount of snow coating the branches.

The scent of cedar was strong, but it wasn't the wood cabin. It was her wolf.

My wolf?

She mentally shook her head. She'd meant, her wolf rescuer. It was obviously his place. She looked at the empty spot next to her with the rumpled sheets and the dent on the pillow. This was obviously his room. Had he slept next to her?

A cupboard slammed in the other room. Sticking her nose in the air, she caught a whiff of food cooking, and her stomach rumbled.

She searched the room for a clock with no luck, and she assumed it was late morning or early afternoon. It was light outside, and days were short in November, so midday was a good guess.

Throwing back the covers, Payton attempted to swing her legs over the side of the bed.

Bad idea.

Pain radiated everywhere. She would need to do this a little slower.

Carefully, she put her right leg on the floor first. She noticed her right leg was bare. She looked down at herself. She could feel she was sans underwear. A man's flannel shirt was the only thing she wore. She grabbed the collar and brought it to her nose. Although the smell was faint, it was the wolf's shirt. It had been washed after he'd last worn it, and now, her scent covered it, too.

She pulled up the shirt to look at her throbbing hip. The wound was bandaged and clean from what she could see. Next, she picked up a chunk of her hair, seeing it had also been washed.

He had bathed her, and she wasn't sure how she felt about that. She appreciated his care, but she knew he'd seen her naked—as if things weren't already awkward.

She lowered her shirt and moved to place her other foot on the floor. She was working up her motivation to stand when the wolf came to the door, carrying a tray of food.

They both froze.

"Payton?"

Wow. Now, this was a man.

It wasn't that she'd expected some hideous creature, but she hadn't expected to feel the pull of attraction either.

He had a strong masculine jaw, showing his virility, which was decorated with day-old scruff, and striking high cheekbones that made him all the more appealing. His hair was dark gray, almost black, with a hint of white at the temples, indicating he was a gray-and-white wolf.

He was older than her, but he couldn't be more than in his early thirties. His hair gave him an almost distinguished look, except he was more chest-thumping masculine than a suit-and-tie sort of guy. But his best feature was his eyes. They were a beautiful clear blue. Cat-shifters and humans didn't have eyes like that, not often anyway. They were pure wolf.

He wore only shorts, giving her an excellent view of his broad shoulders and muscular chest sprinkled with dark hair to match his head. He had a tattoo of a wolf on his pectoral muscle. He was tall and would tower over her if they stood next to each other. He looked vaguely familiar, but she could only picture him younger for some reason.

Not knowing what to say, even after all he'd done, she came up with a weak, "Hi."

"You're awake." He stood still in the doorway, motionless.

"Yeah, I needed to…" She moved to stand, but the pain stopped her. "*Ah.*"

In a flash, he set the tray down on the dresser and squatted at her feet. "What can I do to help?"

He looked so worried that she had to smile, and she almost reached out to touch his face.

"How about you start by telling me your name?"

He cleared his throat and backed up half a foot, still sitting on his haunches. "Damien Lowell." He smiled softly. "You probably don't remember me, but—"

That's why he looks familiar. "Yes, I do," she said.

His smile grew wide.

He was twenty when the pack had left. She remembered he had been good-looking then, too, even though he was thin and gangly. Shifters wouldn't reach full puberty until around their twenty-first birthday. Damien had probably started to fill out right after the pack was exiled.

"Our dads ran L & L Construction together until…"

He lost his smile and stood, putting his hands out. "Yeah. I want you to know that I'm not going to hurt you."

"I know."

"I'm not my father, nor do I—wait." He tilted his head to the side. "You know?"

"Yes. One, if you wanted to hurt me, you would have already. Two, I just"—she shrugged—"know."

And she did. Her instincts told her she didn't have to fear this wolf-shifter despite their parents being enemies. She knew deep down that she was safe with him. She wasn't sure how she knew, but her intuition had yet to fail her.

He ran his hand through his hair. "Huh. That was easier than I'd thought it would be."

She smiled at him.

He smiled, too, until he looked past her to the bed. "I ended up sleeping next to you. You were crying and wouldn't stop unless I was in the room."

She held up a hand. "It's okay."

"You sure?"

"You didn't try anything while I was unconscious, did you?"

"*No.*"

"I didn't think so. Now, stop apologizing." She was more worried about the bathing than the sleeping, but she wasn't going to bring that up.

He smiled again. "Okay." He pointed to the dresser. "I brought you food. Are you hungry?"

"Starving. But first, can you help me get up, so I can use the bathroom?"

He was back at her side again. "Of course."

She put her hands on his shoulders while his fingers circled her abdomen. His skin was smooth underneath her palms, and his hands were a brand around her waist. She felt a current travel through her whole body. Even injured, she felt the electricity between the two of them.

This is going to be interesting.

Once she stood, he helped her walk to the bathroom. When they reached the door, she turned to face him.

"Thank you for rescuing me."

He looked down at his feet.

Was he embarrassed? Shy? It seemed odd that an alpha male, next in line to run his pack, would be shy, but maybe he was modest.

"Hey," she said to get his attention.

He looked at her.

"I mean it. You don't have to be humble. Thank you."

She pulled his head down toward her and kissed his cheek. The corner of her mouth hit the corner of his, and there were sparks.

Wow. Yep, there was definitely an attraction.

By the wide-eyed look on his face, he felt it, too.

She exhaled a deep breath. "Well…I'd better get in there before it's too late."

"Okay. I won't go in with you, but please leave the door unlocked in case you fall or something."

"Okay."

She closed the door behind her and did her bathroom business first. With her injuries, it seemed to take an hour, but she managed on her own. After she washed her hands, she slowly lifted the flannel shirt to remove the bandage. She needed to know the extent of her injuries, but she was scared to look in the mirror. She pulled away the dressing and winced. It wasn't pretty, but it was healing. It would definitely leave a scar, but she was grateful she'd escaped with her life.

She re-covered the wound and really looked at herself in the mirror. *Yikes.* With her hair going everywhere, she looked like Medusa. Damien had obviously washed her hair and hadn't bothered to comb it. She wasn't vain, and she was injured, but she still didn't want to look bad in front of him. That told her more than anything how she felt toward him.

She looked around for a brush or comb, but she came up empty, so she used her hands. She started in the front, and when she got to the back, her fingers brushed against her other injury. Something was off. She slowly lifted her hair to feel around the wound, and she screamed. She couldn't believe it.

Damien burst through the door. "What is it? What's wrong?"

"*You shaved my head.*"

He barely had the decency to look sheepish.

Chapter Six

Sawyer came to with a pounding headache. The assholes had drugged him again.

He opened his eyes to a dirty ceiling that was probably white at one time. The room was dimly lit from a small patch of sunlight coming through a tiny window that was too small to escape out of. The strong odor of a damp basement lingered in the air.

There were two doors in the room. One was made of metal, locking them in the room. The other door was open to what he guessed was a bathroom.

He looked around to see he was on a bed with Kenzie beside him. He'd known she was close because her lemon scent had invaded his senses before he even opened his eyes. But there was more than that.

She still smelled of his scent after a month and a half.

Sawyer tried to forget the way her pores had opened up and absorbed his scent the night he hauled her into the restroom at the nightclub and brought her to orgasm. Just like he tried to forget the way she had opened up and let him touch her. He repeatedly reminded himself that she was human, and he needed to stay away, but his body didn't seem to care.

The next time he had seen her, when he'd broken into her apartment, he'd still been able to smell himself on her from the doorway of her bedroom. He'd been grateful she slept because he needed to compose himself before he woke her to ask about Vaughn and Naya. He'd felt proud of how he could distance himself from her and pretend like nothing had ever happened between the two of them—that was, until he'd caught her watching him like she wanted his cock inside her. His dick had sprung to attention, and he'd had to hide behind her kitchen island. When he'd smelled her lust mixed with his scent, his arousal had gotten so hard that it throbbed in his pants. When she had moved out in the open and he could see her tiny underwear along with her nipples poking out of her tank top, he had thought his head would explode.

Thankfully, it had been dark, and she hadn't found out he was a shifter yet, so she hadn't realized he could see her better than the average human she thought he was. She had dismissed his actions, and he had been able to pull himself together. He had known he had to get out of there before he did something he would regret, like giving away his shifter status, but then he'd almost blown it when she opened her apartment door. The bright light from the hallway had illuminated the tiny outfit she called pajamas, which had made him territorial and jealous. That had only pissed him off.

After that incident, he had vowed to stay away from her because nothing good would come of it. But then, a few weeks later, when Vaughn's bratty cousin had humiliated Kenzie and called her a piece of ass, Sawyer had found himself defending her. The next thing he knew, he'd bitten her again, marking her, right in front of the brat just so the little shit would know he meant what he'd said about her being under his protection. Once again, her skin had opened up and absorbed him. As soon as he had let up, he'd walked away, acting like nothing significant had happened, and he had felt her eyes boring a hole into the back of his head. But he had known he couldn't be near her for another second. He had known she wanted him, and he only had so much willpower.

Thankfully, they had avoided each other since that night—except, here they were now, kidnapped and trapped together. Fate was certainly laughing at him. Kenzie was a temptation he didn't want or need.

Sawyer snorted. He needed to focus because he had bigger things to worry about than being stuck with Kenzie.

Her back was to him, so he leaned over to see if she was awake.

She must have felt the bed move because she rolled onto her back.

"You're awake."

"Yeah. What happened? Do you know where we are?" he asked her.

"Nope. I didn't see anything. I was out the whole time."

She was lying. He could smell it on her, and he wanted to know why she was being dishonest.

"Ken—"

"Can I get you some water? Of course." She scrambled off the bed and walked through the open doorway.

What? Now, he was really confused.

Sawyer sat up on the bed, making the drumming in his head harder. It also made him a little dizzy. Apparently, whatever drug was in his system hadn't left yet. He slowly rose from the bed and followed Kenzie.

The room was a full-sized bathroom and combined closet. It looked like the kidnappers had planned this for quite some time because it was stashed with brand-new clothes. Some still had tags on them.

Kenzie turned around when he entered, and she handed him a cup of water. "Drink."

He downed the water, complying only because he knew he needed fluids to help flush the drugs out of his system. He glanced at himself in the mirror. He could hardly see the amber color of his eyes because his pupils were so dilated. He finger-combed his messy tawny hair, and then he set the cup on the counter.

"Ken—"

She reached up and kissed him. She pulled away and said, "Yes, we *can* take a shower. We're both filthy from the floor of that dirty van."

Did they drug her, too?

She was not acting like the Kenzie he knew. She was usually full of sarcastic comments, but right now, she had her hands fisted in his T-shirt, and her brown eyes pleaded with him to say yes.

"Good idea."

Her shoulders visibly relaxed, and relief rushed across her face. She let go of his shirt and removed hers. She pulled the tie that was holding her blonde hair in a ponytail and quickly rid herself of her bra, pants, underwear, and socks before stepping into the shower.

She turned on the water and shouted, "Hurry up!"

He removed his clothes and got in behind her.

She turned around and faced him. Sawyer always thought he was attracted to full-figured, tall cat-shifters. Kenzie was none of those. Short, thin, and human, she was the exact opposite, yet he always managed to get a hard-on for this girl.

He hated it.

She poked him in the chest and then used two fingers to point to her eyes. "Eyes up here, buddy," she whispered harshly, all traces of the girl outside the shower gone.

Shit. He hadn't even realized he was staring at her chest. He met her gaze. "As long as you don't look down"—and witness his vulnerability to her—"I won't look down. Now, what the hell is going on?"

Kenzie put her hands on his shoulders and pulled him down until her mouth was near his ear. "The two men who kidnapped us brought us to some house. We're in a bedroom in the basement. Since they never saw me wake up, I pretended to be unconscious when we stopped. When we got here, one of the men gave you a shot of something to knock you out again. Do you remember that?"

Vaguely.

He remembered trying to get out of his binds when the van had stopped. One of the kidnappers had stepped into the cargo area, and Sawyer had felt a pinch in his arm. After that, he didn't remember anything until the bedroom.

"Yes," he said into her ear. "But why are we naked in the shower together? And why are you whispering?"

And why do I want to pick her up and rub her body all over mine?

"I thought you had superior vision?" she scoffed. "They have video cameras everywhere. I don't know if they are watching us twenty-four/seven or just recording us. I also don't know if they have sound, but I didn't want to talk where they could hear us."

"And here I thought you just wanted to see me naked."

She snorted. "In your dreams."

If you only knew...

"Look, they think we're Vaughn and Naya, which means..."

Fuck. The drugs had affected him more than he thought. He'd almost forgotten that part. "We need to act like we're them."

"Yep. You and me, happy newlyweds…that's *so* us," she said, her voice loaded with sarcasm.

As much as he hated the thought of pretending like the two of them were in love, he hated even more the thought of the kidnappers finding out that they weren't Vaughn and Naya. He didn't care about himself, but he had sworn an oath to his alpha and his family. Vaughn was the alpha's son and would one day rule the pack. Sawyer would die before he let anything happen to Vaughn, Vaughn's mate, or their unborn children.

Sawyer gripped Kenzie's arms and yanked her back toward him, so he could meet her eyes. "Do you understand how important this is?"

"*Ow.* You're hurting me."

He loosened his grip.

"Yes, I understand." She lowered her voice to barely a whisper. "She's my best friend, too. And I don't really feel like dying today, okay?"

Sawyer closed his eyes with relief. When he opened them, Kenzie was looking down—at his junk.

"Excuse me."

She looked up, her face red and full of guilt. His erection had faded with the thought of Vaughn and Naya being hurt, so at least Kenzie hadn't caught his attraction to her. He felt the smirk cross his face until he focused on Kenzie's shoulder.

What the…

He reached up and outlined the bite mark there. "It's still visible."

She shook off his hand and crossed her arms. "I know, okay? It's not a big deal. It doesn't mean anything."

He lowered his arm. "Yeah, it doesn't mean anything." But it did. *Damn it.*

"Can we figure out what we're going to do before we run out of hot water?" she bit out.

"Fine."

They finished their discussion, and he explained that their captors were human, but he could smell wolf on them, which meant a wolf-shifter or wolf-shifters were probably behind the kidnapping.

She told him that, before they'd carried them into the house, she'd overheard the abductors say that *Vaughn* was very strong, and that was why they had drugged him. They didn't seem to know he was a shifter, but someone had warned them of his extra strength.

The important thing was the abductors didn't realize that they had kidnapped the wrong people, so Sawyer and Kenzie were going to have to pretend to be Naya and Vaughn until they either escaped or were rescued.

After Payton had emerged from the bathroom, Damien had asked if she was hungry. She'd told him she was starved, and now, they were sitting in silence at the table, eating the soup and sandwiches he had made for them.

He was tired of the quiet. "Look, Payton, I'm sorry about your hair."

She set down her spoon and looked at him. "No, Damien, I'm sorry. I know you only did it to clean my head wound. In the overall scheme of things, it's not a big deal. I just wasn't expecting it, you know? As a girl, I take pride in my hair." She smiled at him. "But really, it's okay."

He felt his shoulders sag in relief. He didn't want her to be upset about anything because she would most likely be furious after she found out who was responsible for her attack. Earlier, when she had thanked him for rescuing her, she had mistaken his regret for modesty. But if his father hadn't gone after her, she wouldn't have had to thank him for rescuing her.

He couldn't tell her that now though. He wanted to wait until she was almost healed and in the protection of her parents before he would stress her with that bit of news.

"I really did try to shave off as little as possible."

"I know." She picked up her spoon and continued eating. When she was finished, she pushed back her chair and grabbed her dishes.

He stood first. "Stop. I'll get them. You just sit there. You need to conserve your energy."

She shrugged and smiled. "Okay, thanks."

Damien picked up their dishes and carried them to the sink. When he turned around, Payton was picking at his flannel shirt that she wore, inspecting it. He went back to the table and sat down.

"Sorry. That was the only thing I had for you to wear." He smiled. "I wasn't expecting company."

"I'm fine actually." She fanned herself with the shirt. "I'm surprisingly warm for what little I'm wearing." She tilted her head to the side and then shrugged.

What is going on in her head?

"What happened to my clothes anyway?"

He cleared his throat. "I had to pitch 'em. They were covered in blood."

"Huh." She turned her head to stare out the window. "I suppose that makes sense."

"Payton?"

She looked at him, eyebrows raised.

"What do you remember about your attack?"

"Not much." She squinted. "I finished dinner with some friends. I left the restaurant, and these humans appeared out of nowhere. I don't know why they picked me to rob."

"Did you see anything significant? Did you hear or smell anything?"

She closed her eyes for a few seconds before opening them again. "Not really. Everything was a blur. It happened so fast. They never spoke to me or each other, and the only thing I smelled was oil and grease, like they worked in a garage."

He breathed out a silent sigh of relief. He hadn't smelled wolf on the humans either, but he'd wanted to make sure. He needed Payton to trust him. Her recovery was his number one priority right now, and if she didn't feel safe, it would take her longer to get there.

"They didn't say anything that would help you identify them?"

"No. Then again, I was on the phone, talking to my mom." She jumped forward and gripped the edge of the table. "*Oh my God*. My mom. My dad. My brother. They must be worried about me. I need to call them and let them know I'm safe." She looked around as if she were trying to find something. "*Crap*. I must have dropped my phone and purse when I was attacked." She turned back to him. "Do you have one I can use?"

"Shit. Of course. I'm sorry I didn't think of it earlier." He hurried to the bedroom and grabbed his phone. He flipped it open to a black screen. He returned to Payton and showed her his phone. "The battery's dead. My only charger is my car charger in the truck. Can you wait about ten minutes?"

She gave him a reassuring smile. "Sure. What's another ten minutes?"

Damien grabbed his coat and hurried outside. He opened his truck door and reached for his charger. It wasn't hanging from the cigarette lighter.

What the—

He groaned. He had unplugged it to charge his iPod yesterday. The cell charger had to be here somewhere. He looked on the floor, under the seat, the crack between the seat and backrest, and behind the seat, but he came up empty. "Double shit."

What would Payton think? That he had planned this?

She didn't know about her brother and his mate yet, and she seemed to think her attack was random. Hopefully, once he explained about sending Isabelle to Vance, Payton would feel better. That might be enough to comfort her for now.

He walked slowly back into the cabin. Payton sat where he'd left her, tapping her fingers on the table. He hung up his coat, sat down, and set the useless electronic on the table.

"Payton, I hate to tell you this, but my charger is gone. I don't get it. It was in my truck yesterday."

The corners of her mouth turned down, and her lower lip began to tremble.

"Fuck. I am really sorry."

She hung her head, and a tear fell to her lap.

He got down on his knees, so he could see her face. "Hey."

She looked at him.

"Would it help if I told you that I sent a friend to let your family know you're okay?"

"Wha-what?"

"Last night, I knew your family would worry, and I didn't know when you'd wake up. I thought about calling them myself, but one, I didn't know their number, and two, I didn't think they would just take my word for it."

He pointed to his chest. "Wolf."

The corner of her mouth tilted up for a second in a small smile.

"Anyway, I sent a friend because I thought it would help to have someone show up in the flesh. Your family should know by now that you're okay. I was actually expecting to hear back from my friend, updating me on what had happened, but I guess I know why I never got that call."

Another tear fell down her cheek. Before he realized what he was doing, he reached up and wiped it away with his thumb.

Pure electricity shot through his body.

He hadn't felt it last night when she was unconscious, but when he'd helped her up this afternoon, there had been no mistaking it. Her kiss earlier had been a shock to his system, making him instantly aroused. Now, he felt it again.

She's crying, man.

He moved his hand from her cheek to her shoulder and down her arm, and then he squeezed her hand. "I would drive somewhere and make a phone call, but I don't think your family would appreciate hearing from me, with or without my friend contacting them first. And I just can't risk you going out in the cold and riding in my rickety old truck yet." He squeezed her hand again. "Are you going to be okay?"

She leaned forward and landed in his arms, knocking him onto his back. She wrapped her arms around his neck. "Thank you," she said, her sapphire eyes filling with tears, "for everything."

He rubbed her back. "You're welcome."

He just hoped she would still feel that way once she found out who was responsible.

Chapter Seven

Dante shut the kitchen cupboard. He planned to enjoy the last few minutes of peace before sunset, before the house came alive with activity. As the leader of the Guardians, he was usually up before the others awoke.

He heard footsteps in the hall, and even before she entered, he caught the scent of vanilla that belonged to vampire Princess Anaya. Along with her natural fragrance, she carried the smell of cloves. Her cat-shifter mate had marked her well.

Dante wasn't sure what to think about the pairing yet. Vampire-shifter pairings were not a common occurrence.

"Oh," the princess said with surprise when she entered the room.

He smiled over his shoulder. "Good morning. I'm making coffee. Would you like a cup?"

She sat down at the kitchen island, pushed her dark hair over her shoulder, and rubbed her expanding belly. "Not since I found out about the pregnancy."

"Right." Dante hit Start on the machine. "How did you sleep? Is there anything we can do for you, Princess?"

She smiled. "Dante, please, call me Naya."

"Okay then. How did you sleep, Naya?"

Her violet eyes looked sad. "As well as expected. Everyone kept me up. Poor Vaughn was tossing and turning all day. He finally fell asleep an hour ago. I had to sneak out, so I wouldn't wake him. I could also hear

Phoenix roaming around next door half the night. I hope she's asleep now. Then, the babies...sometimes, it feels like they never stop moving. Of course, they finally seem to be resting, but now, I can't sleep." She put her fingers to her lips and then put her hand down. "I'm sorry. You probably don't want to hear about my problems."

"It's fine, Princess—I mean, Naya," he corrected. "I'm glad you called us for help. You and your mate are safe here."

The night before, when Princess Naya had learned an attempt had been made to abduct her and her mate, she had called the Guardians. Her best friend and Vaughn's fellow sentinel had been mistaken for them and taken in their place. Her mate's sister had also been kidnapped. Knowing her mate and new family needed help and an outside perspective, she had asked for the Guardians' assistance.

"Are you hungry?" he asked her.

"I would love some toast and juice, if you have it."

"Orange, apple, or grape? Take your pick."

Naya put her hands on the counter to get up.

"Naya, please sit. I will get it for you."

She sat back in her seat and smiled. "Thank you."

Dante put bread in the toaster and headed for the fridge. "What kind of juice do you want?"

"Orange, please."

"You got it." He poured the juice and set it in front of her.

She smiled anxiously.

"What are you thinking about in there?"

She laughed nervously. "Can I ask you a question?"

"Sure." He leaned against the counter in a relaxed pose, hoping it would calm the princess.

"How long have you been a Guardian?"

"Since I was twenty-five, so...almost fifteen years. But I began training when I was about sixteen."

She nodded.

"That wasn't what you really wanted to know, was it?"

"No." She took a sip of her juice. "I know you've been a Guardian for some time because I remember meeting you when I was about fourteen or fifteen. You're only about ten years older than me. I guess my question is, have you always known shifters existed?"

Ah, so that's where this is going.

Several months ago, it had been revealed that Naya, an unmated vampire princess, was impregnated by a cat-shifter. But, for Naya, the bigger surprise was the existence of shifters.

Her toast popped up, so Dante grabbed it out of the toaster.

"Butter? Peanut butter? Jelly?"

"Butter is fine."

"Your parents aren't very forthcoming, are they?" Dante asked, continuing their conversation, as he set the food in front of her.

She grimaced. "You heard?"

"We aren't as big as the human population. News travels fast."

Naya used a hand to rub her temples. "How embarrassing."

"Don't be embarrassed. This is on your parents."

She dropped her arm, her eyes wide. "Aren't you supposed to be on their side?"

Dante laughed. "I'm not on anyone's side. I'm simply stating a fact. As royalty, a certain level of shelter is expected, but I think you should have known about the shifters and the fact that we haven't been the best of friends. To answer your question, yes, I've always known about them, even before I was a Guardian."

"I still feel stupid."

"Nobody thinks of you like that if it makes you feel better."

"Really?" She eyed him speculatively.

"Really."

"Well, I'm not sure if I believe you, but since it does make me feel better, I'll go with you on this."

Dante grinned.

The princess was quite courageous. She had stood up to her family and fought for what she believed. She'd turned her crown over to her cousin to appease the Vampire Council and the older vampires, but most of the younger ones thought she should have fought for her rightful spot.

"How do you feel about shifters? What do the other Guardians think? My parents are extremely prejudiced."

He shrugged. "We don't have any beef with them."

He pushed the truth a little, but she didn't need to worry about what the Guardians thought of her mate. She had bigger concerns. He still didn't know if he trusted shifters one hundred percent, but he would keep that to himself. He needed to let everyone know he was behind this mating, including the other Guardians. With the interspecies mating, he supposed the shifters would prove themselves one way or the other.

"Vaughn and Phoenix are safe here. You have my word."

"Thank you again."

They were interrupted by the sound of footsteps and the smell of cat-shifter in the hall. But this wasn't her mate. It was the female sentinel, Phoenix. She had shown up with Naya and Vaughn the night before. From the moment Phoenix had arrived, she'd been on edge. She obviously had control issues and didn't like being in the vampires' domain where she had no authority.

Phoenix narrowed her eyes at Dante.

Maybe Naya should ask if any shifters were prejudiced against vampires.

Dante didn't let Phoenix bother him though. He wasn't going to let some female shifter unbalance him, not in his domain and especially not one who lacked confidence.

She had creamy skin and long dark red hair with black streaks. Her emerald green eyes stood out against her skin and hair, making her looks even more striking. To top it off, she had curves—ample breasts and a generous bottom—that Marilyn Monroe would have killed for, accompanied by long legs any man would love to have wrapped around him, yet she carried herself as if she were the homely girl who would sit in the back of the classroom, trying to blend in. Tonight, she wore baggy dark jeans and a loose T-shirt as if it could hide what she'd been blessed with.

She was insecure with herself, and she hid it pretty well, covering it up with dominance, but Dante saw right through it.

"Good evening, Phoenix," Naya said.

Phoenix walked up to Naya and smiled. "Evening." Phoenix seemed to like at least one vampire. She patted Naya's abdomen and leaned over to speak quiet words to the little ones growing there. She looked up at

Naya. "Vaughn still sleeping?"

"I hope so. Why do you ask?" Naya asked Phoenix.

Phoenix straightened. "I got a phone call that I need to talk to him about."

Naya was immediately on alert. "Did you find out anything? Kenzie? Is she okay?"

Phoenix smiled sadly. "No, honey, I haven't heard anything about Kenzie."

Naya sat back in defeat.

"I'll let you know what was discussed, but let's wait for Vaughn."

"Wait for me for what?" Vaughn asked as he came around the corner. He looked relaxed, but the dark circles under his eyes gave him away.

The princess's face lit up the moment she saw him. He walked over to Naya and kissed her. Then, he rubbed his nose along her neck while he stared right at Dante, his blue eyes firm.

Vaughn didn't have anything to worry about. Dante wasn't going to touch his woman.

Vaughn stood upright, and Dante noticed the bite marks on his neck. So, the rumor was true. Naya did feed from her shifter mate. That certainly put the belief about vampires having to feed only from other vampires in a different light.

Vaughn grabbed Naya's uneaten toast, bit off a chunk, and swallowed it almost without chewing. He looked at Phoenix. "Wha—" he began.

He didn't get to finish because Naya slapped her hand over his mouth.

They all turned to stare at Naya, and she laughed self-consciously.

"I'm sorry. It's just the twins finally went to sleep, or they stopped moving, not that long ago. If they hear Vaughn's voice, they'll wake up." She looked up at her mate. "I'm sorry, Vaughn." She smiled. "They apparently know their daddy's voice already."

Vaughn removed her hand from his mouth and kissed her palm. He leaned over, so they were forehead-to-forehead. "I love you," he whispered.

"I love you, too."

"Why don't you try to take a nap? Maybe you can rest now that I'm not there and the twins are asleep."

"I always sleep better with you, but I'll go try."

He smiled at her and helped her off the chair. "I'll fill you in later." He smoothed his hand down her coffee-colored hair and kissed her on the forehead before she left.

As soon as she was out of the room, his smile fell, and he let the worry he'd hidden from his mate show. "What's up, Phoenix?"

Phoenix stood and nodded toward the hall. "Shouldn't we go in there?"

"No."

Her emerald eyes went wide. "But, Vaughn, what about..." She tilted her head toward Dante.

Not only did she not trust him, but she was also rude. Her attitude was going to get very old, very quickly.

"Phoenix, one of the reasons Naya brought us here is so that the Guardians can help us. They can't help us if they don't know what is going on." Vaughn was unwavering in his statement.

He might not trust Dante to stay away from his mate, but Vaughn trusted him with their private information, and Dante appreciated his confidence.

Vaughn was right to trust him. Whoever was behind this had threatened Princess Naya's life and the lives of her unborn children. He wouldn't live to make the same mistake twice.

"I know you don't know me, Phoenix," Dante addressed the female shifter, "but you can trust us. Princess Naya is important to us. Now that a shifter and vampire have mated, it's time we started working together rather than avoiding each other."

Phoenix pursed her lips and remained silent.

"Spill it," Vaughn told Phoenix.

She wrinkled her nose. "Fine." She threw her long hair over her shoulder and sat back down. "First, Saxon and Tegan went to the restaurant where your sister was last night. They found her purse and cell phone in the grass. They could smell three different male humans, and the humans' blood had been left behind. The smells of the humans were strong, thanks to their adrenaline rush." Phoenix paused.

"Okay. What else?" Vaughn prompted.

She cringed. "They smelled a lone wolf."

"*What?*"

"They tracked the smell to where it ended. All they found was a cell-phone charger that had his scent. This brings me to the second thing."

"What is it?"

"Damien Lowell has your sister."

"*What?*" Vaughn jumped from his seat. "That was the wolf Saxon and Tegan smelled at the restaurant?"

Phoenix held up her hands. "Damien apparently rescued your sister from the humans. He has her somewhere safe. She was injured, but he has patched her up, and he believes she will recover. We haven't spoken to her yet, but Damien sent a female wolf—Isabelle Rand—to deliver his message in person. Zane has her right now. Your dad told him to keep her until we hear from Payton or until she's home."

"Who is this Damien Lowell?" Dante asked.

"He's the son of the Minnesota Pack alpha. Do you know about the rift between the Pride and the Pack?" Vaughn asked him.

"A little."

"About ten years ago, my father kicked Dwyer Lowell and the rest of the pack out of the Twin Cities. When exiled, Dwyer made it known how angry he was. Damien was different from his irresponsible, hotheaded father. He and I always got along. If I had to base this situation on the Damien I knew back then, I would say he's sincere, and he will keep his word. However, considering his pack was kicked out along with his father possibly passing on his hate of us and his brother passing away last year…I just don't know." Vaughn ran his hand across his face. "What does my dad say?" he asked Phoenix.

"I only spoke to Saxon. He says your father is unsure but is hoping for the best. The fact that Damien sent a civilian female to deliver his message in person means that he sent someone he really trusts, and he trusts us to treat her fairly. Your father thinks it's a good sign. That, along with the strong scent of human blood at the area where Payton was attacked, shows a strong possibility that he's telling the truth. Those humans didn't injure themselves, so Damien must have fought them off."

"It also means he knows who's behind this," Vaughn said.

"Why do you say that?" Phoenix asked.

"Because he just happened to be there—in your territory and at just the right time," Dante said.

Phoenix blew out a breath. "Well, shit."

Chapter Eight

Isabelle was looking out the window at the SUV with longing.

The sun had almost set, and she hadn't heard from Damien yet. She had sat around the bunkhouse all day while Zane had made phone calls, like he was doing now. He had never let her out of his sight, yet he'd stayed far enough away that she couldn't hear the person on the other side talking. Also, all of Zane's statements had been so short that they might as well have been in code. She had no idea what was going on.

When Damien had sent her here, she had never dreamed that the cat-shifters would force her to stay. She had assumed that she would deliver the message and leave. Who knew how long she would be stuck here? Soon, she was going to be as anxious to hear from Payton as the girl's parents were.

Isabelle looked down at her watch. It was about a quarter to five, and she was bored. She really wanted to go home, and all she could think about was that if she left now, she'd be home by eight. But that wasn't going to happen. Would she have to sleep here tonight? She'd already called into work for today but not tomorrow. How many days off would she have to take? What a waste of her vacation time.

Zane hung up his phone, so she got up from the couch and walked over to him. He had on jeans and a T-shirt now, but it didn't diminish his attractiveness, and she found it hard to rein in her hormones. His butt looked great in denim.

Zane turned around, and she made sure her eyes were on his face.

"Hey, Blondie, what's up?"

She gritted her teeth. He might be taking the whole situation seriously by keeping an eye on her, but every word out of his mouth made it seem like he thought it was one big joke. And she really hated that he couldn't call her Isabelle. Blondie wasn't any better than Izzy.

Her stomach rumbled almost like it was answering his question because what was up was that she wanted to eat. She put her hand over her abdomen as if it would block the sound. She didn't want him to see any weakness from her. With her luck, he'd probably either starve her or make her beg for food.

He grinned and looked down at his phone. "It is supper time." He looked up. "I'll make us something to eat, but I have to patrol the property first. Why don't we go out to your car and get your stuff?" He smirked. "It looks like you'll be staying here."

"The day's not over yet."

Zane just laughed, tossed her coat at her, and grabbed his. They put on their boots and made their way out into the cold. She hadn't locked the SUV when she arrived, so she opened the door before he could. She wished she could jump in and take off, but he had already confiscated her keys and cell phone.

She grabbed her purse, hit the lock button on the handle, and shut the door. "Ready."

He snorted. "I think I'll just have a look inside first."

"Hurry up. It's cold."

"Keep your pants on, Blondie. You'll have them off soon enough," he said as he used her key fob to hit unlock and opened the back of the vehicle.

"What?"

"What?"

She shook her head. Maybe she'd misheard him.

She buried her nose in her coat and waited for him to finish. She always kept her SUV clean, so it shouldn't take him long.

He shut the last door and came around the vehicle, carrying her winter emergency kit and her extra coat.

"Hey."

"Relax. I'm not keeping it. I just want to give you one more reason not to try to run off." He walked past her and toward the bunkhouse. "Come on."

He still had her keys, so she followed him. If she couldn't get her keys back, she'd have to shift to her wolf and hike back home. But she lived almost three hours away by car. Walking was definitely a last resort.

Back inside, Zane set her stuff on the counter. He made a come-here motion. "Give me your coat and boots."

She shot him a dirty look but complied. She, however, did not like where this was going.

He took off his own coat and boots and grabbed her hand. Once again, they made their way to his bedroom. He opened a dresser drawer and pulled out a T-shirt.

"Okay, Blondie, strip."

"Excuse me?"

He scoffed. "You heard me. Strip."

She crossed her arms over her chest. "Over my dead body."

"Look, I need to patrol the grounds. I can't take you with me, and I can't leave you here alone because you might take off. You aren't a prisoner, and I don't want to lock you up, but I don't trust you not to leave." He shook the T-shirt in his hand. "I'm not going to leave you naked, but I can't leave you with your nice warm winter clothes."

She didn't move.

Zane rolled his eyes and sighed. "Listen, Isabelle, do you have any children? Nieces? Nephews?"

She suspected he already knew the answer, but she didn't accuse him of doing a background check on her. "I have a niece."

"Do you love her?"

"Of course."

"What if someone made an attempt on her life, and you didn't know she was okay?" He leaned forward. "You'd do everything in your power to help her, right?"

She dropped her arms. "Yes," she said reluctantly.

"If you love your niece that much, imagine how much you'd love your own daughter. That's how my alpha and alphena feel. They would do anything. *Anything*. Now, will you please change?"

She understood, but she really, really did not want to get naked in front of him. Her hormones were already out of whack, and even though she wanted to high-five his face, it didn't mean her libido agreed. "Can't you just trust me to stay here and wait?"

"Can you promise me you'll stay?"

She honestly didn't know. Ten minutes ago, she would have said no. However, she didn't know if she could promise him yes.

"That's what I thought. Now, strip."

They stared at each other for a minute.

She finally relented. "Will you please turn around?"

He rolled his eyes again but did as she'd asked. "You sure don't act like a shifter," he said.

She removed her clothes and huffed. "I'm not used to undressing in front of strange cat-shifters. I'm a wolf-shifter, remember?"

That was only a half-truth. Besides being worried about her attraction to him, she was also a little self-conscious to be naked in front of him. She had an all right body, but she was the girl next door—a plain Jane with boring hazel eyes, dishwater blonde hair, and nothing exceptional beneath her clothes. She couldn't tell him that though.

"Here you go," she said, holding out her clothes.

Zane extended an arm behind his back, and she gave him her T-shirt, sweater, and jeans. He separated the items to see what she'd given him.

He held out his hand again. "Bra."

Crap. She figured if she did want to leave, she'd find some clothes to borrow from one of the female sentinels, but underwear was personal. She unclasped her bra and slapped it in his palm. "Happy?"

He didn't say anything. He just passed his T-shirt behind him. She slipped it over her head and was happy to find it hit her mid-thigh. Then, she read the front—*My pen is huge*. This time, she rolled her eyes.

Zane turned around, smiled, and held out his hand again.

"What?"

"Panties?"

"Seriously?"

"Seriously. I'm pretty confident you won't leave without those."

Damn it, he's right.

But at least she could still shift and leave as her wolf. She reached under the shirt and pulled off her underwear without letting him see anything. "You win," she said as she threw it at him.

"I never get tired of ladies throwing their undies at me," he said after catching them.

"Pig."

Zane laughed. "One more thing." He threw her clothes onto his shoulder and reached into his back pocket. He grabbed her hand, clasped a bracelet on her wrist, and turned something on the band.

She pulled her hand free. The silver wristlet was braided with some strong metal, so she couldn't break it, and there was a lock, so she couldn't take it off. Shifters weren't allergic to silver. They weren't werewolves, but the mythology of werewolves and silver did come from shifters. For whatever reason, silver inhibited their ability to shift, so she was now stuck as a human. She wouldn't be able to go home in her wolf form even if she wanted to.

He had taken everything from her—her keys, her coat, boots, clothes, and now, her ability to shift. The only option she had left was borrowing someone else's clothes.

"I'll be back very soon. Don't try anything," Zane said before leaving the room.

She followed him as far as the doorway. He went to every room in the hall and locked it. So much for borrowing clothes. The man had really thought of everything.

Not a prisoner, my ass.

She was officially trapped.

Chapter Nine

"How ya doin'?" Damien asked Payton. "Pain okay? Do you need more meds?"

He had just come in from outside, and he was in the middle of loading firewood into the wood stove. He was unbelievably sweet and sexy.

There was just something about a man working hard and doing…well, men's work. He hadn't shaved, so his five o'clock shadow had come and gone yesterday. He now had a very sexy scruff.

"I'm okay still. A little sore, but that's to be expected."

He finished filling the stove and sat down next to her on the couch. "Sorry there's nothing to do here. This place was my grandfather's, and he liked to be close to nature. The only reason it has electricity and plumbing is because my grandmother insisted on it." He smiled wistfully. "She might have been half wolf, but her human half was undeniably domesticated."

"Was this your mom's parents or your dad's?"

"My mom's. When my grandfather passed away, he left me this cabin with the stipulation that my father couldn't know about it."

"They didn't get along?"

He scoffed. "That's the nice way of saying it. My grandfather almost disowned my mother when she mated my father, but when she became pregnant with my brother, he decided he needed to be around for his grandchildren."

"I forgot about your brother. How is he?"

Damien rubbed his hands up and down his legs. "Um…he passed away about a year and a half ago."

She put her hand on his shoulder. "Oh, Damien, I'm so sorry."

He shrugged. "Don't be. It was a car accident. My brother was an alcoholic. He was driving drunk and ran into a tree. A branch came through the window and pierced his heart."

While shifters were stronger and healed faster than humans, they weren't immortal. She could hardly imagine how Damien felt. She loved her brother and would be devastated if something happened to him.

And that was the second family member Damien had lost. His mother had been gone for about fifteen years, she guessed, and from what she remembered, it had been hard on all three of them.

She moved her hand down to his and wrapped her fingers around it. "Still, it must be hard. At least you still have your dad."

Damien laughed, but it held no humor. "My father and I…we don't get along. We have very different views on things."

"What things?"

He scoffed. "Everything. And it's so much bigger than the two of us." He stared off into the distance for a moment. "Let's not talk about him."

He looked down at where their hands were clasped. She felt her face flush, and she moved to pull her hand away when he grasped it back.

"What about you?" he asked.

"What about me?"

"How's life been treating you since the pack left?"

She rested her head against the back of the couch, but she kept her hand in his. She liked it. "Pretty good. My brother is mated and going to have twins, so I get to be an aunt soon. My parents are good. Things have been relatively calm since the pack left. Business is good. L & L Construction took a hit along with the economy, but it's remained afloat."

Damien chuckled.

She lifted her head and looked at him. "What?"

"Out of all that, you didn't say anything about yourself."

She smiled. "Not true. I said I was going to be an aunt soon."

His brow went up, and she laughed.

"Okay. You want to know about me. Well, I graduated last year from the University of Minnesota with a bachelor's in marketing. I'm currently working on my MBA. I'm really hoping to get a job working for L & L." She sighed. "Right now, that's just wishful thinking."

His eyes narrowed. "Your father won't let you work for him?"

"It's not that he won't let me. I think he wants me to be like my mother. He supports my schooling, but he wants me to get mated and stay home to raise a family. He can be old-fashioned sometimes."

"What do *you* want?"

"Oh. Wow."

No one had ever really asked her that. Her family was great, but they took her easygoing attitude for granted sometimes.

"Well, I want to have a job and be able to support myself. I want to be mated someday and have a family, but I don't want to have to rely on someone else to support me for the rest of my life. I would love to work for the company. It'd be easier to manage time off to work around my family's schedule if I worked for him, especially with the whole shifter thing. Who else is going to understand that I need almost a week off of work twice a year when I go into mating heat and that I can't be out in public because of my raging hormones?"

Damien shifted in his seat, and she laughed.

"TMI, I know, but it's the best example." She held up her free hand. "However, I also want to work for L & L because I want to contribute to and be a part of the family business." She took a deep breath. "Sorry, you probably didn't want to hear about all that."

Damien smiled. "No, I like hearing you talk."

Payton blushed and had to look away.

"So…any boyfriends?"

It was a good thing she was looking at her lap because she knew she looked stunned…and hopeful. Was he asking if she had a boyfriend because he was interested? Or was he just making conversation?

"Um…well, not right now. Truth be told, they don't stick around much after meeting my dad and brother. The shifters are too scared of their alpha, and the humans must sense their dominance and power because they are gone soon after, too."

It was very frustrating, and at this point, she was afraid she was going to die a virgin. She wasn't saving herself for a mate, but she didn't want to give it away to just anyone. Every guy she'd dated didn't last long enough for her to feel comfortable with having sex.

"Either, they make up a lame excuse as to why they are breaking up with me, or I can't handle their...wimpiness, for lack of a better word. I always feel bad, but it's like my attraction to them is gone. It's hard to be with someone who can no longer look you in the eyes."

"That makes sense. You are the daughter of the alpha and alphena. Usually, the daughter of the alpha couple mates outside her pride to an alpha of another pride. Your mother isn't from Minnesota, right?"

"Yeah, she's from Wisconsin. But I don't want to leave Minnesota or my family."

"Maybe you can find an alpha's second or third or fourth son, who would be willing to move to your pride."

She snorted. They both knew that was unlikely. As nature's way of balancing their physical advantages over humans, it was hard for shifters to conceive, so it would be hard to find an alpha who had more than one son. And even if she could, traditionally, the female would live with the male's family.

"Or maybe one of your father's sentinels."

"Ew. Most of them are like older brothers, except Camden and only because he's new."

Camden was newer to Minnesota, and she hadn't known him forever like the others. In fact, she had thought she was attracted to him, but it seemed like nothing more than a tiny crush now that she had felt her attraction to Damien.

"Plus, they're dominants but not alphas." She let her head flop back against the couch. "Maybe I should just become a lesbian."

Damien laughed. "I guess that would work, too."

He stopped laughing, and she lifted her head. He looked at her straight in the eyes, and the crystal blue burned a path straight down to her core.

"It would be a shame for the male population though." All joking had been put aside, and pure sex radiated off him. The whites of his eyes disappeared as his dominant wolf side showed itself.

She sucked in a breath. This was an alpha male, and he wanted her to know it. It was as if someone had thrown gas on the fire burning between them. His rich cedar scent got stronger, and she struggled with the need to rub her thighs together.

"You-you don't say?" She licked her lips and leaned forward. *Please kiss me.*

Instead, his eyes returned to normal and he said, "Ah, you're beautiful, and you know it." With a smile, he let go of her hand, stood up, and stretched nonchalantly as if he hadn't just let his dominance hang all out. "You hungry? I'm going to make supper." He didn't wait for her answer before heading for the kitchen.

Yeah, she was hungry—but not for food.

Walking away from Payton was the hardest thing Damien had done in a long time. Man, did he want her, and he knew she wanted him, too. But now was not the time. She was less than twenty-four hours out from getting shot and suffering a head injury. She didn't need some horny male pawing at her. What had he done, letting her know he was alpha enough to take on her and her family? It was as if he couldn't help himself.

Thankfully, making dinner helped distract him. When he finished, he walked out of the kitchen and saw Payton napping on the couch. He hated to wake her because she needed to sleep, but she also needed to eat.

He woke her, and they ate in comfortable silence. After dinner, Payton insisted on helping him clean up. Even though he thought she shouldn't be on her feet, he didn't protest.

"Thanks for helping me with the dishes."

"You're welcome," she said with a yawn. "I guess I'm tired again."

"That's understandable. Your body needs the rest. Why don't you head to bed?"

"Do you happen to have an extra toothbrush I can borrow?"

"Sure."

He headed into the bathroom, and she trailed after him.

He rummaged through his stuff and found one still in its package. He handed it to her. "Here you go. When you're done getting ready for bed, we'll change the bandage on your hip." Before he walked out, he realized she'd been wearing the same shirt since last night. "Do you want something new to wear?"

"Sure."

"Be right back." He went to the bedroom and grabbed another shirt. He held it up when he came back into the bathroom. "Sorry, I don't have much else out here but flannel shirts. They keep me warm, and they're easy to clean."

She smiled at him, her sapphire eyes lighting up. "That's okay."

He left her to do her thing, and he got out the first-aid kit. She walked out of the bathroom, looking refreshed. She walked over to the bed and lay on her uninjured side. He checked the back of her head first. Everything looked good. Her hip was next. She slowly raised her shirt on the injured side. He almost thought she was teasing him, but when he glanced at her face, she looked serious.

This was the first time he was doing anything with her wound since she'd regained consciousness, and it was torture. Part of her butt cheek was exposed on one side, and on the other, the shirt barely covered her mound, which led to the honeyed spot between her legs. Even worse, he could smell her.

Jesus Christ.

He hoped she couldn't see his noticeable hard-on. His shorts weren't hiding much.

He told himself that he was a disciplined and in-control wolf sentinel, and he had been trained to handle stress and pressure.

Payton closed her eyes, and he got to work. He removed the old bandage, cleaned the wound, coated it with antibiotic ointment, and covered it back up. He did the work with steady hands, and he was proud of himself, but when he taped the bandage, he found himself lingering. He didn't realize what he was doing until she made a noise.

He immediately moved his hands away. "Sorry, did I hurt you?"

She didn't answer. He leaned over her to see her face better.

"Payton?"

She turned her face toward him and opened her eyes. She didn't appear to be in pain, which was a good sign. "Hmm?"

"Did I hurt you?"

She smiled, and rather than answering, she grabbed his shirt, pulled him down, and kissed him.

Chapter Ten

The cat-shifter picked up his prepaid cell and dialed the only number programmed in it. He heard the click of the other side answering.

"Dwyer Lowell."

"What the hell happened out there? I just heard from my source that you sent humans to do your dirty work."

"Look, *cat*, I don't answer to you. I can send whomever I want to do *your* dirty work. You employed us after all, not the other way around. As for humans, you know as well as the next shifter how strong the nose is. I didn't want to risk the cats smelling wolf and having it lead back to us, dipshit."

The cat-shifter gritted his teeth but bit his tongue against telling the wolf off. Dwyer Lowell would get his due.

"Then, why was your son there?"

"What the fuck are you talking about?"

"Your son, Damien? Apparently, he fought off the three humans, and now, he has Vance's daughter with him somewhere."

Dwyer didn't reply, and the cat-shifter could only hear the sound of heavy breathing.

"Are you saying that you didn't plan this?" the cat-shifter prompted.

"No."

"I was hoping you'd set it up to make them think their daughter was rescued."

"That little shit. I knew he didn't approve. Things were coming to a head between us, but I just didn't think he would defy me like this." There was a long pause. "He's going to make a play for alpha," Dwyer said more to himself.

He snorted. "So, you two were having problems, and you let him know what you had planned?"

"Mind your own business, cat," Dwyer hissed into the phone.

The line went dead.

The cat-shifter looked at the *Call Ended* message on his phone and hurled it against the opposite door. Two-thirds of the plan had gone to shit. Payton had been rescued by someone who could point his finger at Dwyer, who in turn would point his finger at him. Vance and Lilith Llewelyn had gone into hiding and weren't telling anyone where they were.

He took a calming deep breath.

At least Dwyer had managed to get Vaughn and Naya out of the way.

Dwyer Lowell threw his phone across the room, making sure it landed on the sofa.

He was going to kill Damien. He couldn't believe his own son had defied him like this. *What am I going to do?* If only Donovan, his rightful heir, were still around, then this would never have happened.

This was all Vance Llewelyn's fault. If the pack hadn't been exiled, Donovan would never have been driving on that back road until he crashed, Dwyer would never have made this deal with the cat-shifter, and his only other son would never have betrayed him.

Everything was spinning out of control.

Dwyer tried to calm his racing thoughts. He had to find Damien.

Damien had left for a few days a couple of times since they'd been in the area, but Dwyer never thought to question where he'd stayed. Dwyer had figured his son found a piece of ass and hung around with her when he'd been absent. Now, it was apparent that he had been up to something else.

Dwyer marched over to the couch and picked up his phone, mad at himself for throwing it in the first place. He dialed Damien. Dwyer would straighten out the situation with his son.

The phone rang with no answer, and soon, there was an echo. Dwyer pulled the phone away from his ear and heard Damien's phone ringing from his bedroom.

"Damn it."

Damien must have left it on purpose and picked up another prepaid phone somewhere along the way.

Dwyer couldn't believe this was happening. He had to find Damien and get rid of him. If Damien challenged him in front of the pack, Dwyer couldn't refuse, and he knew Damien would win. He was younger, fitter, and smarter. Once Damien won, there would be no going back. Damien would be the new alpha of the Minnesota Pack.

"Shit."

Once again, Dwyer cursed the fates for taking away his older son, Donovan, who had always been on board with Dwyer. If Damien had challenged Donovan, it would have been a fair fight.

All Dwyer wanted was his rightful place back where he belonged—in the Twin Cities with his pack and running L & L Construction—but now, everything was going to hell.

He needed a new strategy.

He had to find Damien first. Then, Dwyer could get rid of his son and grab the girl, too—two birds with one stone.

Dwyer ran out of the cabin to the one next door. He didn't bother knocking. He just opened the door. "Lachlan?"

His sentinel turned around from the desk where he had one of his two computers sitting. "Yeah, boss?"

"You alone?"

Lachlan's brow furrowed. "Yeah."

"I need you to find Damien. Run his credit cards. You can't check his cell because he left it here, but there must be some way to track him. Do whatever you have to do to find him."

Lachlan sat forward. "Okay. Can I ask why?"

"No."

"Okay," he said with a nod.

Lachlan knew not to question his alpha—unlike someone else.

"Let me know when you have something."

"You got it." He turned back around and started typing.

Dwyer headed to the door and paused with his hand on the doorknob. "Oh, and, Lachlan?"

Lachlan looked over his shoulder. "Yeah, boss?"

"This stays between you and me." Dwyer opened the door and left.

Lachlan would find Damien, and everything would be okay.

It has to be.

Being alpha was the only thing Dwyer had left.

Payton kissed Damien—correction, Damien was kissing Payton. Once their lips had touched, he took over.

Holy crap, did the man know how to use his lips and tongue.

A minute ago, he'd been re-bandaging her wound, and the simple touch of his fingers on her hip turned her on. She had never been attracted to anyone like she was to him. At this point, she couldn't even remember any of her ex-boyfriends' names.

Damien threaded his fingers through her hair and tilted her head to the angle he wanted. She might be an alpha's daughter and a future alphena, but she didn't want to run the show in bed. She wanted to be dominated. This was one of the reasons why none of her exes had done it for her.

Payton ran her hands down his sides and then up under his T-shirt. He was so warm. She wanted to rip open her shirt and yank off his clothes, so she could take in his heat, his smell, his body inside her own.

She moaned against his lips and opened hers farther for him. He licked inside her mouth and kissed her so deeply that she could barely breathe. She didn't care. Oxygen was overrated.

She shifted on the bed. He was sitting on the edge, but she wanted him between her legs. Once he was there, all she would have to do is lift her shirt and lower his shorts, and then he'd be inside her.

She wanted this wolf to take her virginity.

This new knowledge surprised her for only a second. There was just something about Damien, and she didn't feel the urge to figure it out or question it. More importantly, her cat didn't question it. These thoughts seemed rash, but they also felt right.

Damien broke their kiss and stared into her eyes. He shifted closer to the middle of the bed and then moved down her body, and her hands fell to her sides. He kissed her chest where the flannel shirt was open, and he continued farther. He stopped at her pelvis and inhaled.

She twined her fingers in his hair, barely keeping her claws in.

"You smell so fucking good."

So did he, like cedar, male wolf, and pure sex.

He inhaled again and moved up her body. She was slightly confused at the direction he took, but she released his hair and closed her eyes in anticipation of another kiss.

His hand cupped her neck and cheek, and he pressed a delicate kiss against her lips. "Payton."

She opened her eyes and met his. She swore that they glowed with his desire, which made her passion more intense.

"We can't do this."

What? Disappointment replaced her lust.

Damien chuckled but only for a second. "I want you. God, do I want you. My wolf wants you. But you aren't in any shape to have sex—at least not the kind of sex I want to have." His eyes roamed her face and came back to hers. "Payton, when I'm inside you, I won't be able to control myself, and I don't want anything holding me back from giving you what you deserve..." He leaned down to her ear and whispered, "All of me."

Damien stood in front of the window, staring out. He'd left the bedroom and Payton about five minutes ago. He needed some time to process and to get rid of his uncomfortable erection.

Man, he was getting in deep. He slid his hand down his face and huffed out a breath. *What am I doing?*

He'd always planned that when he became alpha, he would make amends with Vance Llewelyn and the Minnesota Pride. Having sex with Vance's daughter was probably not the way to get the pack home. Damien had basically told Payton he planned to fuck her. He could potentially be ruining the good he had done the last few days—not that he was using Payton to get his pack home, but rescuing her from being kidnapped sure hadn't hurt his cause.

The hardest part was how badly he wanted her, and he didn't know how he was going to keep his hands to himself. Despite the consequences, he wasn't sure if he even wanted to. He had never wanted a female as badly as this one. When they had kissed, she had tasted incredible. And her smell?

Holy fuck.

It was as if her pussy had been calling out to him and inviting him inside. And, boy, did he want in.

He didn't know what to do.

Damien heard the sound of Payton shuffling behind him. Thankfully, her injury gave him some time to figure out where to go from here.

He didn't turn around until she put her hand on his shoulder.

"You okay?" she asked.

"Yeah. You?"

He had come on pretty strong. He knew she'd been into it. He'd felt the shiver travel through her body when he told her what he wanted to do to her, but afterthoughts could be a bitch.

She laughed. "Sexually frustrated, but I'll live." Her face went serious. "I can tell something is on your mind. What's going on?"

He put his hand over hers. He couldn't tell her about the pack and the possibility of them coming home. He didn't want her to get the wrong idea about him saving her, and she still didn't know his father was behind it.

Instead, he told her, "Despite the fact that we are here together, technically, we are supposed to be adversaries."

Payton's eyes narrowed.

Damien opened his mouth to explain better, but she didn't even let him get a word out.

"So, you're saying…what exactly? We're too different? This would never work? I'm not good enough for you?"

Women. Damien controlled his urge to roll his eyes. He felt guilty for being dishonest, but she was mistaking what he had said for rejection.

"You know," she continued, "just because I want to screw you doesn't mean I want you for a mate. Maybe I just want one night."

"Payton," he growled. Now, he was getting pissed off.

"Maybe you're not good enough for me. Did you ever think of that, huh?"

She tried to yank her hand away, but he held on tight and used his free arm to tug her close.

"Payton."

She struggled in his grip, but he didn't let go.

"What?"

"Would you let me finish?"

She stopped moving. "Fine," she grumbled.

"First of all, nobody is too good for anybody. Second, I don't care if I'm a wolf, and you're a cat. You know our bodies are going to be—would be perfect together. Third, you deserve more than one night. Maybe *I* want *you* for a mate, and I don't care what you say because I have plans to claim you."

Payton sucked in her breath.

"But what about your family, your father? Like I was going to say, our families haven't gotten along for years." Damien used their hands to gesture between them. "What would they say? What would they think?" He left it at that. He wouldn't burden her with his problems, and he didn't want her to think he had rescued her for the wrong reasons.

"You're sweet to worry about me."

And selfish because he was worried about himself.

"I honestly don't know how my family would react." She narrowed her eyes again. "Are you sure that's the only thing bothering you?"

"Yes," he lied.

"Do you hate my father for kicking you and your pack out?"

"What?" Damien hadn't expected the question. "No. My father dug his own grave."

The only thing Damien didn't agree with was losing ownership of the Lowell half of L & L Construction. Payton's grandfather and his own had started it together. Damien could understand why Vance hadn't wanted Dwyer involved since he had lost significant industry contracts and tarnished the company's reputation. However, Damien believed the Llewelyns should have bought out the Lowell's half of the business. It didn't seem fair for Vance to just take it away and leave them with nothing.

"I hold no grudge against your father." It was mostly the truth and all Payton needed to know.

"Good." She laid her head on his chest, and they released their hands to wrap their arms around each other. "I guess there are a lot of issues to consider."

"Yes, there are."

He felt her smile against his chest.

"But you are saying you like me, and you think I'm pretty, right?"

Damien tossed his head back and laughed.

Chapter Eleven

$\mathcal{S}$axon entered the living room of the safe house and walked up to Reid. "Got anything yet, man?"

Reid was currently on the computer, trying to find anything he could on the Minnesota Pack alpha and sentinels.

Reid snorted and spun his chair around. His chartreuse eyes were filled with frustration. "I wish. Sawyer's and Kenzie's cells were turned off at Vaughn and Naya's house and haven't been turned on since. You found Payton's phone on the ground outside the restaurant, which does us no good. Because we have Isabelle's phone info, we know the number Damien called from, but that phone is off, and it doesn't have GPS. The only thing I have is the last triangulated position, which is about four and a half square miles. It's going to take me awhile to narrow down the location. The weird thing is, the phone has been active for only a couple of days, and the only phone number he called was Isabelle."

They didn't need the help of the police when Reid could hack into anything he pleased.

"Burner, huh?" Saxon asked.

"Looks like it. The cell phone in his name hasn't been used either. As for the rest of the wolves, Dwyer Lowell and his sentinels went off the grid several months ago. Their credit cards show no activity, and their cell phones haven't been used even though they are still on. Their locations triangulated far from here. They must have left them at home to make it look like they are there. Nothing comes up to show that they've rented or leased anything, and they don't own any property around here anymore. They have to be using cash and burner phones. I'm doing everything I can to find them."

"What about Isabelle's phone?"

"Good news and bad news. The good news is, Isabelle's phone is her phone. She seems legit. She's a high school teacher who, up until today, hasn't even called in sick. She's got a clean record, and her only questionable quality is that she's a wolf-shifter. Oh, and it looks like, she and Damien were an item a couple of years ago. Their breakup seems to be amicable, and they remain friends. That probably explains why he trusts her."

"I don't get trusting ex-girlfriends."

Reid scoffed. "That's because you've never had one. You have to actually date a girl in order for her to be an ex. Fucking a girl for one night isn't dating."

"Ha-ha. You're a fucking riot." But it was true. Just thinking of settling down with someone made Saxon's skin crawl. He was perfectly happy being single. "Anyway, what's the bad news?"

"Like I said, Damien's phone is either turned off or dead. Giving Damien the benefit of the doubt, I'll go with dead. If the phone charger you found is any indication, it's going to stay dead. I'm going to try to find the last known signal and narrow down the area, but it's going to take me a few days."

Saxon swore. He had just left the alpha and alphena, and the whole situation was very hard on them.

"Did you let everyone know they should go somewhere safe?" Reid asked.

He had turned back to the computer, so Saxon was now having a conversation with the back of his auburn-colored head.

"Yeah, Vance's parents along with Gerald were informed."

Gerald Llewelyn was Vance's cousin, and Vance was worried that he might also be in danger.

"We even told Lilith's parents in Wisconsin to be on the lookout just in case."

"And everyone thinks Vaughn and Naya were kidnapped?"

"Yep." Saxon pushed his black-and-blond striped hair out of his face. "I wonder what Vince is going to think when he finds out that we lied to him."

Vince was Vance's father and their former alpha.

Reid turned back around. "I think he'll understand that Vance had to do what he had to do. What I don't understand is why he didn't want Vince to think Payton was kidnapped as well? Won't they be after Payton now?"

"I don't understand it myself. He must trust Damien to keep her safe on some level, but his beef has always been with Dwyer rather than the whole pack. Plus, I think he trusts you to find them before Dwyer does." Saxon smirked. "You'd better not disappoint the boss."

Reid gave him the finger. "I could hack circles around you, asshole."

Saxon laughed. It was true. Reid was hands-down the best tech guy he knew, and the sentinels were lucky to have him on their side.

"What's funny?" Tegan asked as she and Camden came into the room.

"Nothing really," Saxon answered as they both sat on the couch. "Reid's just telling me I'm an asshole."

"Tell us something we don't already know," Tegan muttered.

"Hey," Saxon protested.

Camden ignored them both and asked, "Do you think Sawyer and Kenzie are okay?"

"We have to hope for the best," Tegan said. "Sawyer might not like humans, but he'll pretend one is his mate if it means saving Vaughn. He probably doesn't even care about his own life."

"At least he's with this particular human." Reid snickered.

"Why do you say that?" Tegan asked.

Saxon exchanged looks with Reid and Camden. "Uh...never mind," he said.

"But—"

"How do you think Zane is doing?" Camden asked, changing the subject.

Tegan narrowed her eyes at them but didn't push. "Fine. Why?"

"When we left, he was pretty bummed about having to stay back. He figured we'd get all the fun."

Zane was trustworthy and good at his job, but he was also the resident jokester. He tended to get bored easily and hated missing out on the action.

"And?"

"And Isabelle. It sure would be fun to be a fly on that wall. I bet he's enjoying himself now."

Saxon snorted. Knowing Zane, he was probably making Isabelle's life unbearable.

"I'm sleeping where?"

Isabelle had just finished helping Zane clean up the kitchen after they had eaten. She had ended up cooking because she didn't trust him to make anything edible.

"My bed," he said matter-of-factly as if the answer was obvious.

Isabelle laughed, but it wasn't because she thought the situation was funny. "I don't think so."

Zane shrugged. "Fine. Then, I'm going to have to chain you to the fridge." He tapped his finger against his chin, pretending to think. "Or I could put you in the cell we have in the basement for people we need to lock up." He lowered his hand. "I figured you would at least get a good night's sleep if you slept next to me where it's warm and comfortable. I wouldn't have to lock you up because I'd wake up if you tried to leave." He shrugged. "But, hey, if you prefer a cold hard floor, it's all the same to me."

"Can't you let me sleep on the couch? I promise, I won't leave."

"And I'm going to ensure that…by locking you up."

He was going to win again. She might have to rethink her well-mannered nature. Look where it had gotten her. First, he'd taken her stuff. Second, he'd left her with nothing to wear but his T-shirt. Now, she would have to sleep with him. Why did he always defeat her? Probably because she let him.

"I hate you."

He put his hand on his chest and gasped as if he were offended. "Who? Me?" he said, sounding like a Southern debutant. "I simply don't believe it."

Isabelle rolled her eyes and walked past him toward the hall. Before she could make it, Zane slung his arm around her shoulders. She was peeved that the first thing she noticed was that he smelled great.

"Oh, come on, I'm not that bad," he said in his normal voice as they walked toward his bedroom.

When they got to the room, he removed his arm and held up his hands. "I promise, I won't touch you." He lowered his hands and raised his eyebrows. "Unless you want me to?" he said to her chest.

She looked down. Her nipples were stiff as if they were begging for attention.

Damn cat and her attraction to him. Damn her shifter DNA and her needs.

She crossed her arms over her chest. "Don't flatter yourself. I'm cold."

"Whatever you say, Blondie." He ran a finger down her arm. "Hmm...no goose bumps."

Well, she had some now. She stepped past him, flung back the covers, and got into his bed. She scooted all the way over to the wall, wanting to be as far away from him as possible.

Zane laughed at her. "Oh, Blondie."

She gritted her teeth but otherwise ignored him.

She heard the rustling of his clothes. She really hoped that he would put on pajamas, but she refused to turn around to check. She buried her face in his pillow to stop herself from looking at him, but that was a mistake. Sandalwood invaded her nose. His scent was everywhere, and she reconsidered sleeping in the kitchen while being shackled to the fridge.

She prayed she wouldn't have to use the bathroom in the middle of the night because she'd be forced to climb over him.

The bedroom light turned off, and she felt the bed dip down as Zane climbed in behind her. Despite telling herself to relax, she felt her body tense up. She couldn't let him distress her, and she really needed the sleep. She had to be alert and strong.

She waited for him to say something or touch her, but the next thing she knew, he was fast asleep. Clearly, he wasn't as affected by her as she was by him. She sighed. Life was definitely not fair.

Isabelle looked down toward her feet. Maybe she wouldn't have to climb over Zane. If she moved a little at a time, she could climb down to the bottom of the bed. She wasn't going to try to leave. She just wanted to sleep on the couch. It would not only get her away from Zane, but it would also prove that she meant what she had said when she told him she would stay. Then, maybe she'd get a little trust along with her stuff back.

She peeked over her shoulder. He was definitely asleep.

First, she drew a leg out and waited, and there was no movement behind her. Then, she moved out the other leg. She slowly brought her hand up to push down the sheet and comforter when a strong arm wrapped around her waist and pulled her close.

Damn it.

Now, she had the answer to whether or not he wore pajamas, and it was not the answer she'd wanted.

"I thought you said you weren't going to touch me?"

"I thought you said you weren't going to leave?"

"I wasn't going to leave. I was going to sleep on the couch. You can let go."

There was no response.

"Zane?"

"What?"

"Can you at least put on some clothes?"

"Why?"

She huffed out a breath. "Never mind."

He wins again.

Chapter Twelve

Kenzie had finally fallen asleep beside Sawyer. It seemed to have taken her some time, probably because of their close proximity and their current situation. So far, they had been doing a decent job of pretending to be mates.

After he had left the shower, he had taken some time to study the room. Their captors had to expect that they would assess their surroundings—it was only natural—so he hadn't worried about the cameras watching him. He hadn't made any attempt to escape. Instead, he'd made a mental note of everything.

The door to their room was made of steel, and the walls were cinder block. He was strong but not that strong. Everything was bolted down to the concrete floor, so he was unable to use anything to try to smash through the door. The window was non-egress and didn't open, and it would be too small for anyone to fit through even if it did. It also had glass that let in the light, but it was too thick to see out to gauge their location.

There were four video cameras—two in the bedroom on opposite corners, one in the closet, and one in the bathroom. Thankfully, the kidnappers couldn't seem to hear them. As a test, once Kenzie had gotten out of the shower, Sawyer had told her that their captors had missed a second cell phone he kept on him. It was a lie. Neither of them had an extra phone on them. But if the abductors had heard what he said, he had known that they would want to take it from him. Sawyer and Kenzie had expected the door to burst open any minute, but it had remained closed.

In fact, it hadn't opened all evening, and the two of them were starving. He was sure it was some sort of power tactic to let them know who was in control. It hadn't bothered him because he was a trained sentinel, but Kenzie wasn't. Also, they thought she was pregnant, so it showed that they were major jackasses, leaving an expecting woman hungry. Luckily, Sawyer and Kenzie had water from the bathroom to drink.

The bright spot was, since they weren't being recorded, the two of them could talk freely. They would still have to show that they were a couple, but they wouldn't have to speak like they were. She had called him an asshole half a dozen times while smiling sweetly. Kenzie had lain in his arms before she drifted off, but she had made sure to let him know that she wasn't happy about it.

Yeah, well, neither was he.

Sawyer got out of bed and used his cat night vision to look around the room, hoping that none of the cameras were infrared. Maybe he would be able to find a way to get them out of here before their jailors realized what was going on. He didn't know how long Kenzie and he could be around one another without going crazy.

They had only known each other for a few months, but their history, while short, was complicated. When he had first met her, he had tried to pretend that she didn't do anything for him, but less than ten minutes after they had been introduced to each other, he had pulled her away from some guy who was kissing her. It was as if she were his, and he was jealous.

But she wasn't his, and he didn't want her to be. Sawyer didn't mind humans in a general sense, but he had sworn that he would never date one again. The last human he had dated ended up changing his life forever and not for the better. He would never trust someone like that again. And that was why he resented his attraction to Kenzie.

He hadn't asked for it, and he certainly didn't want it. He felt bad that he was constantly an asshole to her, but he knew she felt the same magnetism he did, and he had to push her away. Any kind of relationship would only end badly for both of them.

At times, he'd been unable to control his attraction to her. One moment stood out in particular. She had told him that she was going to fuck his fellow sentinel. Without even thinking, he had dragged her into the nightclub restroom, stuck his hand up her skirt, and bitten her—all so that Saxon would know not to touch her. Afterward, Sawyer had had to come clean with himself and admit that he used Saxon as a reason to get physical with her. He had known that Saxon wouldn't have had sex with her. Sawyer's actions that night had only made him resent her more even if it wasn't her fault that he had issues.

Sawyer stopped in the middle of the bedroom. Whoever had built and set up the room did a thorough job. There was no way that Sawyer and Kenzie could break out of here. They would have to find some other way to escape.

Sawyer lay down next to Kenzie and pulled her into his arms. She sighed, and despite their problems with each other, he silently promised her that he would get them out of here, one way or another.

Payton dreamed of fire.

For some reason, she had to walk through it. She didn't want to, but she knew safety lay on the other side. She hadn't determined yet why it was safe on the other side, but she knew it would be. She looked behind her and almost fell off a cliff. If she fell, she would certainly die. She looked to the right and to the left.

Then, looking straight again, through the fire, she saw Damien. He beckoned her forward.

Now, she understood. The cliff equaled danger, and Damien equaled safety.

She tried to yell his name, but it only came out as a whisper. She inched forward, determined to reach Damien. The fire licked all along her body. It didn't burn her, but it was hot and made her weak. Sweat poured off her in sheets, and soon, she had to crawl to try to reach him.

Time felt like it had slowed as she put one hand in front of the other—right, left, right, left. Would she ever reach him? Just as she was about to collapse, she called Damien's name again.

Then, Damien swept her up in his arms. "Shh…honey, I'm right here."

The fire was still around them, but at least now, she knew she was safe because she went from hot to cold.

Damien awoke from a deep sleep. At first, he didn't understand what had awakened him, but then he felt the sweat rolling down his neck. He could never sleep when he was too warm.

But why is the room so hot?

It couldn't be the stove. He had let the wood die down, so the temperature would drop, making sleep more comfortable. It certainly hadn't gotten warmer outside.

He threw off the covers, welcoming the blast of cool air, and realized the warmth was from Payton. Damien turned and felt her forehead. Heat rolled off her in waves. She had a fever.

"Shit."

When they had decided to go to sleep, Payton had asked him if he would sleep beside her. He'd been unable to refuse, and he hadn't really wanted to anyway. When they had lain down, everything had been fine, but she was sick now. This wasn't good. A fever meant there had to be an infection somewhere.

Damien jumped out of bed and turned on the light. He pulled the covers off the bed. Payton was covered in sweat to the point that the front of her shirt was soaked, and her face was flushed.

"Damien," she said so softly that he almost missed it.

"Payton?"

She didn't respond.

"Payton, where are you hurt?"

There was still no response.

Damien checked both her wounds and discovered it was her hip. The area around the wound was swollen and red. Everything had looked good earlier, not a hint of infection, and now, her fever was full force. Shifters healed faster, but the flip side was that an infection could set in faster, too.

Damien quickly grabbed the first-aid kit and took her temperature— one hundred and six degrees. Shifters had a higher than average temperature than humans, but one hundred and six degrees was too high.

He stripped off her shirt and carried her to the bathroom. He set her in the bathtub and turned on the water, leaving it set to cold. This was the only way to get her fever down to a manageable level or to break it if they were lucky.

Payton moaned. "Damien," she said. She was barely conscious, her eyes still closed.

"Shh...honey, I'm right here."

"Cold."

"This will make you feel better, I promise."

"Cold."

"I know. I know."

Once the water rose above her waist, he turned off the water. He left her to find some ibuprofen. He didn't know if it would even make a dent in her fever, but it was worth a try. Even if it didn't, she was probably due for the pain reliever anyway.

He brought it to her with some water, and he was able to wake her enough for her to swallow it. He took the glass back to the kitchen, and he realized he needed to change the sheets again. Because the cabin didn't have a washer and dryer and he would have to use a Laundromat, he kept multiple sets of sheets on hand. They were old sets that his grandparents and his mother had accumulated over the years. He had thought it was a little excessive until this situation. Now, he was grateful.

He changed the sheets and found Payton a new shirt. Then, he returned to the bathroom. He sat down on the floor, took her hand, and rested his head against the wall. He planned to stay with her until her temperature went down.

He must have drifted off. The next thing he knew, he was waking up with a sore neck, and Payton was shivering in the bathtub. He quickly removed her, wiped the water off her body, and laid her on the bed. She didn't feel as hot, but her fever wasn't gone. Thankfully, it was down far enough to keep her out of the cold bathtub, so she could rest in bed.

He looked at his watch. He figured that he had given her the medicine about an hour earlier, which meant he had to give her another dose in five hours, probably less. He set the alarm on his watch to wake him up in time. He did not want to go through waking up to her being sick like that again.

Before he went back to sleep, he cleaned out her wound. This time, he used hydrogen peroxide. It bubbled and fizzed, and he was grateful Payton was not awake. He let the wound dry, and then he put antibiotic ointment on it.

He could only hope that it would help.

Chapter Thirteen

It was several days later, and Payton was starting to feel normal again. She sat up in bed and arched her back in the only way a cat-shifter could. She glanced over at Damien. It felt a little weird to sleep with a man yet not sleep with him. His dark hair was messy, and he almost had a full beard, since he hadn't taken the time to shave.

He was out cold.

Poor guy.

He had been taking care of her for the last three nights. Technically, it was four if she counted the first night. She had only had a fever for two nights, and it had broken on their third morning at the cabin, so she had spent the rest of yesterday and last night regaining her strength. It had been worth it because she already felt much better. The pains in her side and head were barely noticeable. She still felt a little hot and achy, but it wasn't the same as before. It seemed a bit odd, but it probably had to do with her injuries. She would most likely be able to go home tomorrow.

She should be filled with happiness, but there was a part of her that was sad.

She got out of bed without waking Damien. He had earned his sleep. She headed straight for the shower, and she stopped cold when she saw what was going on outside the window. Snow was falling in thick flakes, and she estimated a foot of it was already on the ground. The tree branches were covered and sagging under the weight of the snow.

Payton hurried to the front door and yanked it open. Damien's truck was covered, and the snow was almost to the top of the wheels. She closed the door, rested against it, and sighed. She guessed she wouldn't be going anywhere today.

She knew her family would be disappointed, but that didn't stop the smile from spreading across her face. She wasn't ready to leave Damien yet, and the selfish part of her rejoiced.

She went back to the bedroom, grabbed a clean shirt, went to the bathroom, and hopped in the shower.

The water felt wonderful as it flowed down her body. Sometimes, there was nothing better than being clean. While in the shower, she washed the wound on her hip, which was almost completely healed at this point, and she was determined not to get another infection. Once was enough. Her head was back to normal, except for her missing hair. If that was all the damage she went home with, she would consider herself blessed.

Payton finished up in the bathroom and saw that Damien was still sleeping, so she headed to the kitchen. It was her turn to take care of him, and she could start with breakfast.

The bacon and pancakes were finished by the time he emerged from the bedroom. His hair was wet, and he smelled clean. He was dressed in shorts and a flannel shirt, and his face was clean shaven. Payton had never seen him without any facial hair, and she stopped breathing for a moment as she took him in.

"Smells good," he said, oblivious to her thoughts.

She turned her thoughts back to the food and released her breath. She beamed at his compliment and hoped he'd like the taste as well. "Thank you. Why don't you sit down and eat?"

"Let me put some more wood in the stove." Damien picked up a few split logs stacked against the wall and threw them on the fire. "Did you look outside? It's a good thing I brought in that wood last night."

"I know. It's really snowing out there," she said as she filled his plate and carried it to the table.

Damien walked over. "It looks like we won't be going anywhere." He took the plate and set it down. "You're probably feeling better, and I bet you were hoping to go home."

She smiled. "Yeah, but what can we do?" she said with a shrug. "We live in Minnesota."

Damien didn't return her smile, so she grabbed his hand and squeezed tight. "Really, it's okay."

She liked it here with him. It was like they were in their own little world where their cat and wolf differences didn't matter even though she had been sick half the time.

"Now, eat."

Damien sat and picked up his fork. "Thanks for breakfast."

"You're welcome. It's the least I could do to repay you for everything."

She turned to go to the kitchen when Damien yanked her hand, and she spun back around.

The look on his face was very serious.

"Payton, you don't owe me anything."

"Okay." She smiled to assure him.

His face stayed grim. "I'm serious. You don't owe me a single thing."

She dropped her smile. "Okay, I understand."

She didn't understand though, but she'd agreed for his sake. His behavior was strange. She sure felt like she owed him.

"Are you all right?"

He let go of her hand. "Yeah."

She didn't quite believe him, but she moved to go back to the kitchen.

"Payton?"

She stopped and looked over her shoulder. "Yes?"

"I also want you to know that I did all this because I wanted to, not for any other reason. Please remember that."

Again, it was an odd thing to say, but it obviously meant something to him.

"Okay, Damien, I'll remember." She smiled again to reassure him.

He visibly relaxed, and she headed toward the kitchen to get her own breakfast. When she returned to the table, Damien was back to his usual self, and they ate breakfast in ease.

After they finished and cleaned up the kitchen, Damien asked, "Since we're stuck inside, would you like to play a game?"

"A game? Oh," she said, wiggling her eyebrows.

He laughed. "Not that kind of game."

"Oh." Payton stuck out her lip in fake sadness.

Damien simply ignored her and walked over to the built-in cabinet in the corner of the living room. "I'm warning you, these games are old."

"What do you have?"

"Chess, The Game of Life, checkers, Twister—probably not a good idea with your injury—Yahtzee, Monopoly, Operation, and Pictionary, which I think is the newest. Told you they were old."

"Pictionary can't be that new."

Damien picked up the game and flipped it over. "Copyright 1985."

"I wasn't even born yet. See? It's not new."

"Well, I guess I feel old now."

Payton put her hand over her mouth and laughed. "Sorry."

"I'm just giving you shit." He set the game back down. "So, what do you want to play?"

"Hmm…Monopoly, I guess."

First, they played Monopoly, and then Damien picked Yahtzee.

When it was Payton's turn again, she picked Operation.

They were down to only two body parts—the pencil and the leg bone. Damien had two more pieces than her, so if he got this one, he would win. After some thinking, he went for the pencil in Writer's Cramp.

He almost removed it completely when Payton heard the buzzer for a split second.

Damien quickly took the pencil from the tweezers and wrapped it up in his fist. "I win," he said with a smug grin.

Payton laughed. "No, you didn't. I heard the buzzer."

"I think your ears are playing tricks on you."

"I don't think so. It's my turn."

Damien shook his head, grinning.

Payton stood up and put her hands on her hips to show she meant business. It was hard because she really wanted to laugh, but she managed to keep a straight face. "Damien."

"Payton."

She walked around the corner of the table to him. He had been sitting with the side of his chair against the table, so she was now facing him.

She held out her palm. "Hand it over."

"You wish. I didn't know you were such a sore loser."

She huffed. "I am not a sore loser. You cheated."

She reached for his hand, but he was quicker than her.

"You're going to have to be faster than that," he teased.

She could no longer pretend to be serious, and she laughed as she made a grab for the tweezers again. He pulled his hand up high. He might be taller than her, but she was standing. She reached for it again and succeeded this time, except she ended up on his lap, straddling him.

They were both still laughing until their eyes met. Then, it was as if they were both suddenly very aware of their positions. Their laughter faded, and she felt her heart begin to pound in her chest.

Damien whispered her name, and before she knew it, he was kissing her. He took her mouth like a starved man, and it only fueled the flames in her.

She buried her fingers in his hair as he kissed her. It was deep and penetrating, full of tongue, teeth, and lips. No one had ever kissed her like this. The achy hot feeling she'd first noticed this morning intensified. Something told her it was important, but she brushed it aside. Kissing Damien felt too good to waste time thinking about anything else.

He stood up while keeping his hold on her, and she wrapped her arms around his neck to hang on. He swept his arm across the table and pushed the game onto the floor. It landed with a loud thump, but it hardly registered as dirty thoughts took over her brain.

Damien laid her down on the table. Then, he repositioned himself to one side of her legs to prop his hip against the table, and he leaned over her. He broke their kiss and ran his lips down her neck to her shoulder where he sucked her skin into his mouth. He kissed the bare skin on her chest. He paused to unbutton the top of her shirt, and he pulled it aside to reveal her breasts. He studied them for a second before he sucked a nipple into his mouth. She didn't know what was hotter—his intense focus on her breasts or the actual feel of him taking her in his mouth.

While he used his mouth on her, he moved his hand down her side— over her ribs, her waist, her hip, and down her leg. He stopped when he reached the bottom of the shirt. He put his hand underneath and caressed his way up, but then he stopped at her hip. He kept his hand on the spot and didn't move.

It was torture.

At this point, she could hear the sounds that she was making as she opened her legs and arched her hips. She didn't care if she was begging. She wanted him to touch her where it mattered most.

Damien stopped kissing her chest, and he brought his head up to look her in the eyes, his crystal-blue ones almost translucent. Only then did he slowly move his hand until it was between her legs. She held her breath. He gradually eased two fingers into her, and her breath came out in a rush. Her eyes rolled to the back of her head, and she almost came right there.

It was as if he knew she was ready to explode because he didn't move. She locked eyes with him again, and he stroked. Their eye contact was beyond hot.

"You're so wet. I can't wait to get inside you."

She moaned and almost came again.

Damien smiled. "Damn, you're tight. I don't want to hurt you."

Holy crap. This was actually going to happen.

"That's because I'm a virgin," she managed to say through her desire, "but I'm confident you'll fit."

Damien stilled. "Say what now?"

Chapter Fourteen

*P*ayton watched as Damien stopped touching her and stood.

Oh, great.

He was going to act like every other guy she had read about in her romance novels and had seen on TV. He was going to back away because he wanted to do the noble thing. She was a virgin at freaking twenty-three years old, and it was the twenty-first century. The only decent thing to do would be to take her virginity. She'd been making due with everything but sex for long enough.

Payton sat up, pulling her shirt together. She started buttoning it as she prepared herself for some self-righteous speech from him.

The last thing that she'd expected was for Damien to remove his shirt. He threw it on the back of his chair and then slipped off his shorts.

She about swallowed her tongue when she saw the size of his erection. It wasn't the first penis she had ever seen, but there was no wonder as to why he had worried about fitting inside her. It was long and thick, and the head was broader than the rest, thanks to what had to be his wolf genetics.

Damien put his finger under her chin to tilt her eyes up. He tried to hide it, but he had a self-satisfied smile on his face.

She would be pleased, too, if she were him.

"Take off your shirt, Payton."

"Uh…am I missing something?"

Damien started unbuttoning her shirt for her. He pulled the sides apart and pushed it off her shoulders. "Nope. It looks like you have everything we need."

She put her hands on his chest. "Are we really doing this?"

He picked up her hands and kissed them. "Oh, we're doing this, baby girl." He sat down and pulled her until her legs were on either side of him.

"You don't care that I'm a virgin?"

"I care." He rubbed his hand down her cheek, her chest, and her hip where he wrapped his fingers around her waist. "I very much care, and that's why we're doing it this way. I want you to be in control." He drew her closer and looked up at her face. "I don't want to hurt you."

Wow. This was the last thing that she had thought would happen after he backed away from her. She was dazed and full of anticipation.

Damien made no other moves, so she reached down, took his penis in her hand, and stroked him. He closed his eyes, and his head fell back as he moaned. She kept going, and she worried he'd stop her, but he didn't.

She put one foot on the outside rung of the chair. She stopped rubbing but held on to him. He lifted his head and opened his eyes. She positioned herself above him and slowly sank down, feeling him stretching her. There was a slight discomfort, but she felt only a sweet pain, aware that he was the one who filled her.

She let go of him and put both hands on his shoulders. He put his other hand on her waist, but he didn't force her to move. He let her go at her own pace.

It seemed to take forever, but eventually, he was completely inside her. She felt incredibly full, and it was intensely erotic to know that she had this man within her body.

Her virginity was finally a thing of the past.

Payton put her other foot on the opposite rung and used her feet to slowly move up and down. She moaned and uttered the words, "Holy shit."

Damien smiled. "I know, baby girl. I know." He kissed her again.

She wrapped her arms around his neck. She used him and the chair as leverage, and she began to ride him faster. It felt so good. Payton might have been a virgin, but she hadn't been completely celibate her whole life. She had fooled around, and she owned several toys. But nothing could have prepared her for the feeling of actual sex—or maybe it was the feeling of actual sex with Damien.

She felt herself getting closer to coming, and she broke their kiss. There was no way she could concentrate on both. She continued to ride him, but it was as if her orgasm was just out of reach. She could brush her fingers against the promise of sweet release, but she couldn't quite seize hold of it.

Damien moved one of his hands up her spine, and he cupped the back of her neck. He used his other hand to put one of her feet on the floor, and then he brought his arm up to envelop her waist. He took control of her movements. He tilted her pelvis slightly and pushed himself in farther, grinding them together. It was as if he'd hit a detonator deep inside her. After a few thrusts, the bomb went off.

Boom.

"Fuck," Damien muttered.

Her back arched as the spasms racked her body, and she would have fallen off him if he hadn't been holding her. She felt her claws extend, and she scratched Damien's upper back and shoulders, but she wasn't able to hold her grip on him.

She swiftly regained her grasp and clung to him again as he drove into her a few more times before finding his own climax. His seed was hot and wet and filled her to the point of overflowing. But none of him escaped because the next thing she knew, he was expanding. She could feel it. His erection was so large that it almost caused her pain, yet at the same time, it was brazenly carnal.

He was a wolf, and he had tied himself to her.

She had only heard about it, of course. Just like their full wolf cousins, wolf-shifters would create a knot when they ejaculated. The knot consisted of erectile tissue, like the penis itself, which would swell and lock inside a female. In wolves, the male would be unable to separate from the female until the knot subsided. In wolf-shifters, the knot was actually Mother Nature's implement to induce ovulation when the female was in mating heat. The male would withdraw during the knot's presence, causing it to scrape the sides of the female shifter to tell her body that it was time to reproduce. After generations, it no longer worked as it was supposed to—

like cat-shifter barbs—but the knots still existed.

Although Payton wasn't in heat and she had no plans to be pregnant, especially outside of a mating, she couldn't help but feel explicitly bonded to Damien. Possibly, the female part of her that had just lost her maidenhood felt that way. She was so unbelievably tight around him that she doubted he would be able to pull out. That was probably another sign of her virginity.

Damien stood and urged her to grip his waist with her legs as he carried her to the bedroom. He laid them on the bed with her on her back since they were still connected.

He put her arms over her head and twined their hands together. "Are you okay?" His diamond eyes were bright with concern.

She smiled. "Oh, yes."

"Good." He leaned down and kissed her, slow and steady.

He broke the kiss.

She asked, "I thought you were going to let me have control out there?"

The corner of his mouth perked up. "You seemed like you needed a little help." He kissed her again. "Do you forgive me?"

She laughed. "You are more than forgiven."

This time, she kissed him, but she stopped when she felt Damien's knot subside. He was still hard, but the pressure inside her had lessened. She clicked her tongue, making a tsk sound.

Damien chuckled. "Don't worry, baby girl. I'm not done with you yet."

By the middle of the afternoon, Damien and Payton lay in bed, exhausted and satiated. She was on her back with her eyes closed as she purred. The air smelled like sex and lavender—and him. He could smell himself everywhere on Payton.

His wolf was very pleased.

Yet her lavender scent was stronger than normal. He noticed that it was even more powerful than yesterday. Something told him that it was significant, but he didn't know why. He didn't care that much because the scent only made him want her more.

He'd made love to her twice more since the kitchen, and judging by her relaxed state, she was completely satisfied. But he had already figured that out by how hard her pussy squeezed his cock when she came and by how many times she had come. He knew she didn't have anything to compare it to, and that pleased the fuck out of him. His male ego was beating its chest due to the fact that he was the only one to ever be inside her.

He'd be wearing a shit-eating grin if it weren't for one thing.

Damien picked up Payton's hand. "I should probably apologize for not being a gentleman and for making your first time happen in a chair."

She stopped purring and rolled onto her side. She put her hand on his chest and used her forefinger to trace his wolf tattoo. "In case you didn't know, a gentleman is the last thing I wanted." She paused and held up a finger. "I don't want some barbarian though." She resumed her tracing. "But those gentlemen I dated didn't work out, remember? I actually thought that once you found out I was a virgin, you were going to go all honorable on me, call a halt, and leave me high and dry."

Damien turned on his side to face her. "Maybe that's what I should have done, but I wanted you too much."

He ran his finger down the side of her face, and she closed her eyes with a sigh.

"There's just something about you, Payton. I can't figure it out, and I don't even know if I want to." He couldn't even stand the thought of her being with another man, but the reality of a wolf and a cat mating was controversial.

Her eyes flickered open, and she placed her hand over his. "I feel it, too, Damien. I don't know what it is either, but I do know I like it."

He leaned in to kiss her, and she put her hand on his back to pull him close. He wasn't prepared, and he winced. The wound on his back still had not healed. After several days, it should have fully healed, but it felt as bad as the night when he had gotten it. He'd been so consumed with Payton that he didn't worry about it too much, and now was not the time. He didn't want to burden her with his problems. He turned onto his back, so she couldn't see anything.

"What's wrong? Did I hurt you with my claws?"

"No, it's not a big deal. I'll heal." He hoped. "I like your claws." He smiled. "It lets me know I'm doing it right."

Payton laughed, rolled on top of his chest, and kissed him. She seemed to forget about his back, and he was relieved.

"Payton?"

"Yes?"

"Are you sure you're okay with this?"

"What do you mean?"

"Your father. I don't want to cause a problem with your family." Family was important to shifters, and he didn't want her to regret being with him.

"My family isn't here. While I respect their opinions, I'm an adult, and there's nowhere I'd rather be than right here with you." She smiled. "Plus, we can always take multiple showers to wash our scents off of each other."

He growled. He liked his scent on her.

She grinned as if she knew what he was thinking.

"Let's not worry about that now," she whispered.

He flipped her over. "Deal." He kissed her again.

Chapter Fifteen

"Can we go home yet?"

Sawyer didn't bother replying to Kenzie's question. They both knew they weren't going anywhere.

"I think I might die of boredom."

"Not if I murder you first," he said from his spot on the floor at the foot of the bed. He was messing with a clock radio, hoping it would give them some clue of their location.

Kenzie, who was lying on the bed doing nothing, sat up on her elbows. "I heard that."

Sawyer closed his eyes with a sigh. The room was too damn small, and they were getting sick of each other. Four days was too long to be stuck with the same person. In the beginning, they had done a good job of pretending to be a couple, but now, it was getting harder because they could barely stand to be around each other.

He turned around and scowled at her. "Don't tell me you don't feel the same."

"You're right. I do." She flopped back down. "I never thought that I would get so sick of TV, but I would kill to go outside."

"Right now, I would kill for some decent food. The snack bars they keep sending through the hole in the door aren't enough."

"Is that why you're being such a dick?"

Sawyer gritted his teeth.

"Oh, yeah, you were a dick before. But starving you definitely doesn't help your demeanor."

"Well, maybe if you'd quit complaining and try to think of a plan, we'd have a chance of getting out of here."

"I already figured out there were video cameras. It's your turn to do something."

Sawyer flew up to stand over the bed. "Are you fucking kidding me?" He curled his hands into fists because they wanted to wrap themselves around her neck. "I've been trying to get us out of here every night. While you're sleeping your pretty little head off, I'm working."

She looked him squarely in the eyes and raised one eyebrow. "You suck at your job then."

He was pretty sure smoke was coming out of his ears. She was unbelievable. He was grateful there were no microphones because the next sound out of him was purely animalistic.

The smirk fell from her face as her eyes went wide, and her face filled with alarm. She immediately rolled up onto her knees. "Uh…Sawyer, I was just teasing you. I'm just bored, okay?" She lifted her hands as he moved closer. "I didn't mean to make you mad."

"I always knew that mouth of yours was going to get you into trouble."

She scooted back on the bed. "I'm sorry."

"Too late." He lunged for her.

She almost made it off the bed, but he caught her around the ankle.

"Sawyer."

He dragged her to him.

"Wait."

He ignored her and yanked her closer. She looked ridiculous, like a little kid. Their selection of garments was limited, and all of the clothing hung on her like a little kid dressed in her older sister's clothing, too big for her short and slender frame, causing her to drown in them. But Kenzie definitely had the sass of a woman, and she needed to be taught a lesson.

"Stop," she pleaded.

He hauled her over his shoulder and headed for the bathroom. A cold shower might cool off her hot mouth.

Kenzie beat on his back, and Sawyer slapped her on the ass.

"*Ow*," she screeched. "That hurt."

He grunted. "It was supposed to hurt."

When they reached the bathroom, Sawyer pulled the shower curtain open, reached for the faucet—

"Before you do anything rash, remember that I'm your pregnant wife."

He paused.

"*Damn it.*"

The reality that a decent male wouldn't do that to his pregnant mate cooled his temper somewhat. Then, he felt Kenzie relax. She thought she'd won. His irritation rose again. Since he couldn't hurt her, he did the only thing he could think of to relieve his frustration.

He pivoted around and set her on the counter. He didn't give her time to think before he took her mouth in an angry kiss. At first, she didn't react, but then she curled her arms and legs around him and kissed him back.

Desire mixed with her natural lemon scent, giving him a full-on erection. He rubbed himself between her legs, and she moaned against his mouth. She moved her hand down to the front of his jeans and rubbed her hand over his cock. It made his cat go fucking crazy. It was a good thing the man was in control.

He yanked her hand away and put it behind her back. Then, he picked her up with one arm and pulled down her pants with his other. The fragrance of her arousal filled the room, so dark and thick that he could taste it.

Before he even set her down, he had his hand between her legs. Kenzie broke the kiss and threw her head back, panting deeply. He slowly pushed two fingers inside her.

"Oh God," she moaned.

He had her right where he wanted her. In another fit of rage, he had been in a position like this once before, so he knew right where to touch her. He angled his fingers and rubbed while he moved his mouth to her neck. Once he knew she was close, he bit down.

He was prepared for her to come. What he hadn't been prepared for was for her to use her strength to push him away.

She huffed as she jumped off the counter and pulled up her pants.

"What the hell?" He knew her orgasm had been close.

Her pussy squeezing his fingers and the mewling sounds coming from the back of her throat had confirmed that.

She shot him a dirty look. "You're an asshole," she said before she walked back into the bedroom.

He went after her and grabbed her wrist. "Kenzie, what the fuck was that?"

She narrowed her eyes at him and scoffed.

"What is your problem? I know you were close to coming."

She threw his hand off and shoved against his chest. "That's right. *I* was close to coming."

He shook his head and shrugged. "I don't understand. Most women like orgasms."

"Not when they're one-sided."

He dropped her hand and took a step back.

"Oh, that's right. You think that I don't know you, but I do." She stepped forward and poked him in the chest. "You won't let me touch you because you don't want to lose control. You're always so disciplined, always so restrained." She held up her hands and shook them. "God forbid Sawyer ever feels anything or allows himself to enjoy the moment."

He spun, went back into the bathroom, and slammed the door. He took a few calming breaths to avoid the mistake of going back out there and letting her touch him where she wanted.

He couldn't argue with anything she'd said. She was right. His body had loved the feel of her hand on his dick, but he couldn't have let her continue. He couldn't give her that power. It had to be that way. He had already learned his lesson about what happened when he let himself lose control.

And the risk wasn't worth the cost.

Upstairs, Frank watched the monitors. He heard his partner come in behind him. "Wayne, come here. Look, they're fighting."

Wayne whistled. "Looks like there's trouble in paradise. Aren't these two supposed to be newlyweds?"

"Yeah, but they don't act like it."

"For a minute there, it looked like they were going to have sex, but then she pushed him away and started yelling at him."

They both watched the cameras as the husband turned away and stalked into the bathroom. He got into the shower while his wife flopped down onto the bed.

"I actually thought we were going to see some action."

"I know. This job is getting boring."

"Have you heard anything from that Dwyer guy?"

"No. You?"

"Nah, not since the day we took 'em."

Wayne's phone rang, and he checked the screen before picking it up. "Hey, angel."

Frank rolled his eyes and turned his attention back to the monitors.

Wayne got up and left the room. Then, he returned a minute later.

"Hey, man, can I borrow your phone? Mine died on me, and I need to call the girlfriend back."

Frank felt around in his pockets. "Shit, I don't have it."

"Fuck, if I don't call her back, she's going to have my balls."

Frank made the sound of a cracking whip.

"Dude, that's not funny. She's gonna think I hung up on her." Wayne looked around and eyed the two extra cell phones on the counter. "I could use one of theirs."

"No way," Frank protested.

"Oh, come on. One minute. That's all I need."

Frank thought about it for a second. *What would one minute hurt?* In the cop shows, it always took the police at least two minutes to pin the bad guy's location.

"Okay. One minute."

Wayne snatched one of the cells off the table.

"Not that one. It's password-protected."

Wayne threw it down and grabbed the other one. "Thanks, man." Then, he headed into the next room.

Frank only hoped Wayne would stick to the one minute.

From the kitchen, Saxon heard the beeping, and he ran into the living room. Reid was typing furiously on the computer.

"What's going on?"

"Kenzie is using her cell phone—or someone else is using it. Either way, I'm trying to get a location before it goes off again. Thankfully, her smartphone has GPS. If I can't find their location, maybe we can find the person being called by the phone number."

"I'll tell Vance." Saxon turned to leave the room when he heard different beeping. "What's that now?"

Reid picked up Payton's phone. "It's an alert on Payton's calendar."

"What does it say?"

"Just M.H."

"M.H.? What does that mean?"

"I have no idea."

Sawyer stepped out of the shower, got dressed, and walked into the bedroom to tell Kenzie he was sorry. After having time to think in the shower, he felt guilty for his actions and wanted to apologize.

Kenzie had her back to him, so he cleared his throat to get her to turn around. He figured she would still be mad, but her face lit up like a light bulb.

"Sawyer, I think I have a plan."

This was unexpected. "Okay," he said hesitantly.

"You were right. I haven't been helping. But I have an idea."

"Okay. What is it?"

"Um…well, it's kind of disgusting. Since they can't hear us, I think it might be the only way to get their attention."

"Let's hear it." He didn't care if he had to wade through shit. He would do anything to get out of there.

"Okay. First, I was trying to figure out a way to cut myself, but they haven't left us with anything sharp. I'm due to get my period any day now though."

Sawyer curled his lip.

"Hey, I told you that it was kind of gross."

He didn't really think it was disgusting. It was a part of nature, and it was connected with the creation of new life. Half of him was animal. Most humans were the ones who thought it was offensive, but they didn't know how lucky they were to have the opportunity to conceive once a month.

Sawyer's revulsion was with the bastards who had kidnapped them. A female's time was a private matter between mates, and he didn't like her having to involve their captors.

Rather than explain that, he told her, "Sorry."

"So, Aunt Flo is due soon, and when she makes her appearance, I can pretend like I'm miscarrying or having problems with the baby. Our captors haven't hurt us yet, so I'm hoping they will do the right thing, like take me to a hospital. We'll have to get their attention through the cameras, but if they're watching, they will see blood. Hopefully, they'll come and open the door, and when they do—"

"I'll shift and attack them."

"Yes." She slapped her hands together. "Do you think it could work?"

It wasn't the best idea in the world, but it was all they had. "We have nothing to lose by trying."

And everything to gain.

Chapter Sixteen

*D*amien stirred sluggishly, feeling hot, and wondered if it was simply déjà vu. He shook off the sleep and discovered that Payton was giving off an enormous amount of heat again. She moaned in her sleep, and he shot up in bed to check her wounds. They should be fine. After all, they were almost completely healed. He really didn't want her to be sick with a fever again.

He looked at both injuries and discovered that he was right. Her wounds were both fine. She was radiating a ton of heat, but her forehead was cool. It wasn't an infection. It was something else.

He released the breath he hadn't realized he'd been holding, and he noticed the smell. He couldn't believe he'd missed it. The room was pungent with the scent of female and sex. It was now obvious why Payton's scent had been getting stronger and why she was hot.

His dick was as hard as a rock in response.

"Payton"—he shook her arm—"wake up."

"Damien," she spoke his name but remained half asleep. She moved her hand down until she grabbed his naked erection.

"Oh, shit." He closed his eyes and arched up into her hand. He put his hand on her wrist to stop her, but stopping was next to impossible with her pheromones flying and her touching him.

It wasn't until she climbed on top of him and was about to take him inside her body that his senses snapped back to the moment.

He rolled them both over and made sure to lie on her side instead of between her legs. "Payton," he almost shouted.

She opened her eyes but didn't make eye contact. "Damien?" She was in a hormone-induced haze.

"Payton, listen to me."

"Hot." She kicked off the covers as best as she could.

"I know, baby girl."

She finally looked at him and smiled. "Damien," she whispered. She gripped his hand and placed it between her legs.

"Fuck."

She was dripping wet, swollen, and oh-so hot.

"Please. I ache."

Damien flew off the bed. He could barely control his hunger for her. He had to get her attention. She had to know what was going on before they made a mistake.

He grabbed Payton by the shoulders and forced her to sit up. She wouldn't meet his gaze, so he shook her. "Payton, you're in mating heat. You have to wake up."

Her eyes shot open. She looked at him and down at herself before she scrambled to the other side of the bed. She put her hand over her mouth. "Oh no."

"That's putting it mildly." Damien stood up and glanced down at his hard-on. It wasn't going away anytime soon. It was responding to the fertile female in the room, and it wanted to do what it was made for. Walking around fully erect for the next few days was going to make taking a leak a bitch.

But that wasn't the biggest problem. How were they going to keep their hands off of each other? Usually, a male didn't see a female through her heat unless they were mated, and a single female stayed away from all males when she was in heat.

Payton put her hands on her head and groaned. "I should've known. I've been hot and achy, but I thought it was just leftover from my fever."

"Haven't you ever gone through mating heat before?"

Shifters hit puberty around twenty-one years of age, so if Payton was twenty-three, she should have experienced it before and known the signs.

"Only once." She put a hand on her pelvis. "Holy crap, I don't remember it being this bad."

"It's me."

She lifted her head. "What?"

"I'm assuming your mother kept all males away during your previous mating heat?"

She nodded.

"Your first time is about half as strong, and with no males around, there was no one to respond. In turn, you didn't have anyone to respond to. Being a virgin probably didn't hurt either." He ran his hands threw his hair. "Shit, I wish I had known." He wasn't sure what he would have done with that bit of information, but it would have been nice to know.

Payton moaned. "I'm sorry. This is entirely my fault."

Damien walked around to the side of the bed where she sat, and he scooped her up. "Payton, in no way is this your fault. If my—" He stopped himself from saying his father. "If you hadn't been put in this situation in the first place, you would be at home and not here with me."

She studied him. "Thank you for understanding."

She arched and kissed him. It was just a peck, but the contact was all they needed for the kiss to turn fervent. He was so ready to lift her and shove himself inside her that it was all he could do to find the strength to step back.

They were both panting as Damien backed away.

Payton wrapped her arms around herself. "What are we going to do?"

Now, that was the million-dollar question, wasn't it?

Dante turned up the music blaring through his headphones and reached for the barbell to finish his last bench-press set. He hoped listening to Tool while working out would relieve some of his stress, but if the training session he had completed half an hour ago didn't help, he doubted this one would either. He'd thought some time alone would help him clear his head, but it only made him reflect on the current situation.

Despite the conversation he'd had with everyone the night the princess and her mate arrived, the tension in the house was palpable. Naya was wonderful and got along with everyone. Everybody loved her. Though Vaughn struggled with his restrictions, he had started to adapt.

Dante understood Vaughn wanted to be out with the rest of the sentinels, doing something about the situation. Dante could also tell it was hard for Vaughn to be around the male Guardians. Vaughn was an alpha, and the male Guardians were dominant. Dante couldn't imagine how he would feel being confined with a bunch of shifter sentinels in a strange place where he had no authority. Yet Vaughn was courteous and treated them with respect. He'd even worked off some of his frustrations by sparring with some of the Guardians.

No, neither Naya nor Vaughn was the problem. It was the female cat Vaughn had brought with him. Just the thought of her set Dante's teeth on edge. Phoenix had no qualms with showing her distrust and resentment about her alpha's decision to place her here.

Ram had told him the other night, "If she were male, she'd have cojones the size of basketballs."

Dante needed to stop thinking about her because it only made him mad. He didn't want her here any more than she wanted to be here. Her attitude was affecting everyone, and she was so deep in his thoughts at this point that he swore he smelled her. She smelled like the sun, her scent matching her hair and fiery personality. It was a shame because before his conversion into an adult vampire, he had liked the sun.

He finished his last press and set the bar down. Sitting up, he yanked out his earbuds and then grabbed his towel from the floor to wipe the sweat off his face.

"That was pretty impressive."

He stilled at the sound of those words. They sounded like a compliment, but the words dripped with sarcasm. At least he knew why he had smelled sunlight. Phoenix had come down to the weight room and snuck in while he wasn't paying attention.

Dante was grateful that his face was hidden behind his towel because she had surprised him, which didn't help his mood. It took everything in Dante to remain well-mannered when she was around. He had a group of people he was responsible for, and she stirred them up.

Not wanting her to know how he felt, he slowly lowered the cloth and calmly replied, "Thank you."

She ground her teeth and stepped farther into the room but didn't say anything.

Dante turned off his iPod and leisurely stood up from the bench as if he didn't have a care in the world. "Can I help you with something?"

She eyed him up and down as if he were a bug on her shoe. "Yeah, you can put on a shirt."

This time, he gritted his teeth. While Dante knew he wouldn't win a beauty contest, the females never seemed to complain, and he had never wanted for their attention. His brown hair and brown eyes along with his Mediterranean skin tone gave him a rugged, dark look. He was six-three and muscular. The front of his chest possessed a scar that ran from one shoulder down to his opposite hip before disappearing under his workout shorts. Females always told him that his looks along with his scar were attractive.

But a part of him always despised his scar, and her comment made him want to cover it. He hated that she made him feel self-conscious about his body. Just because she was insecure with herself didn't mean she had to project it onto others. If she didn't like what she saw, she could get the fuck out.

"I don't believe I asked you to come down here. You came on your own." He turned away, dismissing her, and headed for the showers.

In the washroom, he went to the corner where his other clothes hung. He had his thumbs in the waistband, about to discard his shorts, when he felt her enter the room behind him. *Now, I can't even shower in peace?* "What?" he snapped. "Can't you see I'm trying to clean up?"

She scoffed. "I'm a shifter. Nudity doesn't bother me."

"If you say so." He pushed down his shorts.

He turned and headed for the first stall, and Phoenix sucked in her breath. He strode past her and smirked. He might be uncomfortable about his scar, but he was definitely secure about his cock. Even flaccid, it wasn't small.

She reached out and gently touched his arm, causing him to stop mid-step.

"What do you want?" he snarled over his shoulder.

Dante thought her touch would be ice cold to match her demeanor, but it was warm. The heat traveled from his arm down to his groin, and he hardened instantly. For the first time, he noticed her pulse beating in her neck. He'd never wanted to feed from a non-vampire before, and he didn't want to start now, yet he found himself fantasizing about the flavor of her blood.

It only pissed him off more.

She must have sensed a change in him because her emerald eyes lost some of their ire. Her next words were spoken softly, "Vaughn is busy with Naya, and I was just wondering if you would spar with me. I should've asked right away. I'm…" For a second, he thought she might apologize. "I need to burn off some energy."

He almost laughed. If she had asked him five minutes ago, he would have said yes. Instead, she'd given him attitude, she'd made him doubt himself, and worst of all, she'd made him want her.

He shook her hand off and flashed a fang. "Go find someone else to play with, and leave me alone. I have more important things to do."

He walked into the stall and closed the curtain. The only other sound was the door closing as she left the room.

Dante turned on the faucet and let the cool water pour down his body. His reaction to Phoenix was unwanted and most likely unrequited. He shook it off as a fluke.

One thing was for sure though. He needed to find a female, so he could feed and fuck—he looked down at his hard dick—soon.

Chapter Seventeen

Payton had experienced a migraine headache only once, but it was something she'd never forget. She'd been sitting in class when she felt a headache coming, and she'd figured she would be able to make it to the end of class, but when the migraine had hit her, she had felt shocked by the intensity. Her head had pounded, the lights had burned her eyes, and she had been positive she'd puke. The coherent part of her had known she only had fifteen minutes left of class, and if she could just make it to the end, she'd be done for the day. But the pain had become so great that it took simply too much effort to concentrate on anything besides the pounding inside her skull. If she'd absolutely had to stay, say if it were life and death, she would have made it, but because she hadn't had to tough it out, she had left class early.

The pain she endured now had the same theme. Her rational side said that she would survive and go on, but the irrational side swore that death was around the corner, and if it wasn't, she wanted it to be just so she wouldn't have to suffer any longer. The ache in her pelvis had gone from dull twinges to sharp spasms, and the pain, the need, inside her was overwhelming. All she could do was lie on the bed and pray that she would black out because she wasn't going to move unless the cabin was on fire or her heat ended.

Payton didn't remember mating heat being half this bad the first time. Sure, she had been sexually aroused, but she had pulled through it. She had actually wondered what all the fuss was about.

Now, she knew and wished she hadn't. The heat was so strong. She felt full and empty at the same time, and her cat scratched under her skin, wanting the misery to end. She was so horny that she was ready to hump the bedpost, yet she didn't have the strength. As humiliating as that would be, she knew it wouldn't help. Her body wanted a flesh-and-blood male.

Mother Nature had really screwed up when she created this process, a process that was now failing. Thousands of years ago, shifters could count on having many children even with the female's fertile time being only twice a year. But the wolf-shifter knot and the cat-shifter barbs no longer really caused a female shifter to ovulate when she was in heat, not the way it had centuries ago, and it didn't seem fair that she had to suffer over something that was nearly broken.

Then, because it was hard for shifters to procreate, there were no contraceptives for them. Hormone birth control only worked on humans, and condoms were pretty much out of the question with their anatomy. Since she was unmated, there were ways to ease her heat, such as keeping all males away, like her parents had the first time. She'd heard about females taking muscle relaxants, anti-anxiety drugs, or sedatives to help them through their mating heat. Unfortunately, she didn't have access to any of those at the moment.

She hadn't realized what a difference it made to be around a male. She would never underestimate the power of pheromones again. To top it off, she was exhausted. She still wasn't fully recovered from her wounds, and she hadn't been able to sleep the night before. Poor Damien had left the cabin after discovering she was in heat. She didn't know if he'd spent the night in his truck or if he had turned into his wolf and slept outside. She doubted he could have gotten very far with the snow being so high, and she hoped he was safe and warm.

Payton heard the front door open. For a second, she felt a quick wave of relief as cold air passed through the room and swept over her hot body. She had spent the night naked and minus any covers. Her body was on fire, and her skin was too sensitive. There was more than one reason it was termed *mating heat*. The wind from outside cooled her, but unfortunately, it didn't last long.

The front door closed, and the breeze from outside was gone. When she smelled Damien, her uterus contracted, and she couldn't control the cry that escaped her lips. She bit her hand to stifle her moans. She didn't want Damien to know she was in pain, especially because she knew he was suffering, too. She grabbed a pillow and curled up into a ball, trying to will away her pain.

"Payton."

She looked up to see Damien standing in the doorway—naked and hard. "Oh God."

He took a step into the room.

She held up her hand. "Unless you have a gun that you plan to shoot me with, you should leave and save yourself."

Damien stepped farther into the bedroom. She saw that his wolf was close. His pupils were larger, and each crystal-blue iris was encompassing the whole eye.

"Payton, I...I don't know what to do," he said as he opened and closed his fists. "I tried to stay away, but I can't get far enough not to smell you, not with all the snow out there."

She dropped her hand and clutched a fistful of the sheet as her pelvis tightened. "Make it stop. Please, make it stop," she begged.

"Fuck. I want to, more than you know, and we both know I can." He ran his hand over his face. "But, Payton, there are consequences. Do you realize that?"

"Am I ovulating? Can you smell it?"

"No, but—"

"Just in case, don't withdraw your knot, and it won't stimulate ovulation. Then, I shouldn't get pregnant."

His penis bounced as if it knew she was talking about it, and he scrubbed his hands through his hair. "You're killing me. Just because I won't get you pregnant doesn't mean there won't be ramifications." He dropped his hands. "Payton, it's more than that. It's called mating heat for a reason. It's intended to take place between mates. If we do this, you are going to smell like me—for a long time, possibly until your next heat— and no amount of bathing is going to make it go away. Not only will your body accept my seed, it's also going to accept my scent, my mark, everything. Do you understand what I am saying?" He paced from one side of the room to the other. "Your family will know that you had sex outside of a mating, and everyone will know that you slept with a wolf. Are you prepared to deal with those repercussions?"

He probably thought that his words would turn her away, but it only made her want him. The thought of him all over her—in her hair, in her skin, deep inside her—only made her desire him more. Maybe it was the hormones talking, but there was no one else she wanted to be with during her heat.

She only had one question. "Will you smell like me, too?"

"Yes, but you will wear my scent longer than I will wear yours."

"Would you care?"

Damien paused for only a second. "Hell no."

Payton pushed herself up, and she got off the bed. She walked over to Damien and pressed her body against his. "I can't think of anyone I want more than you to see me through this. I would be proud to wear your scent."

She didn't have to tell him twice.

The air was scented with her arousal, and her skin was flushed. She was a wet dream come true.

Damien swept Payton up and practically threw her onto the bed. He immediately settled over her. He knew it only made the mating heat worse to orgasm without the male, but her scent had invaded his senses, and he spread her legs to put his mouth directly on her core. Her pussy was hot and puffy, and she came instantaneously.

She tasted incredible, and he didn't want to stop, but he knew he had to. He crawled up her body and knelt between her legs. He wasn't even inside, and he felt her wetness.

He paused, the reality of what he was about to do weighing heavily on his shoulders. Payton's family would know for sure that he had lain with their unmated daughter. They would know he had aided her during her mating heat, risked getting her pregnant, and left his mark on her. The shifter community was less traditional than the vampires but not as progressive as some humans, and she was still the daughter of the alpha. After today, they would know she was no longer a virgin.

There was also the reality that he would most likely be ruining any chance he had of bringing his pack home. He was only one wolf out of hundreds, but he was the alpha's son and heir. He should know better. How would the pack ever be able to look up to him after this? He would be betraying them to lie with a female. When she'd asked him if he cared if he smelled like her, he'd meant it when he said no. In fact, he'd be proud to wear her scent, and he couldn't deny that he loved his scent would be on her to warn other males away. But that had been before the actuality of what he was about to do set in. Now, he was second-guessing his actions.

Then, Payton lifted her lashes and looked at him. Her deep blue eyes were almost feverish. She tried to smile through her pain even though tremors racked her body as her womb contracted.

The man was concerned about the repercussions, but his wolf pushed the man's reservations away. Nothing was more important than Payton and her needs.

Screw her family and his pack. *She comes first.*

He recognized what that meant, but he couldn't dwell on that now.

"It's almost over, baby girl," he told her as he placed her legs over his. He lifted her hand and kissed her palm. Then, he picked up her other hand, weaved their fingers together, and pushed their hands above her head. "I'm going to make you feel good and take away all your pain," he said as he thrust inside her.

His movement pressed her legs up, bending them at her hips and driving him in to the hilt. He cursed at the sweet sensation, wanting to enjoy the way she felt around his thick erection, but he wouldn't let her suffer any longer. He stroked in and out of her to bring himself to orgasm as quickly as possible.

It was a good thing that was his goal because he wouldn't have lasted long anyway. He'd been suffering with a hard-on since the night before, and he was ready to burst from the worst case of blue balls he'd ever experienced.

Payton moaned, arched her back, and exposed her neck. She probably didn't realize what she was doing, but she was offering him the gift to bite her, mark her, show the world she was his.

God, he wanted to bite down, and the need to do it surprised him. He barely resisted, but her invitation to claim her was enough to send him over the edge. His orgasm triggered hers, and she bucked underneath him. The swelling of his cock formed a knot, creating a tie between them, and her pussy clamped down with the strength of her climax. He poured himself inside her, and she absorbed everything he gave.

He let go of her hands and dropped down onto his elbows. Since he couldn't bite her, he kissed and sucked on her neck as she continued to throb around him while he waited for his knot to subside. Despite the fact that scraping a female's walls didn't always cause ovulation like it used to centuries ago, he wasn't going to risk getting her pregnant. He was already going to have to take her home and face her father with the knowledge that he'd had sex with the man's daughter while she was in mating heat of all things. Damien didn't need to bring her home unmated and with child, too.

After a minute or so, the air in the room thinned out. He could still smell her arousal, but it wasn't as rich—for now. He felt her body relax, and she began to purr.

He lifted his head to look at her. "Baby girl, how do you feel?"

Her eyes fluttered open, and a small smile crossed her face. "There are no words."

He laughed. "Everything okay?"

"Mmm…I'm much better." She yawned. "Just tired."

Damien felt his knot recede, and he slowly pulled out of her. She was still swollen and tight, and her body didn't seem to want to let go of his.

He lay down next to her. "You should try to get some rest. You won't have too long before you'll need me again. We probably waited too long, so we'll have some catching up to do."

Payton blinked. "You mean, it's not over? I always understood that it doesn't last as long when you have a male serving you."

The corner of his mouth lifted. "That's true, but it still lasts a couple of days, and you'll need me every few hours until your heat passes."

Her eyebrows arched. "I guess I should've paid more attention when my mother explained the birds and the bees." She wrinkled her nose. "But it was my mom. Who wants to talk about sex with her mom?"

Damien chuckled. "Not me." He rolled on his side and tucked Payton against him. "Sleep, baby girl. We're both going to need it."

Chapter Eighteen

Isabelle looked over her shoulder at the dark blond cat chasing after her. It felt wonderful to be outside even if the snow on the ground hindered their movements. The wind in her hair was cool but uplifting. They had to be quite a sight—wolf and cat running around and playing with each other.

When Zane had asked if she wanted to shift and run around in the new snow, she'd thought that she must have been dreaming. She'd been confined to the house since she arrived, and then it had snowed the whole day before, leaving Zane and her trapped inside together.

This morning, when they had woken up and seen that the storm stopped and the sun was shining brightly, he had suggested going outside. She liked to see it as some kind of truce. He still hadn't given back her things, and she still slept in his bed. However, he seemed to trust a bit more that she meant what she'd said when she told him she wouldn't leave.

She considered asking him if she could sleep somewhere else because he might give in. But she found she liked lying next to him at night, so part of her didn't want him to say yes. It was crazy, but she couldn't help herself. He was male and warm, and being near him at night would keep her needs at bay, especially when she would wake in the morning with his arm around her. Maybe it felt too good to be close to him.

But she was sure she would feel that way about anyone at this point. She wasn't going to stress out about it. Damien would call, she'd go back to her life, and then any thoughts of Zane would quickly fade. As soon as she got home, she would find a nice, gentlemanly wolf to sate her hunger. Everything would be fine soon.

A truck making its way down the driveway interrupted Isabelle's thoughts. She stopped mid-stride and stood still to watch it, wondering who could be here. It had only been the two of them since she arrived.

Zane nudged her, and when she didn't move, he nudged her again. She looked at him, and he roared while swinging his head toward the bunkhouse. He wanted her to go inside. She didn't understand why, but she did as he'd asked.

As they got closer, she could sense his urgency. He shifted when they got to the door, and he opened it for her. Once she was out of the cold, she shifted, too. She hadn't seen Zane shift in front of her, and while he slept naked next to her, he was always covered up, so the sight of him without clothes made her mouth water despite the alarm she sensed coming from him.

Thankfully, Zane didn't seem to notice, and he didn't even pay attention to her nudeness. He grabbed his T-shirt and shoved it over her head along with clasping the silver bracelet back on her wrist. The fun cat who liked to mess with her was gone, and in its place was a controlled sentinel. Except for when she had first arrived, she had never seen him so serious. Something was definitely not right.

Zane, in a hurry, yanked on his jeans, leaving them unbuttoned, and he didn't even bother with a shirt. She wished he would put on all his clothes. Despite the fact that something was wrong, she couldn't stop staring at his muscular chest. He was quite hairless for a shifter until his belly button. A trail of dark blond hair disappeared into his jeans, and she wanted to follow it.

She squeezed her thighs together. With no clothes blocking her scent, he was going to sense her arousal very soon.

She needed a distraction. "What's wrong?"

"Someone's here," Zane said as he went to the window and looked outside. "It's Gerald. He went to the main house first, but this will be his next stop."

"Who's Gerald?"

Zane strode over to her, his sea-green eyes bright with keenness. "He's my alpha's cousin. No one likes him. He's always seemed a little off to me, but he's the alpha's family. I'll explain more later. We don't have much time. He'll be here soon." Grabbing her hand, he added, "He's going to wonder why a wolf is here. There's no point in hiding you because he'll smell you right away." He picked up her other hand. "He can't know about your connection to Damien or Payton, okay?"

She nodded at his urgency, and finally, the panic began to overrule her hormones.

"He can't know that Vance knows you're here. He has to think that I'm hiding you. Let me do all the talking, okay?"

Footsteps sounded near the door, and Zane pulled her close.

He spoke in her ear, "We're going to pretend you're my secret lover. It's a good thing you've been sleeping in my bed, so you smell like me. I just hope it's enough."

Again, she nodded. She couldn't talk if she wanted to. His hand had slipped under her shirt to rest on her bare hip with his fingers resting on her naked bottom. Completely focused on their visitor, he didn't even seem to notice where he was touching her. Even with the importance of the information, she couldn't ignore the feel of him on her unclothed skin.

He pushed her shoulder-length hair off her cheek. Mistaking her wide-eyed look for fear instead of a reaction to his touch, he said, "Don't worry. I won't let anything happen to you."

Why would anything happen to me?

Oh, right. She was a wolf in cat territory. All her thoughts were scrambled by his proximity.

He eyed her up and down. "I don't think he saw us outside. Thankfully, we're both blond, and we hopefully blended in with the snow." He rubbed his hand over his mouth. "Don't hate me for this, Isabelle. I'm doing it to keep everyone safe."

Before she could wonder what he had to do that was so bad, he kissed her.

And it wasn't a peck.

He cupped her head and tilted it to take her mouth in a full-on assault. He nipped her bottom lip, and she opened for him with a gasp. He tasted better than she had ever thought a cat could.

She didn't know why he'd apologized to her. The man knew how to kiss. She wrapped her arms around his waist and grabbed on to his back. She wanted to rub against him, but he held himself slightly away from her. After a second, it didn't matter because the door flung open.

Zane drew away and muttered, "I knew the fucker wouldn't knock," a second before he shoved her behind him.

"Oh, sorry, son. I didn't know anyone was here," the man who had to be Gerald said.

Isabelle immediately disliked him, and she curled her fingers in the back of Zane's jeans. She couldn't see Gerald, but she could smell the deceit on him. He smelled completely fake.

Zane stood with his legs spread, and one hand curled into a fist while the other rested protectively on her side. She could feel the tension in him.

"What can I help you with, sir?"

"Who do ya got there?" Gerald inhaled. "Do I smell wolf? You've been keeping a secret, Zane. Tsk-tsk," he spoke the words with a bit of humor as if he were Zane's friend.

Isabelle could picture him waving his finger, too. It was obvious Zane didn't like him. Zane's hands formed fists but immediately relaxed as if he didn't want Gerald to see.

"She is none of your business, sir."

She heard the shuffling of feet, and Zane backed them up a few steps.

"Pretty lady, why don't you come out here and say hi?"

"Tina, you can stay right where you are," Zane said over his shoulder. He must really not trust the guy if he gave her a fake name. He turned back to Gerald. "She's shy."

Gerald sighed when he realized Zane wasn't going to give in.

"Is there anything I can do for you, sir?" Zane asked again.

"Well, son, do you know where I can find Vance? I wanted to check on him."

Both of Zane's hands moved—*clench, release, clench, release.* "Sorry, sir, but I don't know where they are. They didn't tell me, and I'm the only one here."

"Do you have an update on what is going on? Have they found

Vaughn or Payton? I've been so worried. I hope they get home safe."

"I don't know, sir. My responsibility is here. They didn't tell me so that I wouldn't be able to tell anyone who came along and asked questions."

Gerald scoffed. "Surely, you don't think I'm guilty of anything."

"No, sir. It was just an example."

"Well, if you hear from Vance, please let him know that I'm worried, and I would like an update."

"Will do, sir."

"I'll show myself out."

Isabelle heard the door open and close, but Zane didn't move. It wasn't until the sounds of a vehicle starting and then driving away faded that Zane stepped away from her and turned around.

"I need to call Vance," he said and headed for his phone. He picked it up and punched in some numbers. After a moment, Zane spoke again, "Vance, Gerald was here, asking about you."

"What?" Isabelle heard Vance say through the phone. "He was told to go somewhere safe. Did he say what he wanted?"

"He wanted to know where you were and to tell you that he was worried. He also asked about Vaughn and Payton. I didn't tell him anything."

"He was lying," Isabelle said. She knew she shouldn't have interrupted, but Zane hadn't mentioned it.

He pivoted the phone away from his mouth and looked at her. "What?"

"He was lying. He wasn't worried about your alpha or his children."

Zane put the phone back by his mouth. "Did you hear that, boss?"

"How does she know?" Vance asked.

Isabelle was confused. "I could smell it on him. Couldn't you?"

"Zane?" his alpha said.

"Boss, he smelled like he always does. I admit, I don't trust him, but I couldn't smell any dishonesty."

"That probably means he's been deceiving us for quite some time, if he always smells that way. What the hell is that son of a bitch hiding?"

"I don't know, boss, but we'd better find out—and soon."

Chapter Nineteen

*P*ayton was lying in bed when she felt her need rising again. Damien was asleep behind her with his arm slung over her. She tried to stay still because she hated to wake him. She knew he had to be tired. He had relieved her hunger three times already, and the day wasn't over yet.

She closed her eyes and hoped she'd fall back asleep, but after a few minutes, the first spasms began to rack her body. She pushed her mouth into her pillow, so any noises she made would be muffled. The discomfort was relatively minimal compared to how bad her need could get. She could let Damien rest a little longer.

But her body had a different idea. Her cat wanted its wolf. She could detect the musk of her arousal in the air. Damien remained asleep, but she felt his own arousal growing against her bottom. It only caused her desire to rise. Her womb responded, tightening harder this time in anticipation.

He groaned and moved his hand to her breast and squeezed. She moaned as he pinched her nipple before moving his hand back down to her stomach. Payton glanced behind her. Damien's eyes were still closed, but she knew he wasn't fully asleep, yet he wasn't completely awake either.

His dark hair was mussed from their earlier sessions, and a few locks grazed his forehead. She wanted to brush them off, but she didn't want to disturb him. He looked so peaceful. He hadn't shaved since the day before, and she had the beard burn on her body to prove it. She smiled. To her, he was the most handsome male she'd ever laid her eyes upon, and she was beginning to suspect her feelings went past strictly physical attraction.

He was strong yet gentle. He took care of her but didn't baby her. They had fun, but he was also responsible. He was practically perfect— except for the fact that he was a wolf, a banished wolf.

She didn't care, but she knew her father wouldn't be happy. She frowned. Her father loved her, and she wasn't afraid of him, but she knew he'd be troubled, as would the rest of her family, if she brought Damien home.

At that moment, Damien's eyes opened, and the bright blue of them pierced right through her. She hoped he couldn't read her thoughts. She recognized how imperative it was for him to bring his pack back to the Twin Cities. At this point, he probably thought he had given that up for her, which was probably the biggest reason she was developing feelings for him.

However, if she cared for him, she wouldn't stand in his way. She figured if he just stayed away until her next mating heat, the only thing her family would know was that she had slept with a wolf. Damien had left their area so long ago that she doubted her father would remember his scent. Once her next heat was over and she no longer smelled like Damien, no one would ever know what he had done for her. It would be their secret, something for her to treasure when she was lonely—as long as she didn't become pregnant.

She turned away from Damien's gaze and bit her lip. She felt guilty because part of her wanted it to happen even if she knew it was absolutely ridiculous.

Talk about putting Damien, me, and our theoretically unborn child in a tough situation. Then again, look at my brother.

She mentally shook her head. No, she shouldn't even be thinking about having a baby.

Damien put his finger under her chin and turned her face back to him. She relaxed her expression as he studied her. "What's wrong, baby girl?"

She closed her eyes. That was just another reason to like him. He knew when something was bothering her. Too many guys who she had dated or witnessed her friends dating were clueless as to when a female was upset.

She opened her eyes and tried to smile. "Nothing."

His furrowed brow told her that he didn't believe her, but her body took that moment to seize up again. She hoped that he assumed she was lying about needing him again and not that she was hiding how she felt about him.

He slid his hand back up to her breast and squeezed. She moaned and tilted her head back. She heard his rapid breaths next to her ear, and it only turned her on more to know how she affected him.

He bit her ear and whispered, "Liar."

In one smooth move, he pulled her leg over his own and entered her from behind. She screamed from his sudden but welcome penetration and came immediately. The pleasure from her orgasm only lasted a second before her uterus contracted harder, demanding his essence.

Keeping their bodies connected, he shifted them upright, so she was on her hands and knees, and he pressed her upper body down until it rested against the bed. He placed his hands on her hips and then began to move.

A long deep moan escaped her lips. In and out, he thrust. They had never done it in this position before, and the different sensations were amazing. He withdrew completely, and she cried out. He pushed his heavy erection inside her again. Her core was swollen from her heat and from sex, and the burn from his penetration caused her to cry out again.

She wouldn't change a thing.

She squeezed her pussy around him, wanting him to come inside her.

"Damn," he swore.

So, she did it again. He increased his speed, and she sensed the moment he was about to orgasm. He stiffened and expanded inside her. His knot stretched her to the brink of pain, and she could feel him jerk as he pumped into her, causing her to explode around him.

His semen was hot, yet it cooled the heat inside her. Her orgasm absorbed his seed, her womb instantly soothing as it calmed. All her muscles relaxed, and she would have collapsed on the bed if they weren't still connected by his knot.

He moved them again, so they lay on their sides—her back to his front, him inside her. He drew her leg over his hip again and rubbed her pelvis. He'd told her earlier that massaging her uterus could help it accept more of him and delay her next wave of need.

Once his knot receded, he withdrew and rolled onto his back. She extended her arms over her head and enjoyed her body's state of momentary relaxation. She closed her eyes and let herself go.

"Payton?"

"Hmm?"

"Look at me."

She smiled and turned her head, but when she opened her eyes, she saw the somber look and how close he was to his wolf. Her smile disappeared, and she swallowed hard.

"Don't ever lie to me again."

This was the alpha speaking, and he was not one to be messed with. If she were a submissive cat instead of a dominant, she would have run away, screaming.

He leaned in until they were almost nose-to-nose. "I don't want you to hide your pain from me again. Got it?"

She might have dominance, but his trumped hers. She wasn't scared, but her cat instinctively yielded to him, and she nodded.

"Say it."

"I won't. I promise."

"That's my girl." Then, he smiled as if he hadn't just shown her his power. His wolf retreated, and he kissed her on the nose. He pulled her close and tucked her in next to him.

She tried to hide her grin.

This was the kind of male she'd been looking for—strong, dominant, alpha.

And she knew she shouldn't read into it, but he'd called her his girl.

Damien held Payton as she fell asleep. Once he was sure she was out, he untangled her from his body and got out of bed. He arched his still sore back but ignored his injury.

Since they hadn't eaten all day, finding something for them to eat was his excuse to leave Payton for a while. God knew they needed the carbs and protein. He walked to the kitchen and headed for the fridge.

But his real reason for getting up was the remorse he felt. He had just told Payton not to lie to him, yet he had been lying to her since day one. It was lying by omission but lying nonetheless.

What a hypocrite. Pot meet kettle, anyone?

His wolf had sensed her fib immediately and hadn't liked it. Damien should have told his wolf to shove it.

He sighed.

He had to tell her about his father and his father's role in her kidnapping. He also needed to tell her about her brother. She still didn't know about the attempt made on Vaughn's life.

Damien could imagine how she'd react when he told her, but she was bound to eventually find out who was behind the scheme. It would be better if it came out of his mouth. It would put a rift between them, but once her mating heat was over, he would do it.

He laughed, but it held no humor. He was an asshole. He should have told her before he'd taken her during her mating heat. She should have been given a choice, armed with all the information he had to give her, instead of a bunch of half-truths he'd fed her.

He was selfish. He knew she'd smell like him, and he knew it could last until her next heat. Warning her had meant nothing when he'd figured she'd say yes, when he'd desired her to say yes. He wanted his scent on her, in her. He wanted other males to stay away from her. He wanted to keep her for himself.

Yep, I am definitely a selfish asshole.

She wasn't the only one he was lying to. He was lying to himself, too. With her family and his pack's status, there was hardly even a small chance she would accept him as her mate. It was one thing for them to be together here, in their own little world, but she would go home and return to her old life, one that didn't include wolves. He was fooling himself with the circumstances surrounding her mating heat.

Damien realized he'd been standing in front of the fridge with the door open, but he hadn't taken anything out, so he closed it. He turned and rested his back against the door, letting the cold metal of the old fridge cool his sore back, and he closed his eyes. Regardless of Payton's condition or the situation they were in, she deserved to know.

As soon as her heat was over and she could think straight, he'd tell her even if it meant he would lose her forever. Then again, he never really had her in the first place.

Chapter Twenty

Saxon walked into the safe house.

Reid yelled, "Boss, we've got something! You're going to want to hear this."

Vance jogged into the room. "What did you find out?"

"After you told me to look into your cousin, I couldn't find anything."

"You made it sound like this was important. I suppose this is good news. Perhaps Isabelle was the one lying." Their alpha sighed. "Anything else?"

Reid grinned. "No, boss. While I couldn't find anything on Gerald, which I am still looking into, I did find some stuff on Donovan."

"Donovan? Donovan Lowell? Dwyer's deceased son?"

"Donovan has a savings account under his name, and over the last few months, some big deposits have been made into an account that hasn't been touched since he died. Pretty strange, so I did some more digging. All these deposits are every two weeks like clockwork, and they're always the same amount. Now, I don't know where the money is coming from because they are all cash deposits. Not only is money coming in, but money is also going out from the same savings account to a PayPal account. This account has a generic email address, and the info on file is bogus—fake name, fake address, fake phone number, and so on. But—and it's a big *but*—this PayPal account is making weekly payments to a *real* resort about an hour from here."

"Holy shit," Saxon said. "Did you find a name of someone staying there?"

Reid scoffed. "Ye of little faith," he told Saxon. He turned back to Vance. "A group of nine is staying there. They stick out like sore thumbs because the resort season has obviously passed, and they are the only ones staying there. They must be paying the owner extra to rent the cabins off-season. The biggest red flag is that they are reserved under the name Drew Lowell."

"Damn," Saxon swore.

"Who's Drew Lowell?" Camden asked as he came around the corner.

"Dwyer Lowell's late father," Vance said in almost disbelief.

"This means Dwyer really is behind the kidnappings," Saxon added.

"I knew he didn't have much integrity, but I didn't know he would fall this far," Vance said.

"Why would he do this?" Camden asked.

"Because he still blames me for his failings. I kicked him out, yes, but it was his actions that got him there," Vance explained.

Saxon slapped his palms together and rubbed. "What do you want us to do about it, boss?" He was hoping his alpha would give them permission to go and kick some ass. He was sick of their whole situation, and bashing in some wolf heads sounded like a good idea to him.

"With all due respect, Vaughn, you are not my leader, nor is your father. If we want to go to the resort and confront the wolves, we have just as much right as you," Dante said to the cat he was nearly standing toe-to-toe against.

Vaughn gritted his teeth but remained silent. The two of them had been fighting for the last twenty minutes about whether or not the Guardians had the right to help the cats go investigate some resort where the very wolves who were responsible for Princess Naya's botched kidnapping were staying.

Phoenix was sitting in a chair in Dante's office with her arms crossed over her chest and her foot tapping a rhythm that would soon wear out his carpet. She jumped forward. "Oh, come on, Vaughn! He shouldn't be allowed to go."

Dante looked at her and smirked. "You're just jealous that you have to stay here and sit on your feisty ass while the rest of us get to experience some action."

Her mouth dropped to her chest, and for once, she was speechless.

Dante turned back to Vaughn. "I understand that our alliance is new, and we don't completely trust each other yet, but I believe we have earned a right to help. Our princess, your wife, was almost abducted. We deserve the honor of bringing these bastards down just as much as you do. Now, tell me where the wolves are."

Vaughn threw his arms across his chest and eyed Dante. Dante stared right back. Vaughn wasn't Dante's alpha, and nobody told Dante what to do. He only answered to the king and queen, and that was out of respect. As far as this situation went, they had left the decisions up to him, and he was going to take care of the wolves. Either Vaughn could tell him where to go, or Dante would have his own man hack into the cat-shifters' computers.

"I respect that." Vaughn lowered his arms and pointed a finger at him. "However, I know you need to feed, and I don't want my sentinels at risk because you're not in top form."

Dante was taken aback. He didn't realize Vaughn could sense his hunger. He quickly covered his surprise. "I thank you for your concern, but it is none of your business. I assure you, I am quite fine."

They stared at one another for several seconds when Vaughn must have realized Dante wasn't going to back down.

"Fine. I will get you the details and let my father know you are coming." Vaughn stepped closer to Dante. "But if anyone is hurt because of you—"

Dante held up his hands. "I understand how you feel, but I would not willingly risk anyone's safety."

Vaughn nodded. "Okay."

"Please tell your father it will be me and two others."

Vaughn nodded and left his office. Phoenix stood and followed. Dante turned around to grab his phone off his desk. He heard the door shut behind Phoenix, so he pulled up his Favorites list and hit Send.

"Lennox, I need you and Lexine to suit up. We're going out tonight. Come to my office when you're ready, and I'll fill you in."

Dante hung up after receiving an affirmative from Lennox and tossed his phone on his desk. He leaned over, rested his knuckles on the edge, and hung his head.

Man, he was hungry.

Vaughn was right—not about him being able to do his job though. He'd gone longer than this without feeding although it was rare because it made him a miserable bastard. But it could wait. It had to wait. Thankfully, Dante had a few days left before his feeding situation became critical because that need wasn't even the worst of it.

Blood hunger sucked, but the worst was that he was so goddamn horny. He still hadn't left the compound to find a female, and with the princess and cats here, he didn't want to call on one of his usual females to come to him. But as much as his balls were suffering, he didn't need to have sex to do his job. Once this mission was over, he'd take care of himself.

He suspected that he wouldn't feel so hard up if Phoenix weren't still here. Today, with her attitude on display, he had wanted to bend her over the chair and feed from her vein while he fed her his cock to show her she wasn't as dominant as she thought she was.

He sighed.

The whole thing only fueled his frustrations. Something had to be wrong with him. Typically, he prided himself on being in command of his base desires. He wasn't uptight or a prude, but his mind, not his dick, was the one in charge of picking who he brought to bed.

It must be that he simply needed to get laid. It had to be.

He closed his eyes and took a deep breath to center his thoughts.

His eyes popped open.

Damn. It was like he could still smell her.

"Are you going to ignore me all day or what?" Phoenix said from behind him.

Holy fuck.

With his back facing her, the only response she could see was him lifting his head, but his face had to show shock and embarrassment from not realizing that she was still in the room. How did she keep doing that to him? First, the weight room, and now, this. He'd assumed the door closing meant she left. He was off his game. Maybe he needed to feed more than he'd thought. Thank fuck she thought he'd been ignoring her.

He nonchalantly turned around and sat on the edge of the desk. "Is there something I can help you with?"

"Why don't you feed?"

This again? "I believe I made it clear that is nobody's business but my own."

"Vaughn might be able to let it go, but those are my friends and teammates out there"—she gestured toward the door—"without me to back them up"—she pointed at her chest—"so we are forced to rely on you"—she now turned her finger in his direction—"and you're not at your best."

He slowly stood and put his hand on hers, pushing it down. She had some nerve calling him out like this.

"I will take your concern into consideration." He moved around her with the intent to open the door and show her out.

She stepped in front of him.

"What?" he barked.

"I think we deserve an answer. Why can't you just feed from one of the other Guardians? Why are you doing this?"

He turned away and ground his teeth before looking back at her. "You want to know? *Fine.* Taking one's vein is usually an intimate experience. My fellow Guardians, while my friends, are also my colleagues and subordinates, and we don't have that kind of relationship. Unless it's absolutely needed, we don't feed from each other." That should get her to understand.

Phoenix squared her shoulders. "Then, feed from me."

Dante opened his mouth and closed it.

Then, he opened it and closed it again.

That was the last thing he'd expected her to say.

What is her deal?

He scanned her up and down. Her body language and expression told him nothing, except that she had guts and determination. He sucked in a deep breath. He couldn't smell anything but her natural fragrance—no deception, no fear, no excitement, nothing. She had to be feeling something, but she really knew how to cover up her scent.

"No." He stepped around her and walked to the door.

"Why? Naya feeds from Vaughn."

Dante stopped and sighed. She wasn't going to let this go.

He turned and marched back to her until they were so close they almost touched. "I tried to be polite, but you can't seem to get it through your thick head. When I said it was intimate, I mean, *intimate.* To be clear, when my fangs are buried in a female's neck, that's not the only thing buried inside her."

Phoenix's emerald eyes went wide, and she stopped breathing.

He leaned in closer. "When I feed, I fuck. Understand?"

She swallowed and nodded slowly.

Dante straightened, walked to the door, and opened it. "Now, get out."

Chapter Twenty-One

"I'm going to bed." Isabelle stood from the couch. It was still relatively early in the evening, but she was hoping to fall asleep before Zane came to bed.

He glanced up from his laptop and gave her a two-finger wave. "Night. I'll be there later."

She scurried to his bedroom and crawled into bed before he changed his mind.

And she lay there.

She tried to fall asleep, but all she could think about was her growing need for skin-on-skin contact. Her wolf scratched the surface of her body. It wanted to be touched and give touch in return.

Her thoughts turned to Zane. Was she simply attracted to him because he was the only male around? Or was there more? If they forgot their captor-captive status, she supposed that they could be friends.

He no longer followed her around every second, like when he'd just now let her go to bed without him. Today, they had gone outside and run around in animal form. Isabelle easily could have taken off, but he'd trusted her not to. Then, his alpha's cousin had shown up, and he'd protected her—a cat protecting a wolf against another cat. And his faith in her judgment about what she'd smelled on the alpha's cousin had made her proud because she'd gained his confidence. He'd even called her Isabelle rather than one of the nicknames he had for her.

Yes, they could be friends—except for her attraction to him.

She had been doing so well, but then he had gone and kissed her. It was all she'd thought about for the rest of the day. She'd barely been holding back from touching him as it was. She was about ready to throw herself at him.

If only she knew how long she would be stuck here, if she had some sort of time frame, it would help. Right now, it felt indefinite even though she knew it wasn't.

If only she'd had one more date, a fourth date, with the human she went out with before, then they probably would have had sex or at least done some heavy petting.

Isabelle rolled over. She definitely didn't need to be thinking about sex while she was lying in Zane's bed. She took a couple of deep breaths, and in her head, she started creating assignments for her students. Thinking about work should be enough to knock her out.

She was almost there. She was so close.

Then, she heard Zane enter the room, and she woke up. She could hear the rustling as he removed his clothes, and she gritted her teeth. The cat never wore pajamas. If she called him on it, he'd know he affected her because shifters didn't care about one another's nakedness.

Zane climbed into bed, and as with every night, he fell asleep in seconds. She didn't know how he could do it. Right now, she wanted to punch him for his ability to conk out so fast.

She closed her eyes again and willed herself to sleep, but she couldn't ignore his heat, his smell, the knowledge of him lying naked beside her.

There was only one thing to do.

She had to get out of there.

She would go sleep on the couch, and even though she hated to admit it, she needed to relieve herself. It would not fulfill the necessity for skin contact, but it should hold back her need for a while—hopefully, at least until she went home.

After their first night together, Zane had moved his dresser to the end of the bed to block her in, so her only option was to climb over him.

She carefully lowered the covers to her hips and then nudged them off. She cautiously scooted closer to him until they almost touched, and then she gradually sat up on her knees. Biting her lip, she slowly lifted one leg over him. The beating of her heart was the only sound in the otherwise silent room.

She set one foot on the floor when Zane put his hand on her T-shirt–covered hip. She didn't move a single muscle. His eyes were closed, and she didn't even breathe as she waited to see if he was still asleep.

"Isabelle?"

She closed her eyes as she scrunched up her face and swore in her head. This was where he was going to tell her she had to stay in bed, that she wasn't allowed to leave, that it was for the good of his Pride. *Blah, blah, blah.*

"Yes?" she asked warily.

"What's wrong?"

Her eyes snapped open and searched his face. "What?" she said, surprised.

He watched her, his sea-green cat eyes bright in the dark. "What's wrong? Why aren't you sleeping?"

Their romp outside, his kiss that afternoon, him protecting her, and now, his concern for her—it had been one considerate thing after another. Before she had time to process her actions, she leaned over and kissed him.

He'd never indicated that he had any interest in her, and she wasn't anywhere close to being a bombshell. Not only was she a schoolteacher, but she also looked like one. She was aware that Zane could turn her away, but that hadn't stopped her.

And he didn't. He kissed her back without any hesitation, angling his head to take her better, as if he knew how badly she needed this. He tasted as good as he had that afternoon. Sandalwood filled the air along with her desire. He was an incredible kisser. He knew when to nip, when to suck, and when to give back. However great his kissing was, it wasn't the thing she really needed.

She sat up and lifted her hips just enough to pull down the covers and grab his thick length. Zane hissed and arched his back, but she didn't give him time to grow accustomed to her touch. Her wolf was in charge, and the animal in her knew what she wanted. She placed him at her center and slammed down on top of him.

"Holy fuck, Isabelle," Zane called out as his fingers dug into her hips.

She pressed her eyes shut and barely heard him. His dick hit her right where she needed it to be. She used her leg on the floor to give her extra control over her movements, curling her toes into the rug. It felt oh-so good, and all she could think was, *Right there, right there, right there,* as she rode him. It didn't take her long before she shattered. She bit her lip as she tried not to scream from the strength of her release.

She let the waves of pleasure crash over her until the sensations lulled, and soon, she realized what she'd done. She'd pretty much just used this man's penis as if it were her personal toy. She didn't even know if he'd gotten off or not. She hadn't even asked if he was okay with it.

She reluctantly opened one eye and then the other. First, she noticed she had her claws buried in his chest, so she carefully retracted them. Second, she noticed that she was completely naked. The T-shirt she had worn was now on the floor, the words *Orgasm Donor* ripped in half. She had mocked him when he first gave her the shirt, but it had turned out that he was right. The third thing she saw was Zane lying with his arms behind his head, watching her. She studied him, unable to gauge his mood.

"Uh…" she started but trailed off. *What does one say after practically molesting someone? Sorry?* At a loss for words, she opted to get off him.

"I wouldn't do that if I were you."

She paused. "Why?"

He arched his eyebrows.

Oh. He must be referring to his barbs. She'd never had sex with a cat-shifter before, and she had only heard rumors about the barbs a cat had in place of a wolf's knot, but she wasn't worried.

"I'm nowhere near my mating heat." She wouldn't be getting pregnant—that was, if she'd even given him a chance to have his own orgasm.

"No, that's not it." He sat up. "You had your turn. Now, it's mine."

His change in position shifted him farther inside her, and now, she knew he had come—his barbs hit her in exactly the right spots, and a small orgasm swept through her.

"Oh. *Oh.*" After she caught her breath and could think straight, she told him, "Uh…sorry for using you like that."

"You can use me like that anytime you want, sweetheart," Zane said.

He pulled her close and kissed her again. Once his barbs receded, he broke their kiss and swung his legs off the bed as she still straddled him. Her breasts were small but the taut buds of her nipples rubbed against his chest. Just like that, she was ready to go again. He lifted her and slid her back down on his still hard erection.

She dropped her head back and moaned.

"Damn, sweetheart, you are tight."

Lift and slide.

Lift and slide.

"My name"—she panted from the pleasure—"is not sweetheart."

"Izzy then."

She shook her head. "Old boyfriend called me that."

Lift and slide.

"Belle?"

Another head shake.

Lift and slide.

"Why?"

"Too close to Bella."

Lift and slide.

She moaned.

"What's wrong with Bella?"

"*Twilight.*"

He paused. "Good point."

Lift and slide.

"Before you ask, I don't care for Blondie either."

"You're not leaving me with much."

Lift.

"Why can't you"—*slide*—"call me Isabelle?" The last few words came out in a moan as her orgasm drew closer.

He paused once more—this time, longer—and she looked at him.

"When I'm inside a woman, I don't want to yell out the name her father calls her."

Unconsciously, she squeezed her pussy around him, and he groaned.

He lifted her and slid her down again while maintaining eye contact. She clamped down around him once more. But now, it was on purpose.

"How about Isa?"

Can't we figure this out after we're finished? She was so close to the edge. All she needed was for him to move.

He shook his head and leaned in close, so they were cheek-to-cheek as he spoke in her ear, "I'm not letting you come until you answer me." He shifted inside her just enough to remind her of what she was missing.

She supposed she could live with it if she would get what she wanted. "Fine."

He leaned back. "Yes?"

She nodded and rotated her hips. "Please."

"Whatever you say, Isa."

He stood, pushing his penis deep inside her, and he flipped her onto her back before he followed, arching over her. He began to pump into her so powerfully that she hit her peak within seconds.

This time, she felt him climax, too, as he roared out, "*Isa.*"

Chapter Twenty-Two

*D*wyer paced across the floor of his cabin. Why hadn't Lachlan found Damien yet? He was a computer genius, and he'd had no trouble finding information he needed in the past. Dwyer suspected he wasn't sharing everything with him.

Dwyer stopped. *Are all my sentinels turning on me?*

There was a knock at the door, and Dwyer smelled Lachlan. *It's about time.* Maybe he had judged his sentinel too soon.

He stalked to the door and swung it open, expecting good news, but when he saw Lachlan's face, he knew he was wrong.

"Sir, we need to go."

"Excuse me?"

"We need to pack up and leave. I've been monitoring the resort's computer system. Someone has hacked into it and found our reservation, the one under your father's name."

"Do you know who?"

Lachlan shook his head. "No. If I had time, I could find out, but I'm sure you can guess. I think it's in our best interests to leave."

Lachlan was right. Dwyer could predict who had found them. This was what he had been waiting for.

"Sir?"

"Let them come."

Lachlan blanched. "With all due respect, sir, we are not ready for a fight. We need to find Damien. We didn't plan for the cats to come here. If they find us, how are we going to break our exile?"

Dwyer put his back to him. There was so much that his sentinels didn't know. The only thing he'd told them was that he was trying to get the pack back into the Minneapolis-St. Paul area. They didn't know about his deal with the cat-shifter or about Vance Llewelyn's children being abducted.

Months ago, Damien had gotten into an argument with Dwyer about his plans to kidnap the Llewelyn brats. Damien had disagreed with him, of course, and had told him the idea was thoughtless and irresponsible. Dwyer had told him that the sentinels were loyal to him and would do whatever he told them.

However, Dwyer knew his sentinels were already questioning him, and Damien had only put more doubt upon him. That was why Dwyer had hired humans to take care of the abduction and had never even asked his sentinels. They had no idea what he had done or set in motion. He suspected that if they knew, they would leave, and Dwyer couldn't fight the cats alone.

Dwyer swung back around. "You're right. Tell everyone to pack up and make sure they spray every room. We leave nothing behind. When did this breach happen?"

"Several hours ago."

"Tell the men they have ten minutes."

Saxon was gathered with Vance and Tegan at the meeting point, close to where Minneapolis touched St. Paul. Reid and Camden had stayed back to protect the alpha's wife and to see what more they could find out.

The three of them were waiting for the Guardians to show. In all his years, Saxon had never thought this day would come, and he wasn't sure what to think about it.

He wasn't for or against it. It was just different. None of them, except for their alpha, had had contact with the vampires before they'd met Vaughn's mate.

A black SUV pulled up, and three vampires emerged, dressed in dark clothes. They wore coats loaded with various weapons, much like the sentinels' vests. The two males were large, also like him and his fellow sentinels. The female with them was tall and muscular although smaller than her male counterparts.

The larger of the two males stepped forward with his hands clasped in front of him. He had dark hair, dark eyes, and medium skin tone. Saxon didn't realize that he'd expected all vampires to be pale until he saw this male. Even knowing they weren't the living dead and that Naya had a little color to her skin, he'd apparently still expected ghostly complexions.

"Hello, I'm Dante, the leader of the Guardians," the male said. "This is Lexine and Lennox." He inclined his shoulder at the other two Guardians when he introduced them.

Going by their similar blond hair and names, Saxon assumed they were siblings.

Vance stepped forward. "I'm Vance Llewelyn, alpha of the Minnesota Pride. This is Saxon and Tegan." They murmured their greetings. "Can you tell me how my son and daughter-in-law are doing?"

Dante smiled, and Saxon saw a hint of fang. "Quite well, sir. Vaughn is disappointed that he can't be here tonight, but I'm sure you already know that."

Vance cleared his throat. "Yes, my son made his opinion known. And Phoenix?"

Dante's smile faltered for a second. "I believe she is more disappointed than Vaughn, sir."

"Sounds like Phoenix," Tegan piped in.

"Yes, well, she has her own opinions, too. Please, call me Vance."

Dante nodded once. "Will do." He looked around. "So, where are we headed?"

"About an hour from here," Saxon said. "How about you follow us?"

"No problem. We're ready."

They all moved to get into their respective vehicles when Vance said, "Dante?"

Dante turned.

"Thank you for your help. We're short men and need the assistance. Naya promised we could count on you, but this is my mission, and your support is appreciated."

Dante nodded. "You're welcome, sir. There is nothing we wouldn't do for Princess Naya. You can trust her word, and we'll follow your lead, sir—Vance."

Vance nodded back, and they climbed into their SUVs. Saxon got behind the wheel with his alpha riding shotgun. Tegan rode in the back. They rode in silence, each lost in their own thoughts, and about an hour later, they arrived at the resort.

They parked away from the cabins, which were lined up in a row, and they set out on foot. Vance suggested they pair up, a sentinel with a Guardian. Vance went with Lennox to start with the first cabin, Tegan with Lexine scouted the outer area, and Saxon ended up with Dante to check the last cabin.

They started at the end and continued until they got to the cabins reserved under Drew Lowell's name. The good news was, the wolves were easy to spot since they were the only guests at the resort. Their parking spots and the paths to the doors were the ones where the snow was cleared off. The bad news was, every single spot was empty.

"Damn," Dante said.

"Shit," Saxon agreed.

"They're gone," Dante said.

The pair continued on until they caught up to Vance and Lennox.

"Looks like they cleared out," Saxon told them.

Vance tilted his head back and sniffed the air. "They haven't been gone too long. Somehow, they figured out we were coming."

"What do you want us to do, boss?" Saxon asked.

"Search the cabins. Make sure you keep track of any damage you make, so we can reimburse the owner."

"They rented four cabins, so each pair can take one, and whoever finishes first will take the last one," Dante suggested.

"Sounds good," Saxon agreed.

They each took a cabin, and Dante and Saxon stepped inside the third structure. The first thing Saxon noticed was the horrible odor. He almost gagged from the stench. The wolves must have sprayed something to cover their smell. He had to give it to them. He didn't smell anything but flowery air freshener. It was too bad for them that they couldn't have sprayed outside.

Saxon checked the living room, kitchen, both bedrooms, and the bathroom. They hadn't left anything behind, not even their food. Whoever had stayed in this cabin did a good job of removing any evidence of their presence.

Saxon left the cabin and went to the last building. Again, he checked the living room, kitchen, bathroom, and first bedroom, but he found nothing. The second bedroom's door was closed, and when he got inside, he discovered something.

Saxon heard people come in behind him. It was Dante and Lennox.

"What did you find?" Dante asked.

"Nothing in the first cabin. You guys?"

"Nothing," Dante said.

"Empty," Lennox answered.

"Most of this place was empty, too, except I found a few articles of clothing." Saxon grinned. "And a cell phone." He shook the find in his hand.

"Nice," Lennox said.

"What's on it?" Dante asked.

Saxon opened the phone and scrolled through it. "A bunch of numbers with no contact names and no calls in or out for a while now."

"Do you have someone who can find out more?" Dante asked.

"Yep. If there is anything on it, Reid will find it."

Vance walked into the cabin.

"Hey, boss, I found a cell phone," Saxon said.

"Hmm…who do you think it belongs to?"

"Damien," Saxon answered.

Dante and Lennox looked at him blankly.

"The phone Damien used to call about Payton had only been activated a few days before, and it didn't have any other phone calls on it. Maybe that's because Damien left his phone here."

"If this is Damien's, maybe it could lead us to Dwyer. We can check the call history. There could still be something on there."

Saxon snorted. "Yeah, the dumbass forgot to clean out his son's room before he left."

"Bad for them. Good for us," Dante said with a grin.

Chapter Twenty-Three

*D*amien was drained. It was mid-morning, and he was ready to go back to sleep. It had been a day and a half since Payton's heat started, and Damien thought he might die. Granted, endless sex was a good way to meet death, but he would still be dead.

Although, to be fair to Payton, he suspected that she wasn't the sole reason he didn't feel well. His back was really starting to hurt. He'd been able to dismiss what was a slow ache over the past few days, but this morning, the pain could not be ignored. It was also getting harder to hide it.

"Damien, what's wrong?"

Payton and he were lying on the couch, talking and passing the time until she would need him again, and she had been resting her head on his shoulder. With her back against the sofa, she now propped herself up on her elbow as she stared at him.

"Hmm...what?"

"What's wrong? Did you even hear what I was saying?"

He searched his brain to remember what they had been talking about, and he came up with nothing.

He smiled weakly. "No. Sorry."

She cupped his cheek. "What's going on in that big brain of yours?"

"You don't have to flatter me to get me to talk."

She smiled but only for a second. She wasn't going to let it go.

"My back's been bothering me."

Concern flashed across her face. "Your back? Why?"

"I…" He cleared his throat. "I kind of injured it the night that you were kidnapped."

"What?" She curled her hand into his shirt. "Why didn't you tell me? It must be causing you a lot of pain with everything you've been doing for me. You need to see a chiropractic healer. Why didn't you tell me?"

He felt a small amount of relief. She assumed his back was hurt internally, not that someone had cut him. He'd been very careful about wearing a shirt or keeping his back from her. If he could keep it up, she wouldn't know the extent of his wound.

He put his hands on hers. "Baby girl, I'll be fine. I've been taking ibuprofen." At this point, that was barely taking the edge off the pain, but she didn't need to know that.

She looked at him, her mouth clenched.

"Please." He untangled her fingers from his top and kissed them. "You don't have to worry about me."

"Damien, you are just as important as me. I can worry about you, too."

He grabbed a lock of her black hair. "How about I make you a deal?"

She cocked her head and raised her brow.

"You don't think about my back for now, including how it affects our extracurricular activities."

She opened her mouth, and he held up his hand.

"Just until your heat is over. Hopefully, you're halfway done. Once we get out of here, I will go to a healer. Deal?"

"Halfway? Last time, it was about five days."

He smiled. He couldn't help feeling a little cocky. "That's because you didn't have me."

"So, you, or any male, can service me and make my heat shorter?"

Any male?

Fuck that. Mine.

She was his, and any male who came close to her would recognize that.

He mentally shook his head. Maybe he needed to see a mental healer as well. She didn't belong to him, and he needed to remember the reality of the situation.

"Oh, Damien."

He glanced at Payton. She had a dreamy smile on her face, her sapphire eyes dancing.

"What?"

Instead of answering, she leaned over and kissed him. He breathed her in. He could smell her heat, but her need wasn't rising yet.

She broke their kiss, and this time, her smile was cunning as her deep blue eyes gleamed.

What was she up to?

She threw her leg over him and got up from the couch.

"Where are you going?" he asked.

She spun around and bit the tip of her thumb.

Now, she was being coy?

She angled her head. "The shower."

He groaned. Even though they'd been having a lot of sex, he immediately pictured her wet with water cascading down her amazing body.

Smiling as if she knew his thoughts, she sauntered over to him and pulled him to a sitting position. He hauled her between his legs and put his face against her flannel-covered pelvis. He could smell her and him—lavender, cedar, and the musk of their arousals. He fucking loved it.

She grabbed on to his hair and yanked his head back. "Would you like to join me?" Her indigo eyes glittered with heat.

Do bears shit in the woods? Except—

She leaned over, her face serious. "I won't worry about your back. I promise." She grinned. "Besides, the part of you I'm most interested in is in the front."

He growled at her.

"I love it when you do that."

Huh? He didn't remember ever growling in her presence before. *Whatever.* It didn't matter. He'd growl for her anytime.

"You still haven't answered my question." She whispered in his ear, "I'll make it worth your while."

And, just like that, he was hard as a brick, and all thoughts of sleep and pain faded. It surprised him that, after the amount of sex they'd had, he still wanted her like it was their first time.

He stood, picked her up, and sprinted to the bathroom with Payton laughing the entire way. He turned on the water to warm it up, made a mess of their clothes as he ripped them off with his claws, and dragged them both into the shower.

He resisted the impulse to haul her against him and take her against the wall. He watched her step under the spray of water. It was better than he'd imagined. She put her arms up to wet her hair, and the water flowed down her tan skin, onto her chest, and over the tips of her breasts. He bent and sucked a nipple into his mouth.

She dropped her arms and clutched at him. "Oh…oh," she moaned.

She twisted her fingers in his hair, so he moved to the other breast and sucked on its sweet berry.

She moaned again and then breathlessly said, "Wait."

She hadn't sounded like she meant it, but he complied all the same.

He reluctantly straightened. "What's wrong?"

She arched up and planted a kiss on his lips. "Nothing's wrong," she said, enclosing her fingers around his cock, "big boy."

She pumped her fist on his erection, and he pitched his head back and shut his eyes.

"Holy shit."

"Do you like this, Damien?"

"God, yes."

"Then, you'll like this even better."

He opened his eyes in time to see her getting down on her knees before taking him between her lips.

"Jesus Christ."

She released him with a pop. "What's with the spiritual remarks?" She winked at him and slid him back in her mouth—all the way.

He growled because it was mind-blowing and because he knew she liked it.

It took him a minute to form any words. "I think I'm having a religious experience."

That was the last thing he said for the next few minutes.

It was possibly the best blow job of his life because she knew exactly what she was doing and how to do it. She knew how to use her teeth, and she gave the boys a little play action, too. She swirled her tongue around the head of his cock and then sucked it in deep. It wasn't long before he felt his impending release.

"Payton." He was going to come soon. "Baby girl."

Rather than answering, she placed one hand on his hip and held him in place. It was all he needed to know she wanted him to come, so he let go.

He slammed his hand against the wall to catch himself before he fell over. Payton had moved her mouth to the end of him to avoid his knot, but she looked him in the eyes as she swallowed, and it almost made him come again.

When he was spent, she sat back on her heels. "Wow."

She ran her fingers around his knot, which was about an inch long and stuck out from his penis another half an inch, and he shuddered.

"No wonder you make me feel so full and stretched."

He pulled her up until she stood in front of him, and he took her in his arms. "You say the nicest things," he told her with a smile.

She arched up and kissed him again. He could taste himself on her, so although the knot subsided, his erection did not.

He interrupted their kiss. "I thought you were a virgin?"

She wiggled her arms out from under his and draped them around his shoulders. "I said I was a virgin. I never said I was a saint."

He chuckled and then picked her up, and she swung her legs around his hips. He placed his cock at her core and rubbed.

"*Oh*," she exclaimed in surprise.

He smelled her heat spike from out of nowhere.

"Whoa. How come I need you again so soon?"

"I think your body's upset because you used me in the wrong place."

She laughed, but it quickly turned into a moan as her body told her what it wanted.

"Well, non-saint Payton, maybe your body is telling you that it's time for you to have your own religious experience," he said as he thrust inside her.

Chapter Twenty-Four

Zane knocked on the bathroom door again. Isabelle was presently using the room as a means to avoid him.

"Isa, we have to go soon."

Oh, God, why does he have to call me that?

The night before came whooshing back, and she instantly thought of him calling her name as he'd come inside her. Right on the tail of that thought was embarrassment. Her behavior had been no better than that of a desperate prostitute, trying to make money to score drugs, except the only high Isabelle had felt was an orgasm. So, maybe she had been more desperate. At least a drugged-out hooker had addiction on her side.

She really needed to be fully clothed around the man—or just not be around him at all.

Thankfully, they were leaving for the day, which required him returning her clothes. It felt good to have her jeans and sweater back.

She lifted the collar of her top to her nose. He'd washed her stuff. It was kind of sweet of him. She looked in the mirror and saw a ridiculous smile on her face.

She straightened her spine and gritted her teeth.

No, Isabelle, you idiot. You cannot think of him as sweet.

She needed to remind herself of why her clothes had been taken away from her in the first place.

The only reason she had gotten them back was because the cat-shifter alpha had called that morning and asked Zane to bring her to meet him. Apparently, the alpha had some questions for her. While she dreaded being taken to the Minnesota Pride alpha, she dreaded spending the day alone with Zane more.

She took a deep breath, ran her fingers through her hair, smoothed down her clothes, and opened the door.

Zane straightened from where he had been leaning against the wall. "Finally. I thought maybe you drowned in there." He was his usual self and seemingly unaffected by all the sex they'd had last night.

Isabelle felt her face begin to turn red. *Why did I have to go and think of sex?*

She quickly moved past him, so he couldn't make note of her darkening complexion.

She needed a distraction. *What did he just say to me?* "You're hilarious. You know I was getting ready."

They made it to the front door, and Zane handed over her coat and hat. He must have retrieved it from his hiding spot while she had gotten dressed, which was a disappointment. She'd hoped to find where he had stashed all her stuff.

Once they were in their winter gear, Zane opened the door and slapped her on the ass. "After you, Isa."

She stopped mid-step and clenched her jaw but only for a moment. Then, she continued walking. She wasn't going to let him get to her.

Zane closed and locked the door, and she followed him to the garage. The property was still covered in a large amount of snow from the big storm. It hadn't snowed much since the storm ended, but the snow hadn't melted either, and she was glad that Zane had shoveled a path.

He showed her to a mid-sized SUV, and they got inside. As the two of them left the property, they drove past her vehicle. Staring out the window, she desperately wished she were inside it, heading for home. She would love not to be stuck in a small space with a guy she'd had sex with the night before, so she could avoid having any awkward conversations. She did not look forward to any chitchat they might attempt to make, but it turned out she didn't have to worry at all.

Zane turned the radio up loud and started singing off-key.

Isabelle pulled her hat down over her ears and eyes. It seemed Zane didn't care that she would like to retain her ability to hear. Plus, she was tired since she hadn't gotten much sleep the previous night. She'd been too busy—

She cursed at herself. What was her problem?

Stop thinking about the sex you had with him, Isabelle.

She forced her thoughts elsewhere, and soon, the SUV's heat kicked in. She fell asleep to Zane's tuneless singing, and she dreamed about a naked male cat.

Sawyer was getting very impatient.

When Kenzie had come up with her idea to escape, it was the first time he'd felt hope. But now, his optimism was dwindling.

Two days had passed, and nothing had happened yet. Two days in the real world was nothing, but two days in captivity felt like two months. He was beginning to think they would need to come up with a new idea. Kenzie didn't smell like she was even close to that time of the month even though she'd said she was.

His cat was restless and wanted out of confinement. He was part animal, and he needed to be free to run around in open spaces—not stuck in a small room for a week, which was what the calendar would say tomorrow.

Sawyer heard the water in the shower turn off. Kenzie had been in there for almost an hour. He assumed she had taken her time, so they could be away from each other longer. Despite their truce, they still managed to get on each other's nerves. She bothered his cat more than the man in him. It did not like being locked up with her.

The bathroom door opened, the scents of shampoo and soap hitting his nose first. Then, he smelled it, and he practically jumped off the bed to reach her.

Kenzie screamed and smacked her hand against her T-shirt–covered chest. "Holy crap, you scared me. What's going on?"

"You're close." *Finally.*

She held out her hand. "Close to what?"

"Close to your time." It was as if a weight had been lifted off his shoulders. It was one of many, but it was still one.

Kenzie rubbed her brow and temples with her hands and let out an exasperated sigh. "I already told you that."

"But now, I can smell it. You're close. We are getting out of here soon."

She dropped her arms, and her eyes were wide. "What did you say?"

"We're getting out of here soon."

"Uh…no. Before that."

"You're close?"

"No, before that."

Why was she making him repeat everything? Did she not understand the significance of the situation? They would be getting out of here soon, for Christ's sake. It was his turn to release an irritated sigh. "I can smell it?"

"Yes, that. What do you mean, you can smell it?"

He groaned with frustration. "I'm a shifter, part animal. I can smell that you are close."

When intimate with a female, a human male could often pick up some of the subtle differences in the female's scent, too. Humans just didn't know what the changes meant. But Sawyer didn't need intimacy. Clothes weren't enough to mask a scent from a shifter.

"How?"

He looked down toward her pelvis. "Your hormones change. We can smell when a female is ovulating or menstruating." He didn't understand what the big deal was. This was not important right now.

She crossed one leg over the other.

Sawyer snickered. "Closing your legs isn't going to help."

She swallowed. "Does this mean you can smell other things about me?" She shook her head. "I mean, humans. Can you smell other things about humans?"

What the hell is she getting at? "What things?"

Kenzie cracked her knuckles. "Um…like, physiological changes?"

He shrugged and snorted. "Of course."

Kenzie's face drained of color, and she held up a finger. "Oh my God. I think I'm going to be sick." She went back into the bathroom and slammed the door shut.

Sawyer just shook his head and turned to go lie down on the bed again. *Humans.* He didn't think he would ever understand them.

The cat-shifter had a bad feeling. He couldn't discern where it was coming from, but he didn't dismiss it either.

He'd called Dwyer, and he had insisted that everything was fine and that he was hot on his son's trail. Despite his voice sounding strained, this was good news.

Next, the cat-shifter had tried to reach Vance, but he was still in hiding. If Vance knew he was behind everything, Vance would be at his doorstep, not at some safe house.

No, nothing was different as far as he knew or had been able to find out. *So, what has changed?*

Maybe nothing *had* changed. Maybe something was *going to* change. *But what?*

The cat-shifter rose from his seat and paced the room. He forced himself to stop, and he gave himself a lecture. If he was going to be alpha, he needed to rule with a straight head and not overthink.

He took three calming deep breaths.

There is nothing wrong, he told himself.

There had been no indication that anything was wrong, nor had there been any indication that things were going to change— at least, not for the worse.

Once Dwyer found Damien, he'd have Payton, and he would be one step closer. Then, he only needed to get Vance and Lilith. He was almost finished with the plan.

Yet, he wasn't one to ignore his instincts. Perhaps he should leave town for a while. Yes, that was an excellent idea. He'd get out of town while Dwyer cleaned up the mess he'd made. Once Damien was found and Payton was in their custody, he could move forward.

His brain clicked, and an idea formed. He knew how to get Vance out of hiding. Once he had Payton back in his custody and away from Damien, he would use her as a tactic to bring Vance to him instead of killing her right away. He would demand that Vance trade himself for Payton's safety. Then, he could kill two birds with one stone, or in this case, two cats with one gun. Vance would never put his own life before the lives of his children.

The cat-shifter rubbed his hands together. Things hadn't gone according to plan, but he had found a means to adapt.

He mentally patted himself on the back. *What a brilliant alpha I am going to make.*

Chapter Twenty-Five

Zane shook Isabelle awake.

She pushed her hat up and blinked against the bright sun reflecting off the snow.

"Where are we?" she asked, disorientated from sleeping so hard.

They were in a driveway behind a house. Other homes were nearby, but she didn't recognize the neighborhood.

"The safe house." He opened his door. "Come on."

She exited the vehicle and followed him. When they reached the door, Zane knocked and put her between it and him.

It swung open, and she was met by two cat-shifters. Going by the dominance practically radiating off them, they were sentinels. The first was a female with long white-blonde hair. The second was a large male with blond-and-black hair. Neither smiled, and Isabelle instinctively took a step backward and ran into Zane.

He put his hand on the small of her back. "Shh…it's fine," he whispered in her ear. "They won't hurt you."

"Says you," she whispered back. "They don't look like they agree."

The corners of the female's mouth kicked up for a second.

"Saxon, Tegan," Zane said in his regular voice, "this is Isabelle. Isabelle, this is Saxon and Tegan, two of my fellow sentinels."

Both of the cats stepped back to let her in, and she quickly moved forward. She didn't want them to see Zane's hand on her back. It was a semi-possessive move and definitely a protective one. She didn't want any of the cats thinking there was anything special between her and Zane because there wasn't. Scratching an itch with someone did not a relationship make.

Once inside, they showed her to the main room of the modest house. A couple of computers were set up in the corner, their screens black, and two other cat-shifters were there—both male, one blond and the other auburn.

No one spoke until an older gentleman stepped into the room. She knew he was the Minnesota Pride alpha.

"Hello, Isabelle. I'm Vance Llewelyn."

She smiled uncertainly. "Hello, sir."

Isabelle had never personally met the Pride's alpha. Her family wasn't an important part of the Minnesota Pack, so they weren't involved in the politics or the joint construction business. Her parents were both teachers, like her, and the only time she'd seen Vance Llewelyn before the pack's exile was at functions and celebrations and only from a distance.

"Please sit," he said, holding his arm out toward a couch.

Once she sat, he took a chair across from her.

The reality of the situation began to set in, and Isabelle started to sweat, yet she was cold at the same time. No doubt everyone in the room could smell her nervousness.

Zane sat beside her. He didn't sit close enough to touch her, but it was enough to sweep some calm over her.

"Isabelle, I asked you to come here to answer a few questions," the alpha said. "Please know, we mean you no harm. Just answer as best as you can. Okay?"

"Okay," she answered, her voice slightly higher than normal.

"As you know, my only daughter is with Damien. What can you tell me about him? What did he tell you when he called you last Tuesday night?"

"Um…well, he didn't tell me much when he called. Just that an attempt was made to abduct your daughter, and he intercepted. She was injured and unconscious, and he took her somewhere safe to address her injuries. He didn't have any way to reach you because Payton had lost her phone in the struggle, so he asked me to come and tell you that she was okay. He told me that he intended to call me the next day, but I never heard from him, as you know."

"Do you trust Damien? Is he a truthful person?"

"Oh, without a doubt. Damien would never go back on his word."

"Do you know why he happened to be in the area when Payton was kidnapped?"

"Uh…" *Wow.* She'd never even considered why Damien was coincidentally in the same place as Payton when she was taken or why he was in Minneapolis at all. "No, sir, I don't. Damien and I are friends, but he doesn't tell me a lot of stuff, especially pack business."

"How does Damien feel about his father?"

Isabelle looked down. She didn't know how to answer that. She didn't want them all to think he was a disrespectful son because he truly wasn't. He did the best he could with the father he had.

"Isabelle?"

Her head snapped up. The stern faces of the alpha and the five sentinels, including Zane, were staring at her, and she swallowed hard.

The alpha looked her directly in the eye. "You can trust us. I have my suspicions, but I need to hear what you have to say to confirm them."

Isabelle had to look away. She was a submissive and couldn't continue to look an alpha in the eye. The fact that he'd held her gaze meant that he wanted her to know he spoke the truth. But what suspicions did he have?

She licked her lips. "Damien…" *Crap, there is no good way to say this.* "Please don't think of him as a bad son. He's really a very—" Zane stopped her with a hand on her arm. "Sorry." She took a deep breath. "Damien pretty much doesn't agree with anything his father does," she spit out.

Vance leaned forward. "What do you mean by this?"

She took another deep breath in and let it out. "Damien is a lot like his mother was, and he never understood how she ended up with someone like his father. He thinks his father is irresponsible and the main cause of the feud between the wolves and cats. Damien was the youngest brother, and he has felt helpless when it comes to returning to the Cities, but then his brother, who was a lot like Dwyer, died. As long as no one challenges him, Damien is our next alpha, but with most of our pack feeling lost and being dispersed around the state, he is worried he won't be guaranteed the spot.

"Once Damien realized that he would rule, he tried to figure out how to bring us home. He's never said it, but I believe he plans to challenge his father. I believe he has been patiently waiting for the right time. Like I said, our pack is somewhat broken, and Dwyer has been our leader for so long that most can't see beyond that. Damien has been trying to build up support, especially with his fellow sentinels, so when he does become alpha, his people will trust him."

"Do you know what he was doing in Minneapolis?"

She shook her head. "No. All I know is that his father ordered Damien and the other sentinels to come here a few months back. I know that they've been staying out of the area but closer than they probably should. Damien didn't tell me what was going on, and I honestly don't think his father told him." She sighed.

She knew how conflicted Damien was. He didn't consider his father to have good intentions, and he wanted to overrule the alpha. At the same time, she believed it hurt Damien that his father preferred his older brother and didn't treat Damien the same way.

"The last time I spoke to him, before Tuesday, he said something about finding out some information. If he didn't stop it, there would be no turning back, and the pack would never come home." She shrugged. "That's all I know. I'm sorry. I wish I could be of more help." She hoped she hadn't thrown Damien to the wolves...er, cats.

Vance sat back and rubbed his chin. "Do you think my daughter is safe with him?"

"Yes, sir. I know that he was very worried about her when he called me. He was adamant that I let you know she was okay and safe. He truly didn't want you to worry."

"Hmm...I obviously have my problems with Damien's father, but after what you've told me, I hope Damien doesn't share the same thoughts."

It wasn't worded as a question, but she knew the alpha wanted an answer.

"Damien understands why you kicked the pack out of L & L

Construction and the Cities—" Her cheeks warmed because she almost said more than she should.

"But?"

Uh-oh.

Vance had heard the unspoken *but*, and she doubted he would let her leave until she spit it out.

"Remember, Damien is only thinking of his pack." She laughed nervously. "Damien doesn't understand why you didn't buy his family out of the business or let the pack collect money from the shares they own."

Vance had a good poker face, but she could see a slight flaring of his nostrils. She scanned the room. Everyone's faces showed shock even though they tried to hide it.

Oh no. She didn't want them to think badly of Damien. She had to get them to understand. "He knows his father messed up, but his grandfather, who was a good man, helped start it. They deserved what he put into it. The truth of the matter is that the Minnesota Pack is broke. If we still received the pack shares or had been bought out, the pack might have some money."

The room was dead silent, but the tension in the air was thick.

Isabelle panicked. "Please don't be mad at Damien. He's a good person, a good shifter. He only wants this feud to end." She put her head in her hands. "Oh God, I said too much."

They're going to kill Damien.

"Actually, Isabelle, I believe that you've told me everything I needed to hear."

She whipped her head up.

"It's not Damien I feel anger toward." Vance turned to his left. "Reid, you know what to do."

"On it," the auburn-haired cat said before heading to the computers.

Vance turned back toward her. "Isabelle, you have nothing to fear from me, and neither does Damien. As long as he brings my daughter home safely and he is who you say he is, I offer him nothing but peace."

Peace? Did that mean what she thought it meant? Would Damien get what he wanted so badly?

Vance stood, and Zane followed. She didn't know what else to do, so she got up from the couch as well.

"One more question, Isabelle."

"Sir?"

"Now that you are here, you have the opportunity to stay with us. There are more of us here, so our restrictions will be more lax. Would you like to stay? Or would you like to go back with Zane to the bunkhouse? His position is there watching over the main house, so he won't be remaining here with us."

Finally, this was her opportunity to get away from him. She would never have to see him again, and she could forget about having wild, hot sex with him.

She opened her mouth, ready to utter, *So long and farewell,* to the infuriating cat, except the words that came out were, "I'd rather go back with Zane."

He looked as stunned as she felt.

If she could kick herself in the ass, she would.

Chapter Twenty-Six

The following night, Payton lay in bed as Damien slowly ran his fingers lightly up and down her spine, making her literally purr. She'd never known that she could be so happy and so sad at the same time.

She sensed that her heat was nearing the end. Therefore, so was her time with Damien.

She desperately wished there were a way for them to continue being together.

But there was her father, her mother, her brother, and her pride. When she'd told Damien that she didn't care what her father thought about the two of them being together, she'd meant it. However, she could admit now that her hormones had played a part—not that she regretted being with him in any way.

She would never regret giving him her virginity or picking him to be the first male to take her during her heat.

She knew that her father would be angry and her mother would be disappointed when she returned home, covered with the scent of a wolf. But they would recover, and it would pass. However, taking Damien as her mate would be permanent and something that they might not get over. It had been ten years since the pack's exile. Would her father and the Pride ever accept them back? She was his daughter, and it was probable that she had a certain amount of rebellion, but he was still her father and her alpha, so his decision would be final.

It wouldn't be fair to Damien or the pack if she were the reason they never got to return home. It was obvious Damien cared about his pack. He was proud of who he was. There was a reason he wore a wolf tattoo on his chest. She couldn't live with the guilt if she were the cause of the pack remaining exiled forever.

It probably didn't matter because Damien had never expressed wanting a relationship. But judging from the way he touched her, she was sure he felt something for her. Or was she being a silly female and reading too much into things? She wouldn't be the first.

She turned to her side. There were circles under his clear blue eyes, and his scent had changed as of this morning. He almost smelled…ill. She knew her heat had been demanding on him. It was good that it was almost over. He, as always, had told her not to worry about him when she expressed her concern.

But she couldn't control how she felt, so she used his messy hair from their earlier lovemaking as an excuse to soothingly touch him. She combed through his deep gray locks. The woman, as well as the cat, was pleased to caress and coddle him.

His mouth curved up, and he leaned in to kiss her. He kissed his way down her neck, stopped where it met her shoulder, and sucked. She arched her body into his and rubbed her breasts against his chest. He sucked harder, nipping with his teeth, and she moaned, curling her nails into his side.

Bite me, she pleaded with him in her head.

She froze, her body stiff. "Oh God."

Damien pulled away, concern written all over his face. "What's wrong?"

She couldn't tell him that she wanted him to bite her, that she wanted him to mark her and make her his.

Oh no. This was much more than sex.

She looked up into his face.

She loved him.

And doesn't that just make everything more complicated?

"Payton?"

What was she going to tell him? She couldn't tell him that she loved him.

Think, Payton, think.

"I just realized that my mating heat is coming toward an end." She attempted a smile. "I guess it just surprised me. That's all."

She told herself to relax before he suspected that she was hiding anything from him. It was a half-truth, so hopefully, he wouldn't pick up on her lie.

He took her hand and brought the palm to his lips. "I recognized the change in your scent. I bet you're anxious to get back to your family."

I'd rather stay here with you. "I don't want them to worry about me any longer." She wrinkled up her nose. "How are we going to get out of here? The driveway is still filled with snow." By *driveway*, she meant the extended path leading from the road to the cabin. It was about one-eighth of a mile—far too long to shovel by hand.

"I have an idea. I'm going to take care of it tomorrow as long as your heat is over."

But she didn't want him to take care of it tomorrow. She felt tears pricking the backs of her eyes, and her mouth turned down in an uncontrollable frown. *Oh, great.* This was why guys thought women were clingy. She had given herself to Damien and fallen in love with him, and now, the thought of leaving him made her want to weep.

Damien tugged on her hand. "Payton, hey"—he brushed away a single tear that had escaped—"I promise, I will get you home to your family."

He'd misunderstood her sadness, but she didn't correct him. His concern only made her cry harder.

He pulled her into his arms and held her close, rubbing her back in a comforting rhythm.

"I don't know what's wrong with me. I swear, I'm not usually a blubbering idiot."

He chuckled. "I'm sure it's your hormones combined with our ordeal. After your heat is over and you bleed, you'll return to normal."

After their heat, shifters menstruated similar to humans, but because they were half-human and half-animal, they bled very little and only twice a year.

"Poor humans. I guess there is something good to being diestrus."

Damien laughed again, and Payton crawled farther on top of him. She buried her nose in his neck and breathed him in. She loved the smell of him—cedar and wolf. It calmed and relaxed her, and she soon drifted off, her sad thoughts an ache in the back of her mind.

Flying into a sitting position, Payton awoke with a start. Before she could gain full awareness, she doubled over from the contraction rocking her uterus. Her mating heat must have reached its climax. She'd had friends tell her that the last time it peaked would be the most potent, and they were right. She could barely catch her breath after one spasm ended and the next one began.

She scanned the room. Damien wasn't in bed. The light in the bathroom was off, and the door was open. The room was empty. Where was he? She tried to call out his name, but she couldn't get a sufficient amount of air. The bedroom door sat closed but not for long.

The hinges squeaked as the door was flung open so hard that it bounced off the wall. She didn't have to say anything. Damien grabbed his shirt and wrenched it off. Next went his shorts, his arousal heavy and thick against his muscular belly.

He looked so masculine, undressing in front of her, and the expression of fortitude he wore only made her want him more. Her womb agreed, and the next contraction was so strong that it caused her to bite her lip hard enough to taste blood.

Damien didn't falter in his determination. Gripping the sheet, he hauled it down and off her body. He knelt on the bed as he grabbed her ankles, yanking her into a supine position. He pushed her knees to her chest and entered her in one swift movement.

Without giving her time to adjust, he drove into her over and over until she felt him release inside her. There was a momentary peace before her uterus tensed up again. Usually, his orgasm was enough to make her need go away for a few hours, not a few seconds.

"More," she whispered.

She could feel Damien was still hard as he let her legs drop, and he fell over her, covering her with his body. "I know, baby girl. I know," he said.

He put one arm under her leg, drawing it up so that he could go deeper. He began to thrust again. She wished she could focus on how good he felt moving inside her, against her, around her, but her body's demands were in the way. This time, when he came, so did she. The sensations surged through her so sharply that she saw stars.

When her vision returned, she noticed Damien had dropped her leg, and he was now stroking his thumbs over her cheeks. She couldn't believe how much she would miss him.

Not wanting to dwell on sadness, she said, "Man, that was something."

The corners of his mouth turned up in a wary smile. "It's not quite over yet, baby girl."

"Wh—" Payton didn't even finish a word before a small orgasm trembled through her body.

Her orgasm must have triggered one in Damien because he grunted, bucking slightly, as his seed surged into her core. Their bodies did this twice more before she was able to get a sentence in.

"Wow, this is not what I expected."

"Your body is trying to take in as much of me as possible." He flipped them over, so she lay on him with one knee on each side. "Remember, the goal of mating heat is to get pregnant. Your body is trying to accomplish that by having me release repeatedly into you."

When her friends had mentioned this part, she had thought they were exaggerating.

She felt another spasm. She moaned, and he groaned as their bodies shook.

Clearly, she'd been wrong about the exaggerating.

She pushed herself up, pulling her long dark hair out of the way, so she could see his face. "How long does this last?"

Damien shrugged. "It depends I guess." One side of his mouth turned up. "I've never done this before."

She leaned down and tucked her face back against his chest to hide her grin. At least she had that. It was a minor thing, but it would bring her comfort when she thought of him in the future. They would always have their week here together, a first for both of them.

Her body continued to orgasm, and so did his. Soon, her pelvis began to feel very full.

After about five minutes since their last orgasms, she sat up, careful to keep Damien inside her. She looked down and cupped her lower belly. Her stomach that normally lay flat was now extended, filled with his seed. His sperm had gone through her vagina and settled in her womb where it waited to make a baby.

This was why female shifters always looked pregnant right away and why some of them would show off their stomachs. She rubbed her lower abdomen, imagining a child growing there, and she now understood why those women would flaunt their swollen bellies. They had felt proud. With shifter pregnancies on the rare side, it was a privilege and honor to produce life.

She suddenly realized that she probably looked like an irrational woman high on baby fever. Her head jolted up. She wanted to reassure Damien that she wasn't crazy, but he had fallen asleep with a peaceful smile upon his face.

Payton withdrew him from her body. She pulled up the covers and snuggled next to him. She kissed his jaw and whispered, "I love you, Damien Lowell." Then, she burrowed her face into his neck.

He rolled over to his side, and his hand came to rest on her slightly rounded stomach.

Worn out, she fell asleep and dreamed of dark-haired children with crystal-blue eyes.

Chapter Twenty-Seven

*B*eep. Beep. Beep.

Damien sluggishly awoke to the sound of the alarm on his watch. It was still early, and the sun wouldn't be up for a couple of hours yet. He really didn't want to get out of bed.

Lying in the dark, everything quiet, he could admit to himself that he felt like shit. He was exhausted, and his back throbbed with agony. He'd run out of painkillers last night, and it was becoming more and more apparent that he needed to see a healer soon.

But today was not the day. He needed to get up and focus on getting Payton home. He planned to head into town, and he wanted to leave before Payton woke up, so she wouldn't try to join him. She needed her rest.

He shoved his aches and pains away and checked on her before rising. She continued to sleep. His alarm hadn't woken her. She lay curled up to him, so close that their middles touched. He pulled down the sheet and couldn't tear his eyes away from her abdomen. Her belly was round, full of his seed. He remembered falling asleep the night before after watching her lovingly caressing it. He lightly touched her there and pictured her stomach growing big with his child.

If only…

He shut down any further thoughts. It wasn't meant to be, and wistful fantasies were for schoolgirls. Once he told Payton about his father, there was a strong possibility she'd never speak to him again. He dreaded telling her, but he wanted her to hear it from him before she returned home.

Damien kissed Payton on the forehead, breathing in her lavender scent, and he rose from the bed. From his truck, he grabbed the backpack that he would wear as a wolf, and he filled it with his clothes and money. He put the pack on like any normal human, and he tightened the straps as far as they would go. Then, he stepped onto the porch and gently shut the door.

He quickly shifted into his wolf before he could freeze his most vital parts off, and he headed into town. His backpack was a little loose after he'd shifted, rubbing against his sore back, but he didn't have a choice if he wanted to carry his clothes.

Sprinting most of the way, it took him a little less than an hour to reach his destination. Once in town, he found somewhere secluded to shift back to his human form. Darkness still covered the sky, so it didn't take him long to find a place to change.

There wasn't room for a winter coat in his backpack, but he found he was fine in his T-shirt and flannel shirt. Maybe the temperature had risen, so some of the snow would start to melt.

He went to the nearest convenience store and bought a generic cell-phone charger and more ibuprofen since he'd gone through the whole bottle back at the cabin. He also found some clothes for Payton. She couldn't go home wearing only his flannel shirt and her shoes. The selection was limited, so he picked out a sweatshirt, sweatpants, socks, and some cheap shoes, guessing on sizes. He brought everything to the register and asked for a phonebook and scrap of paper.

The cashier gave him an odd look, but his cell was only a prepaid flip phone. With no Internet at the cabin, an actual phonebook was his only option.

He got the phone number he needed, paid for his stuff, and left. He needed to shift back to a wolf and get out of town before the sun rose for the day.

Unfortunately, his trip back to the cabin took longer. Physically drained, he lacked the energy to run on the way back. The cabin came into view a little over an hour later, and Damien circled, sniffing the ground and checking for any disturbances that might have occurred while he'd been gone.

Assured that everything was safe, he headed to the front of the cabin. The door opened, and Payton stepped out, wearing only his flannel shirt, her legs bare.

"Brr…it's cold out here," she said as she rubbed her hands over her arms and shifted from foot to foot.

Damien shifted back to a man, the cold barely touching his skin. "I guess," he said with a shrug.

"Where did you go?"

"Let's go inside." He ushered her in and slipped off his pack. "I went into town."

"Why didn't you wake me?" She turned to face him. "I would've gone with you."

"I wanted to let you sleep. You looked so peaceful." He kissed her on the forehead, and he walked past her. "I brought back a phone charger and some clothes for you to go home in," he said, patting his backpack.

"Great. Now, I can call my parents," she said with a smile.

Damien unpacked the charger, grabbed his phone, and plugged it in, careful to keep his sore back away from her eyes.

"Damien?"

"What?" He glanced up at Payton, her eyes filled with worry.

"Are you okay? You're sweating."

He wiped his forehead and felt wetness. "It must be from running here. I'm fine." He grabbed his clothes and slipped them on. "Why don't you shower while the phone charges? Then, you can call them when you get out."

"Good idea." She stepped closer, tugged the front of his shirt until he bent over, and kissed him. "Thank you for going and buying a charger and clothes. You're the best."

He kissed her again. "Go."

She turned on her heel, smiling, and went into the bathroom.

He plopped down in the chair and ran his hand down his face. *The best* was not how he would describe himself. He was a jerk. The only reason that he'd told Payton to go shower was because he was a coward and didn't want to tell her anything that would make her hate him.

While he waited for Payton to emerge from the shower, he powered on the phone to make a call, leaving it plugged in, so it could keep charging. He punched in the numbers from the piece of paper. After waiting a few seconds for the other side to pick up, he explained what he needed and where, and the man on the end assured him that they would be there to help him out that afternoon.

Hearing the water shut off, he hung up and turned the phone off, so it would charge faster and just in case someone tried to call. Now was not the time to be interrupted.

The time had come to tell her everything.

Payton walked out of the bathroom, all smiles, until she saw his face and the phone in his hand. "What's wrong?"

Damien set down the phone and stood. He crossed the room to her and grabbed her hands. "I need to talk to you before you call your family. I think you'd better sit for a minute."

"Oh God, something happened to my parents."

He stroked her dark head. "No, baby girl, they're fine." At least, as far as he knew, they were. "Please sit. I have to talk to your father when I take you home, but I wanted to tell you first."

"Okay."

She went to the couch and sat. He followed and sat next to her. He picked up her hands again, wanting to touch her.

"What is it?"

"Remember how I told you that my father and I have different views on everything and that we don't get along?"

"Yes."

"Remember that, please. Promise me."

"Damien...you aren't making any sense."

"Just promise."

She squeezed his hands. "Okay, I promise."

Damien blew out a puff of air. *Here I go. It's now or never.* "My father was behind your kidnapping."

Payton slowly removed her hands away from Damien's grasp. For some reason, this was worse than if she had ripped her hands away.

"What do you mean, your father was behind my kidnapping?"

"A cat-shifter approached my father—I never found out who—and asked him to get you and your brother out of the way, so he could be alpha. In return for my father's help, the cat-shifter would let my father and the pack return to the Twin Cities."

Payton didn't say anything. He'd expected her to jump up and yell, but it was as if an icy calm had settled over her.

He didn't know what to do, so he just kept talking, "Several months ago, my father ordered us to come to Minneapolis. He wouldn't say why. He just said that we had a mission. One night, I caught him right after he had a meeting with another shifter, and I knew something was up. I spoke to the other sentinels, and they didn't know what was going on. I tried to tell them that my father was up to no good, but none of them would listen.

"I finally got my father to tell me what he was planning. I told him he was stupid and crazy and that this was the wrong way for our pack to return, but he wouldn't listen. I already knew the other sentinels wouldn't help me, so I was on my own. I knew when I saw your brother that he could handle his own safety, but you...I worried about you. I felt..." He wanted to say *connected* because it was true. Even back when he'd first started watching her, he'd felt something special between the two of them. But now was not the time to tell her that. "I found out when my father intended to come after you, and I intervened. I didn't know that he had hired humans. I thought it would be his sentinels and that I would be able to reason with them. I didn't know you would get hurt. I didn't know anything would happen between us. I didn't know I would feel this way."

Silence.

Her face gave away nothing as she stared at the wall.

"Payton, please say something."

She deliberately turned her eyes to him. "You saw my brother? Did you see me, too? Before that night?"

He closed his eyes and opened them. "Yes."

"You were at my college, weren't you? You followed me?"

About a month ago, Damien had surveyed Vaughn and Payton a few times. Damien had to see what he needed to do to protect the Llewelyns from his father. There was one time he'd followed Payton to one of her classes, and he'd thought that maybe she suspected something. But she had continued on to class as if everything was normal. It seemed he had been wrong. Payton must have figured out that he had been there, watching her.

"Yes," he answered regretfully. It made him sound worse.

She pursed her lips and nodded. "Does this mean my brother was kidnapped?"

"I honestly don't know. I haven't spoken to anyone in the pack since I've been here. I didn't lie about my phone or getting you home."

She snorted. "At least that's the truth, right?"

Damien hung his head. This was going even worse than he'd thought.

He heard Payton stand, and he quickly followed. "Payton, please, I'm not my father."

She crossed her arms over her chest and clicked her tongue against the roof of her mouth. "Why didn't you tell me right away?"

He thought the answer was obvious—because he hadn't wanted her to be angry with him. But he didn't speak the words out loud. "Because you were hurt, and then your mating heat happened. I didn't want you to worry about anything besides getting better and getting through your heat."

She scoffed and turned to walk away.

"Payton," he called.

She paused.

"I'm so sorry."

She looked over her shoulder, straight into his eyes. "The problem is, Damien, you don't even know what to be sorry for."

She marched to the door, threw it open, ripped off her shirt, and shifted. He glimpsed a beautiful black cat with haunted sapphire eyes before she raced out the door. He followed to see her jump off the porch and run into the woods.

"Payton, wait!" he yelled after her.

Shit. What if she was going home? There was no way she'd make it, human or cat.

She didn't realize how hard the mating heat had been on her body. She'd be fatigued by afternoon.

Damien shifted and ran after her.

Chapter Twenty-Eight

*P*ayton was furious, but that wasn't the worst of it.

The worst was the deep-seated hurt she felt.

She ran through the forest, the cold winter biting at her fur. It was a contrast to the burning rage and the scorching sadness consuming her inside.

She wasn't angry about Damien's father. She knew Damien well enough to know he was a good person, both shifter and human, and he would never resort to such actions. He couldn't help who his father was. She didn't care that he had followed her all those months ago. At the time, she'd felt safe and protected, and she'd been a little curious to know who was out there.

No, what upset her was the fact that he hadn't trusted her enough to tell her. She thought back to this morning when he hadn't woken her to go with him. Maybe he hadn't thought she could handle the news. It was probably both reasons—he hadn't trusted her and hadn't thought she could handle it.

The only reason he'd told her now was because she was going home, and he planned to tell her father, who would tell her. If he'd thought she'd never find out, would he have ever said anything?

Claiming her injuries and mating heat as reasons for not telling her sooner was a load of crap. They were just convenient excuses not to tell her. Here she'd thought she found someone strong, someone who was her equal, and someone who would treat her as such. Her father was an alpha, and her mother was an alphena. Payton was an independent and capable woman. She was not a child who needed to be sheltered from the real world. Her father and brother always protected her more than needed. With Damien, she'd thought she found someone who saw her as strong, not as a little girl who needed her hand held.

The most awful part was that she'd let herself fall in love with him.

Payton slowed her pace. Lost in her head, she hadn't heard anyone following her until that moment.

She swung around and hissed at the dark gray-and-white wolf advancing toward her. If he knew what was good for him, he'd stay back. She was ready for a fight. She'd show him she wasn't a pussy—cat or otherwise.

Damien neared, and she used her paw to strike him in the jaw, warning him to stay away. Her claws were in—for now.

He growled.

He's mad? Good.

She knocked him again—this time, with a hint of claw. His following growl was accompanied with his bare teeth. He was warning her, but he had better think again if he thought she was scared. She roared and pounced on him. She was going to pin him and show him she was stronger than he thought. She wasn't some weak female.

However, things didn't always go the way one had wanted them to go.

She fought dirtier than he did. She used teeth and claws, wanting him to hurt like she hurt, but he still pinned her under him. She was belly up where the entire world could see her loss, if anyone had been watching.

He had his mouth on her throat, but he didn't bite down.

Despite him winning, she didn't want to give up. After all, he was pack, and she was pride. This wasn't about dominance or rank. This was personal. She struggled underneath him, and he shifted, still pinning her with his superhuman strength.

"Damn it, Payton. I don't want to hurt you!"

She followed closely behind him, shifting as well. "Little late for that, don't you think?"

He leaned down until their noses touched. He growled, and she felt a tug in her belly. He knew it turned her on, but she doubted he was thinking about sex right now.

"I already told you that I'm sorry. You have to under—"

She didn't want to hear any more of his bullshit, and since she was trapped underneath him, she did the only thing she could think of to shut him up.

She kissed him.

She wasn't gentle. She nipped and bit, drawing blood. Instead of getting mad, Damien gave her back everything she was giving him. He kissed her with a passion bordering on desperation, and even though she was angry, she still wanted him.

She barely noticed the cold and wetness of the snow underneath her. She was hot with anger, and Damien blazed with heat. She felt his arousal rub her mound. Whether his erection had been caused by adrenaline from their fight or from being aroused by her kiss, she didn't care, and she was able to angle her body enough to settle his cock between her legs before she pushed him inside her.

He broke their kiss. "Fuck."

He turned them over, so she was on top, and he lay in the snow. He was always the gentleman, even when fighting and fucking. This only pissed her off more, and she fueled her fury into achieving an orgasm.

Damien was so hot against the snow and cold air, and she swore that she could feel his heat in her core as well. She sat up and rode him hard, not caring if he was uncomfortable. Going by his groans though, he loved what she was doing to him.

With all the sex they'd had, this was only the second time they had been together while she wasn't in heat. She took in everything around her despite her anger, wanting to watch Damien, as she used his body to pleasure herself.

She knew his body almost as well as her own, and she sensed that he was close. She was on top, so she was going to be the one to control when he came. But she didn't even get a chance to slow her movements to fend off his orgasm. As if he sensed her intention, he flipped her over, so she was on the bottom again.

He wrapped his arm around her back, underneath her, arching her pelvis. He latched on to her breast, sucking hard. Soon, she was ready to come, so when he released her nipple and changed his thrusts from deep to shallow, she tried to increase the pace. But he held her tight and stopped all movements—his and hers. He stared into her eyes, and diamond met sapphire.

She looked away from the authority she saw there.

Damien drove into her, their bodies meeting with such force that she heard the sound echoing through the trees. He sucked on her neck and dragged his mouth back to her breast. This time, he bit down strong enough that she felt teeth, and she shattered around him. He drove into her twice more before he exploded inside her. His seed pumped into her, hot and thick.

Even during her mating heat, she didn't remember it being that warm.

He collapsed on top of her. Normally, she would touch him, caress him, let him know she cared, but this time, she kept her hands at her sides. She was still distressed, and great sex wasn't the solution to everything.

Just when she started to feel the cold, Damien picked her up and headed for the cabin. She wrapped her arms and legs around him to hang on. Neither spoke, but the fact that he was still inside her body conveyed more than any words they could have said.

In her last play for supremacy, Damien had turned the tables. Instead of her directing his release, he'd controlled hers. Despite the tightness of his knot pushing against her walls, he could have pulled out now that her heat had completed. No, he purely didn't want her to forget who the more dominant one was.

Where that left them, she didn't know.

If she said she didn't like the alpha in him, she'd be lying. But could he understand that even though he was stronger than her, she wasn't weak?

Part of her had believed that Damien would eventually find a way to bring his pack back to the Cities, and they might try to have a relationship. But now, she didn't know.

Their fight and sex had taken away some of her ire, and she sighed, resting her head on Damien's shoulder. She could feel his knot inside her as he walked, and such a strong part of her loved their connection.

If shifters had only one single mate who was designed for them, she and Damien were each other's. Shifters were definitely more drawn to their mate. It was almost as if nature wanted them to be together. But there wasn't just one mate per shifter. If a shifter lost his or her mate, the shifter could mate again.

If there were just one mate per shifter, it wouldn't matter what her family and pride or his father and pack said about Damien and her. Her family and pride would have to accept him. It also wouldn't matter if they had problems, no matter how massive, because this would be their only opportunity for happiness, and they would have to work things out. Even if she were pretty sure that Damien was meant to be hers and she was meant to be his, it wouldn't be enough if the rest of the world said no.

What had Mother Nature been thinking, putting a wolf-shifter and cat-shifter together? Maybe she'd thought if she could get a vampire and a shifter together, anything else would be a piece of cake.

Payton rubbed her nose against Damien's neck.

If only…

Damien walked through the open entrance of the cabin and kicked it closed. The main room was cool from the door being left open, but Payton was still warm from the heat Damien was giving off.

He carried her into the bedroom and lay down on the bed with her body draped over him. She waited for Damien to speak because she really wanted to hear what he had to say before she said anything.

He remained silent, and soon, he grew soft inside her. While she had wanted him to shut up earlier when she kissed him, now that her emotions had settled down some, she wanted him to say something. Their problems weren't over just because they'd had sex. She was getting warm, so she rolled off him to read his face, hoping his expression would give something away.

He was asleep.

She couldn't believe it. He had fallen asleep as if nothing had happened. She was just about to get up, march out of there, and slam the door when she saw the sweat covering his forehead.

He shouldn't be perspiring. The excursion outside hadn't been that strenuous, and with the freezing weather, he shouldn't have to sweat to cool down. If anything, he should be a little cold.

She put the back of her hand to his brow and found he had a fever. It was no wonder he was so hot. She felt like a fool for not noticing it sooner.

"Damien." She shook him, trying to wake him. "Damien?"

He didn't move a muscle. He wasn't asleep. He was unconscious.

This was not good. She had to figure out what was wrong.

She thought back, trying to remember anything. He hadn't seemed sick— no coughing, no sneezing, and no vomiting. It probably wasn't respiratory or gastrointestinal.

Did he get hurt?

They had barely left the cabin since they'd been here, except for Damien's trip into town today. He hadn't mentioned getting hurt, and any injury wouldn't be infected this soon.

A light bulb went off. *His back.*

He had mentioned that he'd hurt it the night of her attempted abduction. She had assumed he'd twisted it or something. She rolled him to his stomach.

She was wrong.

She slapped her hands over her mouth. "Oh my God, Damien."

From his shoulder to his hip was a long cut, open and bright red. Something like this should have healed days ago, but instead, it was infected. He needed to see a healer immediately. He needed antibiotics.

A number of thoughts flew around in her head. This was another thing that he'd kept from her, and she was angry, hurt, and disappointed. But the reason she was so upset was because she loved him. Seeing him hurt like this, with a life-threatening infection, only told her how much she really cared for him. If anything happened to him, she didn't know what she would do.

She didn't know what to do now.

With everything that had happened between them, they had never spoken about how he planned to clear the snow and get her home.

Damien was fighting for his life, and they were still trapped.

Chapter Twenty-Nine

"*H*oly shit!" Reid yelled from his perch at the computer.

Saxon shot off the couch to see what he was holy-shitting about.

Everyone else came running, too, even Lilith.

"What? Did you find something?" Vance asked.

"Damien used his cell phone."

Murmurs were uttered throughout the room. Saxon hoped that there was more to the news.

"He only used it for a few minutes before he turned it off," Reid continued, "but he made a phone call to a snow removal company. I just need some time to get into their system, and hopefully, I will have an address. And then—"

"Then, you will find my baby?" Lilith asked, near tears.

"Yes, ma'am."

With her hope confirmed, their alphena started to cry, and their alpha took her in his arms to soothe her.

Vance looked at Tegan. She looped her arm through Lilith's and slowly led their alphena out of the room.

"How long will it take?" Vance asked once Lilith was gone.

"A few hours. By this afternoon probably."

"Can we be prepared to go by nightfall?" Vance asked.

"I don't see why not."

"Good." Vance nodded his approval. "Call Zane and update him, and call Vaughn and have him tell the vampires to be ready."

"I thought you said Damien wasn't a threat, that he was on our side," Camden said.

Vance rocked on his heels. "If we can find Damien, then so can Dwyer, and when it comes to my only daughter, I'm not risking her safety. We're already down Vaughn and Sawyer. If the vampires want to help us, I'm not going to turn them down."

Dante stepped out of the shower, preparing to get a few hours of sleep before nightfall. He wrapped a towel around his waist and walked out of his bathroom to his bedroom. He pulled back the covers on his bed and reached to remove the cloth around his waist when he suddenly smelled sunshine and cat-shifter. A second later, there was a knock on his door.

He didn't bother to dress. In fact, he considered removing the towel just to shock her and make her leave, but he didn't. He had been raised to be more of a gentleman than that.

He swung the door open. "What?" Perhaps he needed a few refresher lessons.

Phoenix, ever tall and proud, paid no attention to his lack of attire while all he could think was how hideous hers was. She wore an oversized sweatshirt and baggy jeans.

"Vaughn sent me. I have news."

The last thing he'd heard was Dwyer Lowell, alpha of the Minnesota Pack, was partly responsible for the attempt on the princess's life, but his son was not.

Phoenix explained what the cat-shifters had discovered and that their alpha wanted to let him know they were asking for the Guardians' assistance.

He was pleased to know they had asked for the Guardians this time, so there would be no strong-arming them to let the vampires help. "Tell your alpha we will be ready at sunset."

He moved to shut the door when she put her hand on it, stopping it halfway.

"Wait."

He opened it again. "What?" he bit out.

"You haven't fed yet."

He grabbed her wrist harder than he had to. He hauled her inside his room and slammed the door closed before anyone else could hear her. "Who do you think you are? The feeding police?"

She stiffened her spine. "No. I'm someone who cares...about my fellow sentinels and alpha."

This again? "My need for blood doesn't concern you. I'm fine."

"If you're fine, why did you bring me in here to have this conversation? So, no one else knows about your condition?"

He opened his mouth to protest, but damn it, she was right.

"I'll feed as soon as I get a chance. Happy?"

She shook her head. "No. You don't have time before tonight." She pulled up her sleeve on her huge sweatshirt and stuck out her arm, wrist up. "Feed from me."

He purposely stared at her breasts, which weren't hidden despite her attempt by wearing baggy clothing. "Remember what I said about feeding?" He immediately became hard at the thought of having sex with her while he drank her blood, and it pissed him off a little that she was the reason he was turned on.

He didn't bother to hide his erection, and for the first time, she seemed to notice that he wore only a towel.

He glanced at her face.

She swallowed, losing some of her resolve. She dropped her arm. "Yes."

"Well then"—he gestured toward the door—"don't let it hit you on the way out."

She didn't leave. She kicked off her sneakers and unzipped her hoodie. She let it fall to the floor, and she reached for the bottom of the T-shirt she wore underneath.

He stepped forward and placed his hand on hers. "What are you doing?"

She lifted her chin. "Undressing."

"Why?"

"So, we can have sex."

"Jesus, Phoenix." She was supposed to leave, not undress and offer her body. "You don't need to whore yourself out to me."

She flinched, and for a second, he felt bad for her. She must really want him to feed, and he had to admit, he really wanted to, too. He'd delayed his feeding too long. She smelled incredible with her blood pulsing fast under the creamy skin in her neck. His hunger hit him full force, and he had to resist attacking her exposed vein.

"Look, I'll feed, but we aren't having sex."

"Really?"

"Really."

Her body sagged as the tension left her body.

Does she have to be that relieved? It wasn't as if sex with him would be bad. She stepped back and bent to pick up her sweatshirt.

"Leave it."

She looked at her bare wrist. "Okay."

She stood, and he didn't bother to hide his hunger or desire any longer. He stalked toward her, maneuvering her backward, until she hit the door.

She held up her arm to stop him. "Here you go."

He cradled her hand in his and brought her wrist up to his nose. He inhaled her aroma and licked at her pulse. Her body shuddered, and she closed her eyes. He couldn't smell any arousal from her, but he couldn't smell any fear either. She knew how to block her scent better than anyone he'd ever met. He ran his fang over her wrist.

She said, "Just do it."

He dropped her arm, and her green eyes snapped open.

"What's wrong?"

He shrugged. "Nothing."

She looked down at her forearm and then back at him. "Why aren't you feeding?"

"Oh, I'm not feeding from your wrist."

He had considered it, but after her reaction to not having to sleep with him, he wanted to make her suffer a little.

"Wh-what?"

He stepped closer. "Move your hair, Red." He nodded at her neck.

She hesitantly bunched up her hair and moved it to one side. He was caught by surprise because he'd thought she'd fight him. She did bunch her hands at her sides, so perhaps her battle was with herself.

He picked up her locks and rubbed the ends against his palm before he put the strands to his nose. Her hair smelled like the sun, too. He wrapped her mane around his hand and gently tilted her head to one side.

She was tall, but he was taller, and he had to bend down to get to her neck. He nuzzled her there, from ear to shoulder. He heard her breathing quicken, and he smiled to himself. He opened his lips and sucked on her skin. Even though she tried to hold it in, a soft moan leaked from her lips.

He lifted his head and blew on her skin. The coolness was a contrast to his next move. He brought his mouth back to her and began to feed. There was no escaping the initial pierce of fangs, but one could be tender or rough, and he did it slowly—just like he would if another part of him were entering another part of her. Her hands moved to his waist, and he felt the scraping of her nails.

She trembled in his arms but not from fear. Perhaps she understood why sex usually accompanied feeding. He drew on her, taking in her blood, and this time, he shivered. Her taste…never had he expected that a non-vampire, a shifter, would taste as good as she did. He could drink from her until he perished, and he would die happy.

Dante had fed on a human before. Human blood was weak and not as sweet when compared to vampire blood. But not Phoenix's. Her blood was strong and thick. While still not as sweet, it had a rich flavor that made his taste buds burst. Her blood flowed through him, and his strength began to return as his erection grew harder.

She moaned and began to rub against him. He still couldn't smell any arousal coming from her, but her body language told him everything he needed to know. He knew his feeding from her would turn her on, and he could likely strip her pants off and thrust inside her. He groaned at the thought, but he'd told her he wouldn't have sex with her, and he wasn't going to go back on his word.

But heavy petting wasn't sex. He lifted her and settled himself between her legs, pinning her against the door. She didn't fight him. She rubbed her pelvis against him, and he cupped her breast and skimmed her nipple. She stilled, so he released her breast. He drank faster, and she ground against him again.

He shifted her, so the seam of her jeans along with her sweet spot were on his cock, and he rubbed. He released her hair and thumbed her pulse on the side of her neck that he wasn't drinking from. The friction from her crotch on his plus her rich blood filling him almost had him coming behind his towel. He held off as her breathing got shallow and fast, but she seemed to have plateaued. Her orgasm was stuck.

He paused in his feeding and sliced his thumb with his fang before returning to her neck. He stuck his thumb in her mouth, knowing what his blood would do to her. Her hand flew up to his, holding it in her mouth, as if she was afraid he'd take it away. She sucked hard and then stiffened around him as she climaxed.

The barrier she used to cover her scent was broken, and his whole room immediately filled with the musk of her arousal. He pulled his fangs from her neck and licked the wound before his restraint was gone. But the air was so thick with her scent that he could taste it, and he lost control of his body. She dropped his hand, and he quickly used it to clutch his towel as he ejaculated into it.

They stood there with him holding her against the door for a minute, both catching their breaths. She pushed against his shoulders. He set her down and stepped back, but before he could say anything, she bolted out the door.

He licked the cut on this thumb, tasting the two of them, and noticed the claw marks on his waist. He hadn't even felt her cut into his skin.

They hadn't had sex, they hadn't even kissed, yet it was the hottest experience he'd ever had in his life.

Chapter Thirty

*D*wyer flipped through the channels on the shitty TV in his crappy motel room. He wasn't really paying attention. His thoughts were concentrated on Damien. They still hadn't found him, and Dwyer was questioning Lachlan's dependability at this point. He was good at his job, but so far, he hadn't come to his alpha with anything new.

Dwyer turned the TV off and chucked the remote on the bed. If only things had gone according to plan. Instead, Damien had Vance's daughter, and Vance was in hiding. The cat-shifter couldn't become alpha of the Pride until Vance was dead and his daughter was out of the way.

The only thing that had gone right was that the humans Dwyer had hired were able to snatch Vaughn and his stupid vampire. Last Dwyer had heard, they were still locked up. He only had to keep them that way until the cat-shifter was appointed alpha and removed the pack's exile status. If Vaughn challenged the new alpha, it wasn't going to be Dwyer's problem. In fact, he might just send an anonymous tip as to who was behind Vaughn's abduction and his father's death. It would serve the cat-shifter right.

Dwyer snorted in the empty room. Damien hadn't thought Dwyer could figure out a complete plan, but he was smarter than his son thought. He just needed to find his son and show him—scratch that. Dwyer didn't have to prove his intelligence to anybody, not even his son. He was alpha of the Minnesota Pack after all.

Suddenly, there was a knock on Dwyer's door, and he sniffed the air. It was Lachlan. He'd better have an update.

Dwyer opened the door and let Lachlan in.

"What do you have for me?" Dwyer demanded.

"Do you remember Redmond Heck owning a cabin up north?"

Dwyer had no recollection of any property owned by his father-in-law. That old bastard had kept this from him. Redmond had never liked Dwyer and had disapproved of his daughter mating with him.

Dwyer hid his irritation at his late wife and her father because he didn't want Lachlan to know he'd been made a fool of. He'd let Lachlan think he had forgotten about it. "I don't remember much about it or what happened to it."

Lachlan cocked his head to the side, but he didn't express any doubts. "How many years ago did he pass away?"

"About twelve. Why?"

"This place was purchased in the seventies, and it has never been sold. Even the utilities are under his name."

This caught Dwyer's attention. "And?"

Lachlan hesitated.

"I know you have more information. You aren't thinking of protecting Damien, are you?"

"I found your father-in-law's will."

"I was there when the will was read."

"I found another part that wasn't supposed to be read when you were around."

Dwyer clenched his fists. "That son of a bitch. What did it say?"

"It named Damien as the beneficiary. Since the property has never been sold, my guess is that you might find Damien there."

Finally, Dwyer received some decent news. He slapped Lachlan on the back. "Good work. Tell everybody where we're going. We'll leave at sunset. I want to go in with the cover of night."

Damien would smell the eight of them coming, so their best defense was darkness.

"Will do." Lachlan nodded and left the way he'd come.

It took about five minutes after Lachlan had left for Dwyer to realize that the sentinel never answered his question. Despite handing over the information, Lachlan hadn't denied protecting Damien.

Payton paced in front of the couch. She was worried sick about Damien. He hadn't woken once since passing out that morning. She had done everything she could think of to help him, including thoroughly cleaning his wound, which had led her to finding out why it hadn't healed.

Whoever had cut him was prepared for a shifter. There had been tiny slivers of silver along the entire length of Damien's wound. If he could have seen it better—or if he had told her—it never would have gotten this bad. It also crossed her mind that the kidnappers hadn't expected Damien to be there, and the knife they'd used was meant for her.

If and when she met Dwyer Lowell, she was going to claw his eyes out for what he'd done to Damien.

She had gone through and picked out every sliver that she could see. Then, she'd cleaned the wound, covered it with ointment, and bandaged it, but his shifter genetics weren't going to get him out of this one. Shifters were stronger, lived longer, and healed faster, but they weren't immortal. He needed antibiotics and more than over-the-counter painkillers. The ibuprofen she'd shoved down his throat probably wasn't doing much for his discomfort, and while it had dropped his fever, it hadn't gotten rid of it.

The only bright spot of the day was that while she'd taken care of Damien, someone had come and cleared most of the snow off the main drive up to the cabin. She had scarcely heard the sounds of the equipment being used because she was so wrapped up in Damien. It wasn't until after she'd finished that she realized someone had been there.

At first, she'd been very excited. They weren't trapped any longer. Then, she'd noticed the location of the sun in the sky. This time of year, dusk along with a plummeting temperature would hit fast. To make matters worse, Payton had no idea where they were. She'd checked the gas tank, and they only had half a tank. Damien had ten dollars and no credit cards, and she didn't know what had happened to her purse during the attempted kidnapping. Payton would need to leave during the day to have the best chance of getting home.

She'd never felt so helpless in her life. Maybe she wasn't as dominant as she'd thought. Damien had never seemed insecure of himself the whole time they were together. Maybe he was right not to tell her everything.

She stopped pacing. *Payton Lilith Llewelyn, quit feeling sorry for yourself and think!*

She resumed her steps, and it hit her. "The phone. How did I forget about the phone?"

The easy answer was they hadn't had one for a week, and with everything that had happened, she'd forgotten.

She raced over to the table, pulled the charger from the cell, and powered it on. The first number she called was her parents at home, but there was no answer. She called her mother's cell, and it went straight to voice mail, which meant it was off. She left a message in case her mother turned it back on. Next, she called her father's cell.

"Vance here."

A minute ago, she had been full of determination, but the sound of her father's voice almost caused her to cry, and any words she'd been ready to utter were stuck in her throat.

"Hello?" her father spoke again.

"Hi, Daddy."

"Payton? Is that really you?"

She heard murmurs in the background and the sound of a moving vehicle. "Yes, Daddy."

"Are you okay?" His voice was filled with such worry that she almost cried again.

"I'm fine. But I need your help."

"What's wrong, kitten?"

"I know you're probably not going to believe me or understand, but please hear me out."

"As long as you are safe and in one piece, I'm all ears."

"I'm in a cabin somewhere outside the Cities. Damien Lowell rescued me from being kidnapped. He brought me somewhere safe and took care of me. Then, we got snowed in with no phone and weren't able to get out.

But I didn't know that Damien had been injured the night he saved me, and now, he's very sick. I don't know where I am, and Damien won't wake up. I don't know what to do," she blurted out everything so that her father wouldn't interrupt when he heard Damien's name. Now, she was in tears. "Plea-please, help us. I'm afraid he might die." She sobbed harder. It was the first time she had admitted that Damien might not make it.

"Payton. Payton!"

It took her a minute to realize that her father had been yelling her name. "Wh-what?" She sniffled. *I am such a softie.* "Please don't say Damien is bad, Daddy. He's not his father. He's—"

"Payton, I *know.*"

Huh? Payton stopped crying. "What?"

"I know he rescued you. I know he took you somewhere safe."

"You do?"

"Yes."

"Are Vaughn and Naya okay?"

"Yes."

She sighed with relief.

"We'll talk more about that later. Right now, I need you to listen."

"Hold on, Daddy." Payton heard tires crunching on the snow. She went to the window and saw a truck and an SUV pulling up. She didn't recognize either vehicle in the dark. She set down the phone and hurriedly yanked on the clothes Damien had bought for her.

She heard her father shouting through the phone, and she picked it up from the table. "I'm here."

"What's going on?"

"Two vehicles pulled up."

"Shit," her father said.

She was momentarily shocked. Her father never swore in front of her.

The doors opened, and eight individuals got out. The moon was bright, and they'd left the car headlights on. The eldest of the group had dark gray-and-white hair and looked like an older version of the wolf passed out in the bedroom. *Damien's Father* might as well have been stamped on his forehead.

"Shit is right, Daddy. The wolves are here."

"Payton, you listen to me," her father said, his voice full of urgency. "Stay inside. Lock the doors and windows. Do not let them in. All you have to do is stall them. We're about five minutes away."

"You are?"

"Yes. Five minutes. Please, just stay safe. Your mother will kill me if anything happens to you."

The moment was serious, but her father managed to put a smile on her face. She pictured her mother going after her father with all the fierceness of a mama bear.

"Okay."

"Promise me that you'll do as I say."

"I promise. See you soon."

"See you soon, kitten."

"Oh, and, Daddy?"

"Yes?"

"I love you."

Payton hung up the phone, but she didn't wait for Dwyer and his sentinels to come knocking. She had to protect her wolf, and she wasn't going to let them get anywhere near him.

She put on the shoes Damien had bought her, even if they were a little big, and she stepped outside. She left the door open a crack in case something happened to Damien.

"Payton Llewelyn, I presume?" Dwyer asked as he approached.

His sentinels had fanned out behind him, but they didn't seem to be on alert. They looked more confused than anything.

She lifted her chin. "Who wants to know?"

Dwyer clenched his jaw. She'd purposely pretended not to know who he was just to piss him off.

"Dwyer Lowell," he said through clenched teeth. He tried to smile, but it came off as fake. "Is my son here?"

She straightened her back, trying to make herself taller. "He's busy."

Dwyer stepped forward. "I don't care. He owes me an explanation."

"You mean because he didn't let you kidnap me?"

"You got a mouth on you, little girl. I see your father could've done a better job in raising you."

This wolf. What a piece of work. "You don't talk about my father like that."

Dwyer came closer, taking the two steps to the porch. His sentinels stayed where they were. They didn't move any closer, which seemed odd, but she was grateful because she could only be so brave.

"Where is my son?"

Payton looked Dwyer straight in his ice-blue eyes. "You can't see him."

Dwyer looked behind her and then grabbed her upper arm. "Fine. It's you I wanted in the first place. Either he left, or he's injured. Otherwise, he'd be out here. I'll come back for him later."

"Let go of me."

He ignored her and tried to pull her along, but she kicked him in the balls. He let go of her and grabbed his crotch.

"You bitch." The look in his eyes was malicious. He was done being nice.

Payton stepped back. She was scared, and she hoped her father would show up soon.

Dwyer slowly straightened and stalked toward her when she heard the door swing open behind her.

"Don't you fucking touch her."

Chapter Thirty-One

*S*omething was wrong.

Damien blinked his eyes open. *Man, I feel like shit.* His back burned, and so did his skin from fever and infection. He should probably still be sleeping, but he knew something had awoken him.

Something wasn't right.

"Let go of me," he heard from the living room.

Payton. Who was she talking to?

He heard a scuffle and then, "You bitch."

Ah, hell. His father was here.

Damien used every ounce of energy to get himself off the bed. He had to protect her. He realized he was naked but didn't care. He had shifted in front of his father plenty of times, and nudity was unimportant when Payton's life might be at stake.

He stumbled to the bedroom door, paused to regain some of his strength, and walked to the front door.

He flung it open and looked directly at his father. "Don't you fucking touch her."

Damien stepped outside to stand by Payton. He noticed his fellow sentinels stood back, away from the porch. Lachlan, Chase, Kendall, Ranulf, Bowden, Quentin, and Raven—none of them looked happy to be here.

"Why? Because she reeks of you?" Dwyer leaned toward her.

"Couldn't resist the wolf cock, huh?"

Payton gasped.

"Or maybe my son couldn't resist the pussy? After all, he is one."

"He's more of a man and shifter than you will ever be," Payton snapped at Dwyer, fists clenched and fierceness in her eyes.

His father ignored her, looking back at Damien. "Speaking of rotten, you don't smell too good, boy."

"You leave him alone, asshole," Payton spoke up again.

His father continued to ignore her. "Your bitch has a mouth on her, son."

Damien stepped forward and punched his father in the jaw and then the stomach. Dwyer clutched his face with one hand and his abdomen with the other, bending at the waist.

Damien stepped back to Payton, still looking at his father. "You are not allowed to talk to her like that."

His father uncurled. "You seem to have forgotten who is alpha and who isn't."

"Maybe it's time to remedy that."

"Are you challenging me, son?"

"It's about time, don't you think?"

Payton put her hand on his arm. "Damien." Worry filled her eyes. His infection wasn't going to make this an easy fight, but she didn't speak the words out loud. "Kick his ass."

He knew he wasn't out of the doghouse with her yet, and they still had a lot to talk about, but it gave him strength to know that she still cared for him.

Damien brushed his thumb over her cheek. "My pleasure."

"My God, you love her," his father spit.

Payton froze.

Dwyer unbuttoned his shirt. "This must be my lucky day. You're injured and in love. I'm barely going to break a sweat. When I win, I'm going to take your pretty cat, and you won't be able to do anything about it. Nothing is going to stop me from moving forward with my plans."

The sentinels looked at one another, bewilderment on their faces.

"I see you still haven't told them anything. Do you enjoy keeping your sentinels in the dark?" Damien spoke loud enough for all the sentinels to hear.

"What are you two talking about?" Chase asked, clearly unhappy.

The others nodded in agreement.

Damien opened his mouth to answer when three more vehicles approached. The first person to exit was Vance. Damien felt immediately intimidated. It wasn't because Vance was the Pride's alpha. If Damien defeated his father and became alpha, he and Vance would have equal standing within their groups. Damien was intimidated because Vance was Payton's father.

His own father stood looking at the cat-shifters, but Damien saw his smirk. Damien couldn't let Vance's presence affect him. He needed all his concentration to win. And if his father thought his feelings for Payton were a hindrance, his father was wrong. She only made him stronger, especially when she slipped her hand into his instead of running away from him and toward her dad.

Behind Vance stood four cat-shifter sentinels and four non-shifters— three males and one female. He knew they were vampires because they didn't smell human. Instead, they had a sweetness radiating from them. They must have come due to the vampire princess, Vance's new daughter-in-law. Damien sincerely hoped his father hadn't succeeded in kidnapping the princess and Vaughn.

"You okay, kitten?" Vance asked.

"Yes, Daddy."

"What are you doing here?" Dwyer asked Vance.

His father was now exposed to Vance, and the two of them were evenly matched, but Dwyer was too proud to admit defeat. His stupid pride was what had gotten them here in the first place.

"I could ask you the same thing," Vance responded.

"Well, I'm here because my son has challenged me for alpha, and I have accepted." Dwyer held out his hands and scanned the area. "You will all be my witnesses to his failing."

When a challenge was issued, shifter law prohibited anyone from interfering. The shifter who lost would not be allowed to challenge the same alpha again, nor would he be allowed to be the alpha's successor. If his father won and Damien lost, this would be the end. Damien wouldn't be alpha, even after his father died or retired. This was his one chance. This fight would be to the death or until one of them surrendered. His father could kill him, but Damien had to try. He couldn't let Dwyer continue to destroy the pack.

Damien watched his father out of the corner of his eye as Vance asked, "Is this true?"

Damien didn't respond because his father, still in his human form and without warning, attacked.

He never fought fair.

Saxon watched as Damien sidestepped Dwyer, away from Payton, and leaped off the porch. He shifted to wolf mid-jump and landed on all four paws. Dwyer removed his pants and followed. The two growled at each other.

Both of them were almost identical in color, but Damien was bigger and younger. However, Vance had filled them in on Damien's infection and fever. Saxon didn't know if Damien could win, but it would be a very good thing if he did.

Payton stood on the porch, wringing her hands. It was obvious by her agitation and the way she'd held the wolf's hand that she cared for him.

Dante approached Saxon's side. "Why doesn't anyone stop them?"

"We can't. Shifter law," he said.

"Even though Dwyer attacked without warning? That doesn't seem fair."

Saxon finally glanced at Dante and did a double take. The first time he'd met Dante, he would have thought of him as weak or lacking, but seeing him today, it was apparent that something had changed. "It was a dirty move. Technically, they should be in a ring or an open space, and both would be given plenty of time to prepare, but it's not illegal." Saxon, not known for tact, blurted out, "What's different about you, man?"

The vampire cursed. "If you noticed, I guess I was worse off than I thought."

"Worse off?"

"I waited longer to feed than I probably should have."

Saxon was confused. He thought vampires ate daily, like shifters and humans. "How long can you go without food?"

"Not that kind of fed. Blood."

"Oh." Saxon eyed him up and down, wondering what drinking blood was like.

Dante stepped closer and leaned into him. "Shouldn't you be watching the fight?"

Saxon had to hide his reaction to Dante's smell. It was subtle, but he smelled like Phoenix. Saxon was all kinds of surprised. As far as he knew, Phoenix was asexual, but he was quite sure that Dante hadn't had sex with her because the smell would be stronger. But something had happened.

Saxon's brain clicked. "Ho-ly shit."

Dante, who had turned to watch the challenge, jerked his head in Saxon's direction. "What?"

Saxon shook his head. "Nothing."

He turned his head back to the battle, and Dante did, too, but that didn't stop Saxon from taking a quick peek at Dante. Saxon was shocked that Phoenix had let a vampire feed from her. It wasn't sex, but from what Vaughn had told him, feeding was pretty damn intimate.

Saxon turned back to the vampire and eyed him once more. Dante had better not hurt her. Phoenix was like a sister to Saxon, and if she got hurt, Dante would have him to answer to.

"What?" Dante asked when he noticed he was being watched.

Saxon shook his head and locked away that news for later, choosing to focus on the fight.

So far, Damien and Dwyer had been taking swings and nips at each other, but the small wolf suddenly jumped on the bigger one's back and had him by the back of the neck.

Payton yelped and slapped her hand over her mouth. Damien sagged down on his stomach, and his father placed himself over Damien.

Out of nowhere, Damien broke Dwyer's grip and escaped. His side dripped with blood from where his father's teeth had broken the skin, but it didn't stop Damien. He launched a full attack, knocking Dwyer on his side. Damien went for his throat—literally.

Dwyer struggled to get away, but Damien bit down. Dwyer rolled onto his back, exposing his belly. It was his surrender. Everyone watching sighed with relief, releasing the air they'd been holding while watching in anticipation.

Damien stepped back, and they both shifted back to human.

Damien stood over his father, panting. "Swear your loyalty to me," he said, demanding the respect he had earned and deserved.

His father sat to catch his own breath. He opened his mouth. "I, Dwyer Lowell, swear—" He didn't finish. He extended his claws and swiped, aiming for Damien's legs.

Damien must have been prepared for his father to do something sneaky because he jumped back before his foot shot out, kicking his father in the face and knocking him out.

"Was that allowed?" Dante asked.

"Dwyer, no. Damien, yes. Dwyer lost, surrendered, and then came after Damien. If Damien wishes, he has the right to kill Dwyer."

Dante nodded in approval.

Damien faced his sentinels, his shoulders back and head held high. He was covered in cuts and bruises. The largest was an infected one running across his back, and the second largest was where his father had taken a chunk of skin out of his neck and shoulder. Both bled heavily. "Do you swear your loyalty to me?"

All seven of them got down on their knees without hesitation.

The first one spoke, "I swear and pledge my loyalty to you, Damien Lowell, alpha of the Minnesota Pack." He used his claw to cut his right wrist. "I will fight with you and bleed for you."

"Once the sentinels acknowledge Damien as their new alpha, the rest of the pack will follow," Saxon explained to Dante.

Each of the wolf sentinels spoke the words and cut their arms to show their allegiance.

When they finished, Damien said, "I accept each and every one of you as part of my pack. Your position of sentinel, however, has yet to be determined."

The seven nodded in understanding.

Then, as if he couldn't hold on any longer, Damien passed out and collapsed on the ground.

Payton ran off the porch, screaming and crying, and shivers ran down Saxon's spine at the strength of her anguish. She reached Damien and spoke his name over and over, demanding that he wake up. The sound of her agony was haunting, and Saxon vowed that he would never let someone care about him like that, or vice versa. After all, no one could take away what wasn't his in the first place.

Chapter Thirty-Two

$\mathcal{F}$illed with a mix of dread and anticipation, Vance Llewelyn reluctantly descended the stairs to his basement. Along with most of his sentinels, he had returned home. He'd left his mate and Tegan at the safe house and made Vaughn and Naya stay with the vampires until he could be sure it was safe for them to come home. He'd tried to get Payton to join her mother, but she'd refused. He'd deal with that situation later. Right now, he had bigger fish to fry—correction, he had a bigger shifter to fry.

Vance walked past the entertainment room, past the door to the workout and training room, past the bathroom, and to the door of the one unfinished room in the back. He pulled out a key and unlocked it. He left the door open just in case he needed reinforcement, but he highly suspected that it wouldn't be necessary.

The room had no windows and held only a single cot, toilet, and sink. On the cot lay Dwyer Lowell. He wasn't in good shape after the challenge with his son, and he had a few injuries that needed healing before he'd be back to his normal self. He was, however, in better shape than his son.

Damien lay unconscious upstairs with Payton at his side. As soon as they had returned home the night before, Vance had called a healer. Dr. Bennett had stitched up Damien's back and neck. After the doctor had hooked Damien up to an IV and given him antibiotics, Dr. Bennett's outlook seemed hopeful. But Damien had yet to awaken.

"Your son is going to be okay," Vance said to Dwyer. "The doctor says he will recover to his full health."

Dwyer curled his lip. "You brought a healer here and didn't have him see me?"

"I didn't think you deserved it. After all, you're a nobody now, whereas your son is the new Minnesota Pack alpha."

Dwyer growled but remained seated. He was no match for Vance with his current condition while in Vance's home where Vance's sentinels waited a floor away.

"Why did you do it, Dwyer?"

Expecting some flippant answer, Vance was shocked when Dwyer bellowed, "*You killed my son.*" The words were spoken with such malice that Vance almost took a step back.

"Donovan? I had nothing to do with his death."

"If you hadn't kicked the pack out of the Cities, he'd still be alive."

Vance pointed a finger at the self-centered wolf. "If you had been the alpha you should've been, I never would've had to kick the pack out. I even gave you the choice to step down, to leave and let the pack stay, but you were too stubborn. You and your stupid, stupid pride had to take everyone down with you. As far as your son goes, I heard he was drunk and ran his truck into a tree."

Vance held up his hand before Dwyer could say anything. "If you think the pack leaving was the reason he drank, you're delusional. I recall one of the reasons I asked you to leave was because of Donovan. What you were doing to the business was only part of the problem. He was out of control, Dwyer. He and his friends were drinking and getting arrested, putting humans in the hospital because he'd get into fights, shifting in front of humans and exposing our kind to them...the list goes on. Your son was an alcoholic long before he left the Cities."

"That's just what you told those bloodsuckers, so they would believe you."

Vance had hoped Dwyer would feel some shame instead of lashing out. At one time, the two had been good acquaintances, almost friends, but now, the man sitting before Vance was a stranger.

When Vance had given Dwyer an ultimatum—step down as alpha, get Donovan help, leave L & L Construction, and the pack stays—he'd thought Dwyer would go along with it. Dwyer had refused, and when Vance had gone to the king and queen of the vampires, he had been able to exile the pack from the Cities.

As the Minnesota Pride alpha, Vance had had no more authority than the Minnesota Pack alpha because they were equals. Vance had had to go to a third party, the vampires, and explain that if humans found out about shifters, the vampires would be next. It had taken some convincing, but the vampires had eventually seen his side. They'd realized the risk Dwyer, his son, and a handful of pack members were to anything that talked and walked on two legs but wasn't human.

The night that the cat-shifters and the vampires had banished the wolf-shifters was the last time Vance and his wife had seen the king and queen until they'd come banging on his door a few months ago with the news that his son had impregnated their daughter.

"You should really watch what you say. Those bloodsuckers are now my in-laws."

The vampires and the cat-shifters were still working on their alliance and learning to get along with one another, but he was confident that it would happen in due time.

"I suppose now that my miserable excuse of a son is fucking your daughter, you'll let the pack back in?"

Vance had yet to speak to his daughter. She was obviously in distress over Damien, so there was no denying their involvement. The wolf-shifter's scent was very strong on his daughter, even after she had showered, which meant she'd slept with him while she was in mating heat. As a father, Vance didn't want her smelling like any male—he wanted her to be his little girl forever—but Lilith had warned him that it would happen sooner or later. He still thought Payton should have waited until she was properly mated before she risked having young though. Vance had also noted the absence of the wolf's mark on her. They'd already had one shotgun mating in the family. They didn't need two. He wasn't happy with Payton or the situation, but he wasn't going to allow Dwyer to goad him or to speak about his daughter that way.

"It's funny that you would say that, Dwyer. I believe, when I asked you to step down, I suggested you make Damien the pack's new alpha."

Vance had seen that Damien, even at twenty, was better suited for the role. He was different from his father and older brother. "But you told me that you would never do that." Vance held up his hands. "And now, here we are. The very thing you'd tried to prevent is the very thing you caused to happen. It might have taken ten years, but it happened." He let his hands fall, and he took a step forward. "Was it worth it?"

Dwyer growled and charged at Vance, but Vance was ready. He sidestepped and swept his foot out behind Dwyer, knocking the wolf flat on his back. Vance kicked his side, and Dwyer rolled over. Vance pushed Dwyer onto his stomach and put him in a choke hold.

It took everything in Vance not to break Dwyer's neck. He was behind the kidnapping of his only daughter and the attempted kidnapping of his son and his sweet daughter-in-law, who was carrying his grandchildren. Because of Dwyer, one of his best sentinels along with his daughter-in-law's human best friend were still out there. If they didn't find her, the humans would start investigating, which would only lead to trouble.

"Why did you do it, Dwyer? Why did you go after my children?"

He clawed at Vance's arm, trying to get free, but Vance only tightened his grip.

"I wasn't going to kill them."

Vance squeezed harder.

Dwyer coughed. "I swear. I was only getting them out of the way."

Vance's grip loosened. "Out of the way for what?"

"Shit," Dwyer said, realizing his mistake.

Vance retightened his hold.

"It wasn't my idea. I was hired. None of this was my idea."

Vance let him go, pushing Dwyer away, before standing over him.

Dwyer kept on rambling, "If it wasn't for me, your brats would be dead. That's what he wanted. I was just going to get them out of the way until he killed you. I only agreed to do it so that the pack could return. Yes, I hated you…still hate you, but I wasn't going to kill anyone. He was."

Vance sat on his haunches. He grabbed Dwyer by the hair. "Who is he? Who hired you?"

Dwyer didn't say anything.

Vance forcefully shook Dwyer's head. "You son of a bitch, tell me

R . L .   K E N D E R S O N

who had the audacity to threaten my family."

When Dwyer spoke the name, Vance was shocked. This was someone he cared for and trusted.

"He contacted me for help. He wanted you gone," Dwyer taunted. "He planned to kill you and take your place. That's why he wanted your kids killed, too. He didn't want anything to stand in his way of becoming alpha."

"Enough." Vance threw Dwyer away from him before standing and heading for the door, but he paused and turned before reaching it. "One more thing. What happened to the money?"

The instant look of guilt across Dwyer's face told Vance he didn't have to expand on what money he spoke of.

"You don't have to tell me. I already know. You should be ashamed of yourself," Vance said and put his back to Dwyer.

"Wait. What are you going to do with me?"

Vance turned around, his hand on the knob. He was struck with how pitiful Dwyer looked. The former wolf alpha sat on the floor, full of scratches and welts from his fight the night before. Snot ran from his nose, and his face was red from Vance choking him. It was hard to believe that this shifter used to be a leader. Now, he resembled nothing but a sniveling, pathetic excuse of a man.

"It's not my decision. That is for the pack alpha to decide. He can kill you for all I care." Vance exited the room and silently shut the door behind him.

Chapter Thirty-Three

*P*ayton made her way to the bedroom where Damien slept.

Unconscious was probably a better word for his state. Damien was very sick, and she was still upset that he'd kept his condition from her.

She couldn't believe Damien had challenged his father last night. He was lucky that his father hadn't killed him. He shouldn't have been out of bed, much less fighting, yet he had taken his father on. She was so glad that he had won. If he had lost, Payton had no doubt that Dwyer would have killed his son.

Damien was fortunate, especially with how ill he was. It was as if he'd held out for his sentinels to swear their loyalty before he passed out. Payton thought she had been worried about him before, but after he'd fainted, she'd never been more afraid in her life. She'd thought he was dead until she ran up to him and saw his chest rising and falling.

Mercifully, her father had promptly arranged for Damien to come back to her parents' home, and he'd called on their healer, Dr. Bennett. Now, Damien was thankfully on the mend, but he still had a ways to go.

Payton had refused to leave his side, even when her father had told her to go to bed. She had seen the look of disappointment in his eyes when he'd smelled Damien on her. Vance Llewelyn wasn't stupid, and with her lack of Damien's mark, her father had put two and two together. She'd hated to distress her father more than he already was, but she'd insisted on staying with Damien.

She must have fallen asleep, and someone—probably her dad—had carried her to her own bed because that was where she'd awoken a few minutes ago. It was after eleven in the morning, and she had wasted almost half the day sleeping instead of watching over Damien.

Payton opened the door, ready to resume her position at his bedside until he woke up, but she was surprised to find someone else in what she had already come to think of as her spot.

"Oh." Payton paused in the doorway.

The female wolf stood. She had shoulder-length caramel-blonde hair and hazel eyes. She was pretty in a girl-next-door kind of way, except for her mouth. She had thick dark lips that looked like they belonged on a movie star. They were the kind that women would pay good money for. She wore a simple sweater and jeans, and she stood several inches shorter than Payton.

"You must be Payton."

"Yes. And you're Isabelle?"

The female nodded.

On her ride home, Payton had found out that her father had made Isabelle stay with Zane until her father found out where Payton was, and that explained why Isabelle smelled a little like Zane. Last night, when Payton had asked who Isabelle was, Payton had felt a little stupid when her father told her that she was Damien's friend. She had assumed Damien's friend was a male, and he had never indicated otherwise. She'd had a small knot in her stomach ever since.

"Yes. I just wanted to see how he was doing."

Payton motioned Isabelle back into the chair she'd been sitting in, and then Payton sat at the end of the bed. Payton knew Damien didn't belong to her, but she didn't want Isabelle sitting on the same bed that Damien lay in.

"How's Damien doing? I haven't seen him since last night," Payton said.

Isabelle shrugged. "The same. He hasn't moved since I came in here. What did the doctor say?"

"He has an infection. Dr. Bennett cleaned Damien's wound, stitched it up, and gave him antibiotics. He was close to being taken to the infirmary." She was glad he hadn't been, so she could be closer to him. "Now, we just wait I guess."

"Poor Damien." Isabelle leaned over and brushed his hair off his forehead.

Payton stiffened and held back a gasp. Her anger had quickly turned to dismay. Isabelle obviously cared for Damien, and he must feel something in return if he'd trusted her to come to the cats with the news that he had Payton. The knot in Payton's stomach got bigger.

Isabelle still had her eyes on Damien, so she'd thankfully missed Payton's reaction.

"How long have you known Damien?" Payton asked in a casual voice—at least, she hoped it sounded casual.

Isabelle looked at Payton and smiled. "Oh, gosh, I don't know. Since we were kids." She sat back in her chair, but she'd grazed Damien's bare shoulder with her hand before she did so.

Payton felt her heart sink, and the knot flared to life. She'd never asked Damien if he was involved with anyone, and like a dumb girl with stars in her eyes, she'd assumed the boy she liked would tell her if he was taken.

Payton gulped, afraid to ask the next question, but she knew she had to. "How long have you been together?"

"Oh, we're not together. We dated for about a year, but that ended about three years ago."

Yet, here she was, at Damien's bedside.

"You're obviously still good friends," Payton said with what she hoped was a steady voice. She tried to smile, but she knew it must look fake, so she gave up.

Isabelle grabbed Damien's hand. "Very. Damien is quite special. He's a great guy, and you can count on him for anything."

Isabelle smiled at Damien as if she had a secret, and suddenly, Payton felt like a voyeur, intruding on an intimate moment between two lovers.

"He's even helped me out a few times when he really didn't have to, if you know what I mean."

She might be speaking in generalities, but Payton knew what she had meant. All she could picture was that when Isabelle felt the need for skin-on-skin contact or when she was flat-out horny, she would go to Damien, and he'd fulfill her need.

Isabelle smiled secretly again. "But I suppose I did the same for him."

Payton prayed she could disappear. She felt like she was going to throw up. The thought of Isabelle kissing Damien with those porn-star lips made Payton feel sick.

Isabelle looked at Payton and sat up straight as if she'd just remembered that Payton was in the room and that she'd been talking out loud. "I'm sorry. I shouldn't have shared that information. It was too much. I don't even know you." She put her head in her hand before looking at Payton again. "Please don't think of me as a bad person. I really don't sleep around."

Sure you don't, you harlot. Payton held up her hand. "It's fine. It's hard to think when you're concerned for your...friend."

Isabelle tilted her head and smiled. "I guess you don't realize how much someone means to you until you think you might lose him or her."

Translation: She hadn't realized how much she loved Damien until now.

"Please forget I said anything."

Yeah, right. Not in this lifetime.

"Damien would kill me if he could hear me."

Why? Because he doesn't want anyone to know he services some hussy when she needs sex?

Payton held up a hand. "It's okay, really." *Just, please, stop talking about it.*

Isabelle reached over and squeezed Payton's hand. "Thanks. I guess you understand where I'm coming from."

Isabelle's smile was kind, and Payton immediately felt ashamed.

Damien wasn't Payton's, and Isabelle had known him in an intimate way long before Payton had. She was getting distraught because she had thought Isabelle was intruding on Damien's relationship with her, but it now seemed that Payton was interfering with his relationship with Isabelle. Isabelle had to smell Damien all over her and know what had happened between the two of them. Isabelle was probably just as upset as Payton was.

Damien had never made any promises to her, and she herself had thought that they would go their separate ways. Apparently, subconsciously, she had thought they might have a chance to try something long-term. But if he still had feelings for Isabelle—it was obvious she still had feelings for him—and he wanted to be with her, then Payton wouldn't stand in his way. Damien was the new wolf-shifter alpha, and it made sense that he would want to be with another wolf. Payton was silly to think Damien would be with her, a cat-shifter.

Back at the cabin, he had really seemed to like Payton, and when she had spoken of other males and he'd growled, she'd thought he was jealous. Then, his father had said Damien was in love. She'd only seen what she wanted to see, and she'd only heard what she wanted to hear.

What a fool I've been.

She'd thought she might have a future with him, but it was no wonder Damien had kept so many things from her. Beyond their stay at the cabin, he'd never intended for them to be together.

Silly, foolish Payton, blinded by love.

With a heavy heart, she sighed. The saying went that if you loved something, set it free. She wouldn't make any demands on Damien or get between Isabelle and him, but Payton sure didn't have to sit there any longer and torture herself.

She cleared her throat to keep the tears at bay. "I'd better get going. It's getting late, and I haven't even showered yet this morning." She stood. "Nice to meet you," she said before walking out the door.

She hurried to the bathroom, hoping the water would mask the sound of her crying.

Isabelle watched Payton fly out of the room, and she instantly felt guilty. Why had she let Payton think that she and Damien were more than they actually were? Isabelle hadn't lied, but she had stretched the truth.

Damien was her dear friend. She hadn't realized how much she cared about him until Zane told her what had happened this morning. If anything, it only showed her that Damien really was a friend and would be nothing more than that.

As for Damien and her having sex, that hadn't happened for about two years. After they'd broken up, they'd slept together a few times, especially when their need had gotten too great, but it had only happened two or three times before they firmly moved into the friends-only department.

"Damien, you're going to kill me when you wake up."

While the scent of Damien on Payton was stronger to males to warn them away, Isabelle had still noticed it the second Payton stepped into the room. She hadn't missed Payton's smell on Damien either, even with the scent of his infection thick in the air.

Isabelle hadn't been lying when she said Damien was a good guy. Damien would never have taken Payton during her mating heat if he didn't care for her. He'd dated Isabelle for a year, and he had courteously stayed away the two times she'd gone into heat. Yes, Damien definitely had feelings for Payton.

So, why the heck didn't I tell Payton that?

There was a knock on the door, and the answer to her question walked into the room.

"How's he doing, Isa?" Zane asked.

"Fine. The same."

"That's good. The way Payton ran out of here, I thought maybe something had happened to him."

"Uh…no, everything's okay."

Zane glanced out in the hall, looking both ways, before stepping back into the room. He grasped her hand, hauled her out of her chair, and kissed her as if his life depended on it. Only after he took her breath away along with her senses did he release her.

"Sorry, Isa, I couldn't resist." He swiped the wetness off her bottom lip with his thumb. "I missed you last night."

After Zane had found out that most of the sentinels were on their way home, Isabelle had asked if she could sleep somewhere else. She'd no longer needed to be watched over since Payton was safe, and Isabelle had needed the space to think. She had been given Vaughn's old room since Damien was in the guest bedroom. The bed had smelled of clean sheets. It hadn't smelled like Zane, and she hadn't slept well. She had missed him, too.

Isabelle studied Zane. Ever since she'd come back to the bunkhouse with him after her talk with Vance, they had continued to have sex, and she was becoming far too attached.

That was why she knew that the minute Damien woke up and she was sure he'd be okay, she would be out of here. She had just broken a young girl's heart because she was trying to deny any feelings for Zane. She'd acted as if making up a relationship with Damien would cause her hunger and longing for the infuriating cat-shifter to go away. Only distance would do that.

It was definitely time for Isabelle to get out of here and go home.

Chapter Thirty-Four

Damien hated waking up and not recognizing where he was. Usually, after a minute or two, he could identify his whereabouts. Tonight was different.

He sat up and looked around. He was no longer at the cabin. He was obviously in someone's home. The only light came from a digital clock on the nightstand that told him it was a few minutes after three in the morning. The queen-sized bed he lay in had soft sheets and a comforter with a spring theme that matched the curtains on the wall. The room was decorated to be a comfortable space. The smell of the numerous cat-shifters told him he was probably in the Llewelyn home.

Suddenly, his urge to piss grabbed his complete attention. There was an open door leading to a darkened room, and he really hoped it was a bathroom.

Getting out of bed was tough. He was sore all over and felt like he'd been in a fight. As he shuffled to the bathroom, he remembered that he actually had been in a fight—with his father. And Damien had won.

He was alpha now.

He recalled their altercation and how he'd used the last of his energy to keep himself upright while *his* sentinels had sworn their loyalty to him. After that, his memory went blank. He needed to find out what had happened.

After Damien emptied his bladder, he turned on the light and inspected his back. It was on the mend. Someone had stitched him up and already removed his or her handiwork. He was healing fast. His fever was also gone, which was a good sign. He faced the mirror. Of course, he didn't know how long he'd been out. That was another reason he needed to talk to someone.

Damien shut off the light as he left the bathroom, but he didn't get back into bed. There was no way he'd fall asleep. Instead, he headed for the hall. The cool air washed over his naked body, but he overlooked it. He was on a mission.

This wasn't the house that he remembered the Llewelyns living in ten years ago. To his right was a staircase. Past the stairs, on the opposite side of the hall to him, was a single door. Going by the desk he could see through the partly open door, the room was an office. Double doors were at the end of the hallway, and it had to be the master bedroom. On his side of the stairs, there were three doors besides the one he was standing in. There was a door directly across from the bedroom he was staying in, and he peeked in. It was a laundry room and bathroom combo. Excluding everything else, Damien lumbered his way down to his left to the last two doors, located at the end of the hall directly across from one another.

As he got closer, the scents of Payton and Isabelle got stronger. When he reached the end of the hallway, it was apparent who was in each room. He opened the door on the left. Isabelle's blonde head poked out from underneath the covers. The greens and blues of the room had a masculine feel, and Damien guessed it was Vaughn's old room.

Damien stepped inside and walked up to the bed. "Hey, Izzy. Thanks for everything. I owe you one," he whispered to her, not wanting to wake her.

He didn't know how he'd ever repay her because he'd never expected her to still be here. Of course, he'd never called her back, and she was the only connection to him and therefore Payton. If he were Vance, Damien would have made Isabelle stay, too.

Damien exited the room and gently shut the door. He opened the door to the room across the hall. The first thing he noticed was the light blues and purples. It was definitely a female's room. He entered and quietly shut the door behind him. He approached the bed and saw only a few strands of long dark hair sticking out from under the comforter.

He drew back the covers, and Payton immediately curled up, trying to conserve warmth. She wore thin pants and a camisole. While the outfit was appealing to the eyes, it didn't hold in the heat.

Even though she was asleep, she had fatigue written all over her face. After her attempted kidnapping, mating heat, their fight, and his infection, she must have been exhausted.

Damien winced. Most of that stuff was his fault, and he should walk out of here, go back to his room, and leave her alone because she'd be better off without him. But he didn't. He slid into her bed and pulled the covers over them. She uncurled now that she was warmer, and he scooted closer. He moved her hair off her neck and buried his face there. He inhaled her lavender scent, and he was instantly comforted. He almost jumped when her hand landed on his bare hip.

Her fingers pushed into his skin, trying to draw him closer to her, so he kissed her neck and settled back onto the bed. He pulled her close, and she began to purr. Pleased with her contentment, Damien fell asleep to the sweet vibrations coming from her.

Payton awoke to the sounds of a frantic conversation in the hallway. From all the commotion, it sounded like something was missing, but she didn't have the ambition to open her eyes and help search. The thin stream of light coming through her curtains told her it was still early, and she wanted to go back to sleep. She was sure they'd find what they were looking for, and it probably wasn't a big deal anyway. Plus, she was warm and comfy in her bed, and she swore she could smell Damien's cedar scent, which soothed her. She didn't want to wake up and face reality yet. If the people in the hall wanted her help, they would come and ask, but until then, she was staying put.

She was surprised to discover she wasn't as tired as she'd thought she'd be. The first night home, she'd been worried about Damien. She was still worried about Damien, but yesterday evening, the healer had removed the stitches, and Damien's fever had broken, proving he was on the mend. Her fretting last night had come from the constant images of Damien and

Isabelle as a couple assaulting her brain. She remembered dreaming about them and awaking several times, wishing she could banish all thoughts of them together.

She could still picture the two of them. That was why, even though she felt refreshed, she didn't have the motivation to get out of bed and help anyone. She knew it was selfish, but the thought of seeing them together hurt too much. She'd rather hide in her room.

She licked her dry lips and felt wetness on her cheek. She'd slept so hard she drooled. Thank God she'd never done that in front of Damien. She would have been terribly embarrassed. She moved to wipe away her spit, and her hand met hard flesh. She stopped, not moving a muscle— except for her head that was moving up and down as the chest underneath her inhaled and exhaled. How had she missed the fact that she was using a naked male chest as a pillow?

She heard the voices in the hall getting closer to her room, and she suddenly understood that they weren't missing just anything. They were looking for Damien. She rose slowly from the bed, trying not to wake him. He needed his rest still, and she would be absolutely mortified if he found out she'd salivated all over him. She groaned at the likely humiliation.

She crept from the bed and tiptoed to the door. She opened it and stuck her head out just as her father and Saxon knocked on Vaughn's door, the room where Isabelle was staying.

"Hey," she said.

They spun around to look at her.

"He's in here. Be quiet. He's still sleeping."

Both of their faces showed relief, but a second later, her father's tightened up. She didn't know where his thoughts were, but she could guess it had to do with a male asleep in her room. Her father still hadn't talked to her about Damien and her mating heat. She had thought her father might bring it up a couple of times yesterday, but it was obviously a conversation he was putting off. She wasn't exactly looking forward to it either, but at this point, she just wanted to get it over with. However, now was not the time, and they were saved from any further exchange when Vaughn's door opened.

They all looked to see a sleepy Isabelle standing there, rubbing her eyes. Payton froze. Why hadn't Damien gone to lay with Isabelle? Would Isabelle be hurt to find out that he was in Payton's room?

Payton avoided looking Isabelle in the eye.

"Sorry," her father said. "We couldn't find Damien, but he's—"

"In Payton's room," Saxon finished.

Isabelle shrugged. "Okay." She looked behind her back into the room. "It's still early. I'm going back to bed."

Isabelle stepped back into the bedroom, and right before she shut the door, Payton looked up. She expected to see anger or resentment, but Isabelle had a knowing smile on her face. When their eyes met, Isabelle winked at Payton.

Payton was so stunned and confused that she barely muttered good-bye to her father and Saxon before she shut the door. She made her way back to her bed and sat with her head in a jumble of thoughts.

How did Damien feel about her? How did he feel about Isabelle? Had he come to Payton's room because he didn't realize Isabelle still loved him? But if Isabelle still loved him, then why the grin and the wink when she'd found out Damien was in Payton's room?

"Quit thinking so much. I can hear you from over here."

Payton jumped. "Huh?"

She glanced at Damien. He had woken up enough to roll onto his stomach, but his eyes were closed. From her sitting position, she saw the long wound on his back. It was closed and light pink now, and without thinking, she traced her finger over it from his shoulder to his hip. She paused where his back curved into his bottom. She hadn't recognized before that he was completely naked.

He was a gorgeous specimen, and her thoughts turned to her mating heat and how he had serviced her. She felt her skin heating as she grew wet between her legs. There was no way he could miss the scent of her arousal.

She shouldn't be thinking of sex. They obviously had things to talk about—not just Isabelle, but also why he'd kept things from Payton back at the cabin.

Damien growled as he snatched her from her spot and placed her beneath him, his blue eyes bright next to his healthy skin. "I thought I told you to quit thinking."

She opened her mouth but didn't even know where to begin. Seconds later, it didn't matter because Damien kissed her. His tongue raided her mouth as if he hadn't kissed her in forever instead of just kissing her a mere two days ago. Although, the events of the last few days did make it seem like it had been longer. He kissed down her neck, and then he pulled one strap of her camisole over her shoulder, so he could suck her nipple into his mouth, causing her back to arch.

She shook her head. "Damien?"

He momentarily paused in his admirations to say, "Shh...no talking," before he resumed his task.

She shut up. Even though they needed to talk, she wasn't sure what the outcome would be. And the last time they'd had sex, it'd been angry sex. It would be much better that this be their last time if that was how things were going to end up.

"Okay," she sighed.

Damien looked up. The corners of his mouth were stretched from one side of his face to the other, and his eyes were filled with humor. "That was easy."

"I seem to be when it comes to you."

He wiggled his eyebrows and moved over to her other breast until he had her panting. He rolled onto his side and removed her pants and underwear. Her shirt had ridden up, so she was naked from the belly button down, and he paused at the sight of her bare midriff. Her abdomen had already started to return to the way it was before her mating heat. She tried to read Damien's face, but she had no idea what he was thinking. Was he worried that she'd accidentally gotten pregnant? She hadn't bled yet, but by her flattening belly, she was pretty sure that she wasn't pregnant. It was just another thing they needed to discuss.

Before she could reassure him, he spread her legs and placed his mouth where she was hot and ready for him, flicking his tongue over her tight knot of nerves.

Yes, there was absolutely no reason that any conversation they needed to have couldn't wait.

Chapter Thirty-Five

Damien stared up at the ceiling, feeling content. After finishing their early morning sex, Payton rested her head on his chest as he combed his fingers through her dark mane. He couldn't see her face, but the tension in the air was thick.

"I can hear you thinking again," he said to her.

"I'm just listening to the sound of your heart beating and how I almost—how the world almost lost you."

"Hey," he said, gently tugging on her hair so that she'd look at him. When she met his eyes, he said, "I'm fine. I'm right here."

"Did you come here to say good-bye?"

"What?" Damien was taken aback. "You think I would just come in here to sleep next to you, so I could fuck you in the morning and then…what? Just leave?" The fact that she would think that about him pissed him off a little.

Payton sat up and used one hand to hold the sheet to her bare breasts while she held herself up with the other. "Damien, I'm not judging you. I'm just asking."

"Do you think I'm that callous? That I care for you that little?"

"Well…*no*. But…"

"But what?"

She sighed and looked down, almost like she was embarrassed. "I met Isabelle."

He was not following. "Okay?"

"You're going to make me say it, aren't you?" she said quietly.

"Damn right I am because I have no idea what you're talking about."

Payton swung around so that her back was to him, and her legs hung off the bed. He was ready to snatch her if she tried to leave before their conversation was over.

"It's apparent that you trust Isabelle. She's the only one you called to help you, and she came here, possibly risking her life, to talk to my family—for you. I saw the way she looked at you when you were comatose. Now, you're alpha…"

"And?" he asked when she didn't finish.

"You're alpha of the Minnesota Pack."

"Baby girl, you're just telling me stuff that I already know."

She exhaled with a huff and turned to glare at him. He could sense her frustration, but he wasn't being purposely obtuse. He really didn't know what she was hinting at.

"I'm the daughter of the Pride alpha." She stared down at her hands. "And Isabelle's a wolf, like you."

"Payton?"

"Since you two obviously care about each other—"

"Payton."

"And you and I never talked about what would happen to us after the cabin. I thought—"

"*Payton.*"

She looked up at him. "What?"

"Will you shut up"—he growled—"and let me get a word in?"

She wrinkled her nose. "Fine."

"One thing at a time."

"Okay."

"First, what about your brother?"

"What about my brother?"

"Whom is he mated to?"

"Naya."

"Who is…"

"A vampire." The duh expression on her face said she wasn't getting his point.

"Exactly."

"Exactly what?"

Now, who is being obtuse?

"Your brother and future alpha of your pride isn't mated to a cat-shifter. Hell, he's not mated to any kind of shifter. So, why do I have to be mated to a wolf-shifter?"

"That's different."

"How is that different?"

"I don't know. It just is." She shrugged. "Maybe because our pride hasn't gone through what your pack has. I would think they need more stability. And my brother is only the *future* alpha at this time. As of right now, you *are* the alpha."

"Okay." He nodded. "I see your point. However, I will be with whomever I want to be with."

He saw the corner of her mouth slide up for a split second.

"Was there a second thing?" she asked.

"Second thing? Oh, yeah. Isabelle and I are not romantically involved." She opened her mouth, and he held up his hand to stop her. "Yes, we had a romantic relationship in the past, but we are now strictly platonic."

"What if that changes?"

He looked to the ceiling as if it had any answers. He needed somebody to save him from the female mind. "It's not going to change."

"How do you know?"

He seized her so fast that she yelped as he hauled her down next to him. "It's not going to change because I've already been there with Isabelle. I dated her for a year, and not once did I want to take her during her mating heat. We got along, but toward the end of our relationship, we both realized we treated each other more like brother and sister than boyfriend and girlfriend. Even if I didn't have feelings for someone else, I wouldn't choose to be with Isabelle, nor her with me." He got right in her face. "We don't think of each other like that."

She smiled coyly at him. "So, whom do you have feelings for?"

"Let me see if I can find her."

He pulled the sheet off her breasts and thumbed her nipple. She bit her lips and moaned.

"I like her." He leaned down and sucked it between his lips, nipping the tip as he lifted his mouth. He moved over to her other breast. "Of course, I have a crush on her twin." He sucked on her there, too. He slowly slid his hand down her chest, over her abdomen and pelvis, and to the hot center between her legs. "Then, there's their cousin downstairs. I'm especially infatuated with her." He slipped his fingers inside.

She was hot and slick from their earlier lovemaking.

She rocked her pelvis against his hand. He paid special attention to her G-spot while he rubbed her clit with his thumb. Soon, he had her panting and writhing on the bed. He removed his hand before she could come and tugged her underneath him. He slowly entered her. His shaft was hard, and she pulsed around him as she stretched to accept him. Once he was fully seated in her core, he stopped.

"Payton, open your eyes."

Her sapphire eyes blinked open, bright with arousal.

"In case you haven't figured it out, the one I feel the strongest for is the owner of the twins and their cousin. Because she is not only beautiful, but she is also smart and strong."

"Oh, Damien, I…"

He knew what she was going to say, but he didn't ask her to finish her sentence. He didn't want to pressure her. They'd been through a lot over the last week, and she would tell him when she was ready. It was enough to know she felt that way because he loved her, too.

Payton let out a satisfied sigh as Damien withdrew from her body and drew her into an embrace. They'd made love twice now, and while she felt better about some things, there were still a few topics she needed to discuss with him. For the moment, she wanted to relax in her post-coitus glow.

"Payton?"

"Hmm?"

"If you thought I came into your room to say good-bye, why did you have sex with me?"

She drew circles on his chest. "Because the last time we had sex before this morning, we were fighting. I didn't want our last time together to be angry sex." She chuckled uncertainly. "I wanted something good to remember you by."

He grabbed her hand and brought it to his mouth to kiss. He set it on his chest and covered it with his own. "I suppose we should talk."

She lifted her head and rested her chin on his chest. "Yeah, we'd better." She took a deep breath and exhaled. "Why did you keep things from me?"

He squeezed her hand as if he was afraid she'd leave. "You have to remember that, at first, I didn't know you that well. I had no idea that we'd…become involved. I needed you to trust me, and telling you that my father was the reason you were in the position you were in probably wouldn't have gone over well. You were injured and needed help. I couldn't risk you trying to leave and hurting yourself further."

"Okay. Then, why not later?"

"Well…I guess I didn't want you to hate me."

"Oh, Damien." She scooted up on the bed and looked down into his face. "I could never hate you."

He grinned.

"But I can get very, very angry with you."

He lost his smile. "Point taken."

"I'm still a little disappointed. Not telling me about your father was not your only secret. Why didn't you tell me you were injured? That one I can't understand. I wouldn't be mad or blame you for anything. So…why?"

He looked up at the ceiling and sighed. "When we first got to the cabin, I knew I was cut. From what I could see in the mirror, it seemed long but pretty shallow. It wasn't a serious wound, and I thought I'd be halfway healed before you even woke up. It didn't heal, but it didn't get worse either—at least, not until the last few days. I didn't want to worry you because I didn't want to make your mating heat worse. It was almost over, and then I could get you home safely. I knew I could worry about myself after."

Payton growled at him, and Damien's eyes rounded.

"Didn't I tell you back at the cabin that you are just as important as me? Actually, you're *more* important than me now. You're the alpha. What if my father hadn't come? What if you had died? Your pack would have been stuck with your father." She trembled at the thought.

He cupped her cheek. "You are gorgeous when you're fierce."

She tilted her head and shot him her best look of annoyance.

"But you're right. I should've told you when I realized something was wrong."

"Do you know why you didn't heal?"

He shook his head.

"You had slivers of silver in your wound. I don't know what kind of knife they used, but it left silver behind."

His eyes rounded.

"If you had told me, I could've removed the slivers before it got to the point of infection, and the whole situation would've been avoided."

His jaw clenched, and his breathing picked up.

"Hey. Hey. You're okay now," she reassured him.

"Payton, I don't give a crap about me. That weapon was meant for you."

"Yeah, I realized that back at the cabin."

"I'm going to fucking kill him." His nostrils flared with his anger.

Who is the gorgeous one now?

He looked at her like she was crazy. "Why the hell are you smiling? You're supposed to be angry."

"Because you're so sexy when you're all irate because someone might have hurt your woman. You Tarzan. Me Jane."

Damien lost some of his wrath. "You're a smart-ass, you know that?"

"Believe it or not, that's not the first time I've heard that."

He ran his hand down her hair with a serious look on his face. "I don't like the thought of someone hurting you."

"Ditto. You can't keep things from me, or this will never work. I realize that you are more dominant, but a relationship is still a partnership, and I need to know when something is wrong."

"I understand, and you're right. I promise not to hide anything from you, and you won't hide anything from me." He held up his hand. "Deal?"

She placed her palm against his and shook his hand. "Deal."

He yanked on her arm, pulling her closer. "Then, let's seal it with a kiss."

Chapter Thirty-Six

*D*ante walked toward the great room of the manor, looking for Vaughn. Dante had been told the cat-shifter was looking for him to discuss something.

Suddenly, Dante stopped dead in the hallway.

The deep hum in his blood warned him that Phoenix was in the great room, and he had no doubt that seeing her again would be awkward.

He hadn't seen her for the past two days, not since she'd run out of his room after he fed from her. She had avoided him, and quite frankly, he had avoided her, too. Thanks to her blood, it was pretty easy for him to do. He didn't know what to expect when he saw her again. She was usually hostile toward him and kept up a wall that seemed to keep everyone at a distance, and he knew her well enough now to know that she didn't appreciate the vulnerability she'd let slip in his room.

He could still taste the strength of her arousal in the back of his throat from when it had exploded around him—along with her. How she managed to cover up her scent all the time baffled him. He'd never met anyone who was as closed up as she was.

As he reluctantly got closer to the great room, Dante was amazed at the strength of her blood in his veins. He had been feeding since his conversion, and he had never felt a connection like this before.

Soon after vampires learned to feed, they were taught how to block their emotions from one another. Feeding from others always gave them the ability to sense the presence of the one they had fed from when that one was close, but it would only last for about a month or so. The strength of the bond would lessen over time until it disappeared completely.

However, Phoenix didn't know about the blood connection and had never been taught to put up that wall. He could restrict her a little from his side of the bond, but she was like a radio blasting down the hall. Inside him, she was a deep vibration in his blood. She was a jumble of emotions, and he found it hard to decipher how she really felt. Only one thing was for sure. Whatever she was feeling was strong. If she knew what he could sense from her, she would be pissed.

As he neared the room, he picked up on the conversation there.

"Are you sure she's going to be okay with—" Phoenix stopped mid-sentence. "Do you feel that?"

Her voice and her blood in Dante were suddenly filled with panic.

Dante stopped and stepped back against the wall. He really wanted to hear what she had to say.

"Feel what?" Vaughn asked.

"I don't know. It's like…like a buzz inside me. It started two days ago, and it's kind of freaking me out."

He dropped his head back and closed his eyes. *Could she possibly feel me the way I feel her?* He didn't know what this meant, but he figured it couldn't be good.

Damn it. He should have never given his blood to her. He'd done it because the vampire blood of the opposite sex was an aphrodisiac. Yeah, he was an asshole. He'd known that giving Phoenix his blood would turn her on, and he had wanted her to suffer as much as he had. He really hadn't expected her to come from his blood and the simple friction between their bodies.

He looked down at his hand and realized he'd been rubbing his thumb—the one she had sucked his blood out of—with his forefinger. He dropped his hand to his side as if it were a hot poker.

This blood-link thing between the two of them was a huge shock. He'd thought it was only between vampires. Of course, he'd never let a non-vampire drink from him. He frowned. Actually, he never even let vampire females drink from him. His excuse had always been that he needed to be in top form, so he couldn't afford to spare his blood, and he didn't want to get a female pregnant.

Liar, liar, pants on fire.

"Are you sick?" Vaughn asked.

"No. Except for the buzzing, I've never physically felt better."

Dante swore quietly and thumped his fist lightly against the wall. That was because of his blood.

"Did you hear something?" Phoenix asked.

Dante stilled. For an instant, he'd forgotten that shifters had even better hearing than vampires.

"No," Vaughn said after a second. "Phoenix—"

"Shh…" she said. "Wait a sec." Her last sentence was getting louder. She must have been moving closer to the hall.

Dante slid farther away, hoping she wouldn't catch his scent. Thankfully, he lived there, so his scent was in all the common areas. Hopefully, she wouldn't pick up on the fact that he was in the hallway.

"Vaughn, um…"

Her voice was quieter, so Dante moved back toward his original spot.

"What?"

"Do you ever drink Naya's blood?"

Damn, the female is smart.

"That's kind of a personal question, don't you think?" Vaughn responded.

"Please. I wouldn't ask if it wasn't important."

She obviously trusted Vaughn to talk to him about something like this, and it kind of pissed Dante off. Then, it pissed him off that he was pissed off. Who cared who Phoenix was close to?

Dante could hear the distress in her voice, and apparently, so could Vaughn because he sighed. Dante cringed. Vaughn was going to out him to Phoenix, and if Dante had thought she was a problem before, she was probably going to make his life a living hell once she found out that he'd known what his blood would do to her.

Dante was completely surprised when Vaughn replied, "Besides the drop at our mating ceremony, which was from a cup, not her, no. Naya's pregnant, so I would never take blood from her when she needs it so much. I've never bitten her hard enough to break the skin because of the pregnancy. Why do you ask?"

Dante was confused for a moment. Then, it dawned on him that the princess probably had no clue what her blood would do to the opposite sex. She had been very sheltered. Hell, she hadn't even known that shifters existed. So, she wouldn't know what her blood could do to a male.

"Are you blushing?" Vaughn asked.

Phoenix answered with an abrupt, "No."

"Why do you want to know about Naya and me?"

"I think vampire blood might..." She paused and laughed nervously.

"Phoenix, spit it out."

"I think vampire blood might be an aphrodisiac."

She really was smart. She had figured it out all on her own. Dante should probably watch his back.

"Interesting. Naya and I might have to try that after the babies are born, not that I need another reason to be turned on. We have plenty of sex as it is," he said more to himself than to Phoenix.

"Gross. I don't want to know that."

Dante grinned. She thought Vaughn having sex was gross. This was good.

Wait.

Dante dropped his smile. He didn't care who she did or didn't want to have sex with.

"You brought it up in the first place."

"Forget I said anything," she said.

"You're not getting off that easily. How the hell do you know this little tidbit of information? Does this have anything to do with the fact that you smell like a certain vampire?"

The gagging sound that followed had to be Phoenix, and Dante entered the room before she was forced to answer the question. The thought of Vaughn, or anyone, knowing what had happened in Dante's room between Phoenix and him made his guts twist.

"Vaughn?" Dante said.

Vaughn swung around. He looked at Phoenix and then him. Then, he looked back to Phoenix and back to him.

Due to their close proximity, Phoenix's blood was like a freight train inside Dante now, but he gave no indication that anything was amiss. Phoenix, on the other hand, looked like her head was about to explode. It didn't take a blood link to know that she was in fight-or-flight mode.

One thing was for sure. He needed to talk to her before she left the manor. He couldn't have her walking around freaked out and mad at him.

"You wanted to see me?" Dante asked, drawing Vaughn's attention away from Phoenix.

Yuck. As usual, she wore a hideous outfit—a giant sweater and shapeless jeans.

"I'm going home today, and Phoenix is going to stay with my mother at the safe house, but I want Naya to stay here for a few more days. Is that okay with you?"

Shit.

The sun was already up. He had to talk to Phoenix this morning before she left. He looked over Vaughn's shoulder. She wouldn't look Dante in the eye. He had never seen her like this. She usually glared at him. He really needed to get her alone, so they could speak.

"Dante?" Vaughn said.

What were we talking about? "Sure, it's fine if Naya stays here. You know we'll keep her safe."

"Thank you. She's not going to be happy."

"Is that why you waited until the sun was coming up?" Dante asked.

Vaughn looked slightly embarrassed. "Yeah."

"Don't worry too much. She knows that you care about her," Dante said.

Vaughn took a deep breath. "Now, I just need to tell her—"

"I'll do it," Phoenix broke in. By the sound of her voice, she was eager to leave the room.

She stepped around Vaughn and made her way toward the hall. She worked so hard to avoid Dante's gaze that she accidentally bumped into him.

The zing in his blood started where they touched and fanned out across his body. Phoenix gasped. Her eyes were huge, and her breathing sped up.

"We need to talk," he said.

"No, we don't."

"Phoenix—"

"I have to go."

She rushed out of the room, and Dante looked at Vaughn, who stood there while raising his eyebrows in a silent question.

Dante ignored him and asked, "Anything else you need?"

"Uh...no."

Dante could tell the shifter was still waiting for an explanation. *Fat chance of that happening.*

"Okay. Talk to you later," Dante said before he pivoted and left the room almost as fast as Phoenix had.

Payton smiled back at Damien as she opened her bedroom door to exit the room.

"Damien, I would like to speak to you."

Payton turned around and squeaked. She hadn't expected her father to be standing outside her door, waiting for her to open it.

She was thankful she'd already showered—with Damien—and grabbed some of her brother's clothes for Damien before they'd decided to leave the room. Isabelle had already risen for the day, and since a Jack-and-Jill bathroom—hidden behind the end of the hallway—connected Vaughn's and Payton's bedrooms, it made for easy access without going into the hall.

But showering and clean clothes weren't going to erase Payton's and Damien's scents from one another, especially after what they'd shared during her mating heat. It didn't help that her room also smelled like sex. Why couldn't her father have waited until they were downstairs?

"Daddy, don't you want to speak to me first?"

He gave her a quick glance, his face stern, and then he transferred his focus back to the wolf-shifter behind her. "No, I need to speak with Damien."

Payton had a sudden moment of panic. Her father was going to confront Damien about her mating heat. She'd known that her father was upset, and he had been avoiding her, but she'd never dreamed he would go around her and speak to Damien first. It was just another way her father babied her. She was twenty-three years old—an adult by human *and* shifter standards. *Why can't he see that?*

"Daddy—"

Damien stopped her with a hand on her shoulder. "It's okay, Payton. I know your father and I have some things to discuss."

She turned around and shot Damien a look, but he was staring at her father and didn't seem to notice her displeasure with the situation. She was displeased with not just her father. Damien should be supporting her and telling her father to speak with her first. She didn't need to be coddled, and she didn't need decisions to be made for her.

Damien looked at her, and the warmth in his eyes said to trust him. Because she'd talked about relationships being a partnership and because she did have confidence in him, she nodded her acceptance.

Damien's hand slipped down to the small of her back. "Where would you like to speak, sir?"

Despite her father and Damien now being equals, he was wise enough to show her father respect. In this case, it was more of a boyfriend speaking to a girlfriend's father rather than an alpha-to-alpha conversation. Some things were the same, no matter the culture, race, religion, or species.

"My office," was all her father said before he walked away.

She didn't miss the grim expression that had crossed his face. What that meant she didn't know, and she was worried.

Damien grabbed her hands and gave her a quick kiss. "Don't worry, baby girl. I won't let him rough me up too much."

That was why she loved this male. He knew how to make her smile when she needed it.

Why hadn't she just told him how she felt earlier?

Because I didn't know my father would pull him aside and demand to talk to him.

It was on the tip of her tongue to tell Damien now, but she thought better of it. She'd tell him after.

"It's not you I'm worried about," she said with a smile.

He grinned. "Well then, just for you, I'll make sure not to hurt him too badly."

She laughed. "Thanks." She kissed him again. "Good luck."

He stepped back, still holding her hands. "I don't need luck. I have you." He let go and followed her father.

Payton silently wished Damien luck again. There was no way her father would go easy on him.

Chapter Thirty-Seven

*P*ayton waited until Damien and her father both stepped into his office before she moved near the door. She stopped when she could just barely hear them, not wanting to get so close that they might smell her. She lived in the house, so thankfully, her scent was pretty much everywhere, but she wasn't going to risk getting caught.

She'd planned to go downstairs and let them have their conversation in private. She really had, but with the door ajar and her curiosity piqued, she'd stopped and pressed her back against the wall to listen.

"Sit down, Damien."

Payton heard her father's leather chair whine, and one of the wooden chairs across from her father's desk creaked as Damien must have done as he had been instructed.

"Do you know why I asked to speak to you?" her father asked.

Payton closed her eyes. It seemed like a no-brainer that her father wanted to question Damien about sleeping with his daughter. This was going to be painful.

"You want to speak to me about Dwyer, the pack, and my role in everything that happened this past week, sir?"

Payton's eyes flew open. Of course her father wanted to talk to Damien about this stuff. This was why Damien had told her to trust him. She felt silly. With everything that had happened, Damien sleeping with her was the least of her father's concerns.

Payton had seen males practically run in the other direction when they met her father, and right now, she was so proud of Damien. He sounded confident and not nervous in the least.

Now that she knew her father wasn't questioning Damien about having sex with her, she had a nagging feeling that she should leave, yet she didn't move a muscle.

She heard her father's chair squeak again, and she pictured him leaning back in it.

"What can you tell me about everything that happened?"

Knowing her father, he wanted to give Damien the illusion that this was a casual conversation. She knew that it was anything but.

"I know Dwyer was running L & L into the ground. Some accidents happened. You were losing business and getting sued. Then, Donovan and some of his friends were causing problems as well. I know it got so bad that you had to make a few payouts, go back and do work over, and cover up the sightings of shifters. I also know Dwyer left it all up to you." Damien's voice suddenly changed. "I wasn't living with them. I was at college." He sounded ashamed. "If I had known sooner, I would have tried to do something about it, help you to some degree. It wasn't until we had been kicked out that I learned of it all."

Poor Damien. It wasn't his fault that his father was a jerk.

"What's happened to the pack since then?"

"About a third of them left for other packs around Minnesota. The rest scattered to various cities and towns. It was decided that such a large number of people moving into the same city would be hard to explain."

"How have things been?"

Damien cleared his throat. "We've made do."

She heard her father's chair snap forward as he sat up.

"I'm going to ask again, and this time, no sugarcoating it. How have things been?"

Damien moved in his chair. "Sir, honestly, not good. Many places don't pay like they do around here, and a lot of us had to take pay cuts. The last few years have been bad. The pack doesn't have any money. Our healers have had to go work in human hospitals and clinics because we can't afford to keep our own open anymore. Families have had to move in together. The country's recession hasn't helped."

"What do you know about the pack's exile?"

"Just that you and the vampires knew exposure was too much of a risk, so we were all kicked out."

"What can you tell me about what happened to my son and daughter and their abductions?"

"A few months ago, Dwyer brought us to a resort about an hour from here. He wouldn't explain why. I caught him right after he had a meeting with someone—I never found out whom—and he wouldn't tell me anything. I spoke to the other sentinels. They didn't know what was going on either. It took a few weeks, but I finally got him to tell me his plan. I thought about telling you what was going to happen, but I didn't think you'd be inclined to believe another wolf. I honestly didn't know if anyone else would help me stop him. The pack is so fragile, and I didn't know how they would react. Would they tell Dwyer that I planned to stop him? In hindsight, I realize I should've just challenged him. Then, none of this would've happened."

There was a long pause before her father said, "Damien—"

"Sorry, sir. I did the best I could with just myself. I scouted out Vaughn and Payton. I thought maybe I could stop both of their kidnappings, but then I discovered they were happening at the same time. I knew Payton was more vulnerable, so I arranged to intercept her kidnapping. I figured I would fight the captors off, and she would go home to tell you what had happened. I figured Vaughn would be strong enough to stop anyone. After you heard what had almost happened, you'd be on alert. I never planned for her to get hurt so badly. I never planned for my phone to die and to also lose my charger. It all sounds like a pathetic excuse now, but I want you to know, I never agreed with this plan. I'm glad Vaughn and his mate are okay. I'm sorry about Sawyer. I'm sorry I didn't fight Dwyer harder."

When Payton and Damien had gotten ready for the day, she had filled him in on her brother and Naya.

There was a heavy pause in the office.

Why was her father torturing Damien?

Her father had asked Damien question after question, and Vance was giving Damien nothing in return.

She was ready to bust into the room when her father finally spoke, "Damien, did you know that, ten years ago, before I helped exile the pack, I gave your father the option to resign as alpha, to take himself and your brother away from here, and to turn the pack over to you?"

From the hallway, she heard Damien's deep inhale.

"Can you repeat that, please?" Damien's voice was firm.

"I saw what your father was doing and that he wasn't fit to run the pack. I knew your brother wasn't either. But I knew you'd do just fine even though you were only twenty."

She heard the groan of Damien's chair as he burst out of it, and then she could hear his strides as he paced the office. On one hand, she felt bad for Damien and his pack. Dwyer was incredibly selfish. On the other hand, she was so proud of Damien. Her father had recognized his abilities ten years ago.

"What else didn't he tell me?" Damien asked.

"When Isabelle first mentioned the pack being broke, she also said that you were upset about losing the Lowell part of the business, the shares, since your grandfather had helped to start it."

Damien's steps stopped. "She shouldn't have told you that. I understand why you did it. It was just hard because I respected my grandfather. He was a good alpha. There have been times the money would've helped."

Oh, Damien. He was trying so hard not to offend her father.

"The thing is…your father still owns half the business. Well, actually, he *did* own half. It now belongs to you. He won't be making any more money off the business and hiding it from your pack," Vance explained.

"Wait. I don't understand. He always said there was no money."

Her father sighed. "After speaking with Isabelle, we did some digging. We know your brother was an alcoholic, and it appeared he wasn't the only one with an addictive personality. Your father gambles—a lot. It seemed that all the money he earned from L & L would get gambled away within days. I'm sorry."

Payton put her head in her hands. Finding a father had turned on his own was awful. She couldn't imagine how Damien felt. If someone had told her that her father had done those things, on top of everything else he'd already done, she'd be devastated.

"Where is he?" Damien said, his voice low. He was pissed.

"I'll be happy to take you to him, but I think we need to discuss something else first."

There was no response.

"Please," her father added.

She heard Damien sit back in his chair. It must be killing him right now, not to find his father and beat the crap out of him.

"You're right. I need to calm down before I see him. Thank you."

"You're alpha now. Your sentinels swore their loyalty to you. Do you believe the rest of the pack will follow?"

"Yes."

"Do you trust your sentinels?"

"Yes and no. I think they need to earn my trust. I need to make sure they know who their alpha is now."

Nothing was said, but she could picture her father nodding his approval.

"Do you want the pack to return to Minneapolis?"

"More than anything."

Payton stood stiff with anticipation. This was everything Damien had wanted for him and his pack. From what it sounded like, they deserved it. If Damien were allowed to return, it would make everything easier on the two of them.

"I need only three things from you for the vampires and the Pride to consent to this."

"Name them."

Payton had been squeezing her hands together so tightly that her knuckles were now white. She released her hands, but it didn't stop the anticipation.

"One, you need to assure me that your sentinels are loyal to you and nobody else. Two, you have to kick Dwyer Lowell out of Minnesota completely. Three…I need you to give up Payton."

She held her breath. How could her father do this to them? What was Damien going to do now? She knew how important his pack was to him, and that was before he was even alpha.

"Done."

Payton gasped and felt light-headed. Damien had spoken the word without any hesitation. He hadn't even tried to fight for her.

She heard Damien's and her father's chairs squeak. *Did they hear me?*

She looked around in a panic, momentarily frozen. If she stayed in the hallway, they'd catch her eavesdropping. Damien would look her in the eyes and tell her it was over, and she'd promptly burst into tears in front of him.

There was a sudden wetness on her cheeks. It was too late. She had already started crying. This wasn't how it was supposed to go. Everything Damien and she had talked about in bed that morning was all moot.

Sounds coming from the office knocked some sense into her. She needed to stop feeling sorry for herself. They'd walk out any second and find her weeping like a baby. Her father already thought she was fragile. Apparently so did Damien because if he'd only asked, she would have stood up to her father beside him.

She forced herself to stop crying, and she wiped at the tears. She couldn't let Damien see her like this. She *wouldn't* let him see her like this. *Damien could go fuck himself.* She wasn't some weak female that he could walk all over.

She hurried to her room as quietly as she could. She snatched a few things and threw them in a bag. She peeked into the hallway to make sure it was clear, and then she sprinted down the stairs.

She ran into her brother as he was coming through the front door.

"Payton?"

"Vaughn!" She threw herself into his arms. A hug from her big brother was exactly what she needed at the moment. "I'm so glad you're okay."

"You, too, kiddo. You, too." He held her at arm's length. "Do you want to tell me why you smell like a wolf?"

She loved her brother, but here was another person who thought of her as delicate.

"It's a long story. Listen, Daddy is upstairs with Damien. If Dad asks, tell him that I went to my friend's house for a couple of days while they get things settled here."

244 | R. L. KENDERSON

She had stayed at her friend Alaina's house more than once and could count on her to take her in. Hopefully, Damien would be gone by the time Payton came home.

Vaughn gave her a sideways glance. "Payton?" The cobalt blue of eyes that mirrored her own were filled with concern.

"I can't explain right now. Please let him know, okay?" she insisted.

The office door opened upstairs.

"I've gotta go." She gave him another quick hug, and she was out the door in a flash before Vaughn could even answer.

Chapter Thirty-Eight

Damien shook Vance's hand as the cat rose from his seat behind his desk.

"Thank you for your assistance. I'm glad we were able to come to an understanding," Vance said.

"You're welcome," Damien said as he stood. "Do you think Payton will ever forgive us?"

They had just finished their meeting, and Damien was a mix of emotions. He'd found out some things about his father, and Vance had told him that he would be allowed to bring the pack back to Minneapolis— as long as some requirements were met.

"Once she understands why it had to be this way, she'll come to terms with it," Vance said.

One of the stipulations for returning to the Twin Cities was for Damien to end his relationship with Payton. At first, he was surprised by the request, but now, Damien understood why her father had made the demand. Vance was a smart man and only wanted what was best for his daughter.

Vance walked to the office door and opened it. "Your father is downstairs whenever you're ready to see him. I understand this is hard, so I'll give you until tomorrow."

The second condition was that Damien had to force his father to leave Minnesota forever. It was fine with Damien. If it wasn't against the law, he'd probably kill his father.

"No, it's not hard. But I need to speak to my sentinels first. I think it would be good for them to help me escort Dwyer over the state line. It would be a little finality for everyone."

If any of his new sentinels questioned the decision they'd made to swear their fidelity to him, now would be the time to find out. It would show him and his father who had their loyalty now.

The corners of Vance's mouth twitched with approval. "Your sentinels are staying at the nearest hotel. I'll get you the name."

"Thank you."

Vance and Damien exited the room and went downstairs. Vaughn was there, waiting.

"Hello, son."

"Hey, Dad."

Vance and Vaughn hugged.

"How's your female?"

Vaughn chuckled. "Miserable. The babies make it hard for her to get a good night's sleep, and she wasn't happy that she had to stay behind."

"It's for the best," Vance said.

"I know." Vaughn smiled. He was clearly enamored with his mate.

"I'll get everyone together, and we'll have a meeting this afternoon."

"Sounds good." Vaughn lost his smile and motioned with his chin to Damien, who stood behind Vance. "What are you going to do about him and Payton?"

"It's all taken care of."

"Good," Vaughn said with a smirk. "I thought maybe I'd have to go all big brother on him and kick some ass." He held his hand out to Damien. "My father filled me in before he talked to you. Welcome back, man."

Damien shook Vaughn's hand. "Thanks."

They dropped their arms, and Damien looked around.

"If you're wondering where Payton is, she took off to stay with one of her friends for a couple of days."

"What?" Vance and Damien said at the same time.

"She just got home safely," Vance sputtered.

"Oh, relax, Dad. The danger's over. She'll be fine. She's tougher than she looks."

Vance lost some of his incredulity. "I know, but the danger is not quite over. There is one more thing we need to take care of, which is something I wanted to talk about at the meeting."

Vaughn frowned. "Should I have stopped her from leaving?"

Vance sighed. "No, it should be fine. In fact, she might be safer with her friend. Plus, I know where this other individual is at the moment."

Upstairs, Vance had explained to Damien that he had found out the cat-shifter who had helped Dwyer and betrayed him.

"Do you know who or where Payton's friend is?" Damien asked.

They had some things to discuss.

Vaughn clicked his tongue and shook his head. "Nope. She was in a hurry, and I didn't get a chance to ask."

"Damn. I really need to find her."

"You can try calling or texting her," Vaughn offered.

Damien was speechless. He didn't even have her phone number. It seemed strange that he'd been inside her body repeatedly, yet she wasn't in his phone.

The two cat-shifters must have read his expression.

"Don't worry, son. I'll give you her number," Vance said. "But you might want to tend to your other business before you speak with her."

Vance was right. Damien needed to take care of the former alpha, his sentinels, and his pack before he talked to Payton. A day should be enough time to manage things, and then he'd be ready for her.

Isabelle drove up to the Llewelyns' house for the last time. She was ready to go back to her real life. The only thing left was to talk to Damien and grab what little stuff she had there before she headed for home. She still hadn't seen him since he'd woken up, and she knew she'd feel terrible if she took off without saying good-bye and telling him how proud she was that he was their new alpha.

She could only hope that she wouldn't run into anyone else before she left. She hadn't seen Zane since he kissed her in Damien's room while the wolf alpha was unconscious. Zane had told her to find him after dark, but she had made sure that she went to bed early. She'd managed to avoid the cat ever since.

Isabelle knocked on the front door just to let anyone near know that she was back before she entered. Damien walked in from the back of the house where the kitchen was.

"Hey, Isabelle. I was looking for you." Damien grinned.

She smiled back at her old friend. He looked good. His hair was longer than when she'd last seen him upright and walking, and his crystal-blue eyes were bright with health.

"Hey, Damien. I was just getting ready to head home."

When he reached her, he pulled her into a hug. When he drew back, he had a slight frown on his face. "Let's go in here." Damien directed her into the sitting room off the foyer where they could sit on the couch. "You smell like cat, Isabelle."

She snickered. "Yeah, well, so do you, Damien. I've been their prisoner for a week and a half. What's your excuse?"

She sensed that Damien suspected something more had happened during her stay here, but he didn't press the issue.

"Sorry about that, Izzy. I lost my charger, and my phone died. I never thought they'd make you stay. But I really appreciate everything you've done for me and the pack."

She waved her hand. "Don't worry about it. If I were a parent, I'm sure I would have made me stay, too. Now, it's time for me to get back to the real world."

Damien narrowed his eyes. "Your job okay?"

"Yes. I got a *doctor's note* saying I was very ill."

"I'm glad the Llewelyns took care of you."

It was actually Zane who had taken care of her. *Tomato, tomahto.* "Me, too."

"Are you sure you don't want to stay here with the rest of the pack?"

"What?" Isabelle couldn't believe her ears. "We were granted permission to come back?"

Damien nodded as he grinned from ear to ear.

"That's wonderful news."

"Isn't it? I'll have to fill you in on all the details sometime soon. So, do you think you'll come back?"

She shrugged. "I don't know. Not right now. I like where I am." *Without any cat-shifters.* "I can't wait to tell my parents though. They'll be so proud."

"Send them my best. Will you at least consider moving back?"

She smiled. "For you, yes." She leaned over and hit him with her shoulder. "Alpha."

Damien laughed. "That sounds weird."

"Nah, you earned it."

"Thanks, Izzy."

She gave him a hug, and he kissed her on top of her head.

"I'll miss having you close."

"Me, too, but that's why phones were invented." She pulled away. "Well, I'd better go make sure I got everything before I head out."

"Okay."

She rose from the couch and walked toward the stairs, but she stopped when she remembered she needed to own up to her mistake. "Damien, I might have given Payton the wrong impression about something."

Damien raised his brow. "You mean that you and I still have feelings for each other?"

She chuckled nervously. "Yeah, that."

The corner of his mouth arched up. "Don't worry about it. I know you were looking out for me. I already talked to her about it."

"Whew." She pretended to wipe sweat off her forehead.

"See you later, Izzy."

"Bye, Damien."

She went upstairs to the bedroom where she'd spent the last few nights. The day after Payton had come home, Isabelle had gone shopping for a few extra clothes and things, so she only had a few things to pack and take home.

Almost ready, she went to the bathroom for one last walk-through. When she walked out, she almost screamed.

Zane stood with his back to the closed bedroom door, the one she had left open when she'd come in, and he didn't look happy. His expression was cool, but he still looked sexy in his worn jeans and tight long-sleeved tee.

She slapped her hand against her chest. "You scared me."

He didn't so much as smile. "Close the door." He gestured toward the Jack-and-Jill bathroom.

She cursed under her breath as she put her back to him. She'd almost made it out of there. She shut the door and turned back to him.

"Is there something you needed?" she asked.

Zane sauntered up to her, put his arm around her waist, and jerked her close. "Were you just going to leave without saying good-bye?"

"No, you were my next stop," she fibbed.

"Liar."

"I don't like good-byes."

"Nobody does. It doesn't mean you avoid them."

She put her hands on his chest. "Look, Zane, it's—"

Before she could finish, he took her mouth in a scorching kiss. Opening his mouth, he pressed his tongue against her closed lips. She wanted to be strong and push him away, but he was like her kryptonite, and she had no idea when she'd see him again. She wrapped her arms around his neck, opened her mouth, and kissed him back. He tasted amazing, and his kisses alone sent heat to the secret place between her legs.

Zane kissed his way down her neck, pausing when he got to her neckline. He ripped her shirt over her head and yanked her bra straps down. He took her nipple between his teeth, not even close to gentle. She moaned deep in her throat from the almost pain.

He paid the same attention to the other breast before kissing down her stomach. He stopped when he reached her jeans but not for long. He opened her fly and pushed her pants and underwear down, and he quickly removed one leg at a time before flinging her pants aside in a pile.

He was on his knees now, and he lifted one of her legs onto his shoulder before putting his mouth directly on her clit and sucking it into his mouth. She grabbed on to his hair, but it was difficult with her bra straps around her arms. Zane grasped her butt and pulled her even closer to his waiting tongue. She started rubbing herself against his face, not caring how she looked because it felt so good.

Right before she was about to explode, Zane threw her down onto her back, laying her on the floor. Without further warning, he ripped open his pants and entered her. Her internal muscles immediately clamped down around him. She heard him mutter something before he plunged in and out with long, deep movements.

He kissed her again, and she could taste herself on him. His tongue was like his cock, moving in and out of her body. He slowed when she was close again, and she wanted to beat on him or scratch his back, but her arms were still trapped.

He broke their kiss. "Do you want to come, Isa?"

She arched her pelvis. "You know I do."

He didn't say anything back, and when he held himself still inside her, she pleaded, "Please, Zane. Nobody makes me come the way you do."

He smiled at her, but she couldn't tell if he was actually happy.

He grabbed on to her hair, which was conveniently in a ponytail, and pulled her head back. He began to thrust again, and at the same time, he sucked where her neck met her shoulder. He didn't use teeth, but she knew she'd go home with one hell of a hickey. It seemed like a childish thing to do, but rather than turning her off, it only fueled the flames.

He slipped his hand between them and massaged her engorged clit. With two more pumps, he sent her over the edge with him right behind her.

After a few seconds, he released her neck. It throbbed from where he'd sucked. It wouldn't be a mating mark, but it was pretty dang close. He looked down to her face, but he spoke no words. He pulled out, and she immediately missed the feeling of having him inside her.

He pulled her bra straps up and handed over her clothes. She dressed in silence, neither of them speaking, while he straightened his clothes.

She fixed her ponytail and watched Zane walk to the door.

He opened it and spoke so low that she almost didn't hear, "Goodbye, Isabelle."

He walked away and didn't look back.

It wasn't until she was at the end of the driveway, headed for home, that she realized her cheeks were wet with tears.

The SUV was filled with silence.

No one spoke as Damien rode in the back next to an unconscious Dwyer. The former alpha hadn't been happy when he found out that he had to leave Minnesota. Damien had told him that he was lucky he wasn't going to Canada. Once again, Dwyer's ego had gotten in the way, and he'd started smarting off, so Damien had punched him in the face, knocking him out. That had been about an hour and a half ago, and Dwyer hadn't woken up since.

Instead of heading north to Manitoba, Canada, they were headed south to Iowa. Lachlan drove with Bowden in the front, and Quentin sat on the other side of Dwyer. Once they reached the state line, Damien would complete another thing he'd promised Vance in order to reverse their exile.

Damien had already accomplished one of them. After his meeting with Vance, Damien had met with the sentinels to determine their loyalty to Damien or Dwyer. It had turned out that Dwyer was abhorred, but with the pack's status, the sentinels had felt trapped. They had sworn allegiance to Dwyer, and if they had formed an uprising, they would have risked losing their reputations as trustworthy sentinels and pack members.

This information explained why Dwyer had hired humans to abduct Vance's children. The wolf sentinels would have refused to participate. When they found out what Dwyer had done, they were disappointed and disgusted with his actions.

Damien had never been more proud of them.

Damien felt quite confident in his sentinels' fealty, especially when they had agreed to help him escort Dwyer out of state immediately.

"Wh-where am I?" Dwyer stuttered after waking up.

"Oh, good. You're awake. I didn't want to have to leave you on the cold hard ground," Damien said.

"You're still taking me to Iowa?"

"It's either that or death. You pick."

"You would kill your own father?"

Damien slowly turned his head toward Dwyer. "You lost that title when you tried to kill me."

Dwyer looked around at his former sentinels. "You're just going to sit back and let him do this?"

No one replied.

"Aren't you going to answer me?"

"We no longer report to you," Lachlan simply replied.

Dwyer tried to lunge for him, but his hands were tied. Damien yanked him back by his collar.

"Sit still before I knock you out again."

Dwyer huffed and puffed for the last fifteen minutes of the ride but didn't say anything.

They crossed the state line, and Damien hauled Dwyer out of the vehicle. The others reached for their door handles, but Damien held up his hand.

"I have to do this alone."

"Holler if you need help," Lachlan said.

Damien nodded.

Dwyer looked around. They were outside of a casino, off of I-35, in the middle of the night.

"Why am I here?"

It was cold, and their breaths created fog with every exhale. Dwyer was lucky they weren't leaving him out there to freeze to death.

Damien untied Dwyer's hands. "Because this is where you and I part ways. Someone from the Iowa Pack and Iowa Pride will meet you here. I suggest you don't wear out your welcome because you can never come back to Minnesota." Damien grabbed the bag out of the back of the SUV. "You have everything you'll need in here."

Dwyer's face was filled with wonder. "You're actually going to leave me here?"

"Yes."

"Why didn't you just kill me?"

"Because I'm not you."

Damien tossed the bag, and Dwyer caught it.

"One more thing before you go. Where did you take Vaughn and his mate?"

Dwyer snickered. "As if I would tell you that now."

Damien spun Dwyer around and yanked his arms behind his back, forcing him to drop his pack at their feet.

"You're going to break my arms."

"I don't care. I only said I wouldn't kill you, not that I wouldn't hurt you." Damien tightened his hold. "Now, tell me the fucking location."

"Okay, okay, okay."

Damien released him, found out where to find Sawyer and the vampire princess's friend, and hopped back into the SUV without a second glance.

Dwyer could rot in hell for all Damien cared.

Chapter Thirty-Nine

The next morning, Saxon rapped his knuckles on Vance's ajar office door. His knocking caused the door to open all the way, and he saw Vaughn already there, looking over some papers. Vaughn looked up when Saxon entered.

"Hey, man. How's it going?" Saxon asked.

"Not bad. Ready for all of this to be over. The mate wasn't happy that I had to leave her again this morning."

Saxon looked around. "So, your dad called another meeting."

The meeting the afternoon before had been to discuss what Vance had discovered in his interrogation with Dwyer and how they planned to move forward.

"Yeah. He said something about having news on Sawyer and Kenzie."

"That's good."

As of yesterday, they had still been trying to find the whereabouts of the missing sentinel and human.

"What's good?" Zane asked as he walked into the room. His hair was a mess, he had bags under his eyes, and he hadn't shaved.

"Dude, you look like shit," Saxon told him.

"Fuck you."

"Something's got his feathers ruffled," Vaughn said to Saxon before looking at Zane. "Rumor has it, you were in the company of a cute wolf-shifter over the past week."

Zane slumped into a chair. "Can we not talk about her? Please?"

Zane was rarely in a bad mood. Saxon was slightly curious as to what had happened between the two of them. It was something besides the sex they'd obviously had. Zane still smelled of her. The bad thing about being a shifter was that none of them could hide private matters from one another.

"Well, I would like to meet her and tell her thank you for helping us out," Vaughn said.

"She left." Zane closed his eyes and rested his head against the back of the chair.

Vaughn looked at Saxon. Saxon shrugged. He didn't know any more than Vaughn did.

Everyone else filed into the room, essentially killing the subject of the female wolf.

Vance brought up the rear. "Good news. I've found the location of Sawyer and Kenzie." Their alpha nodded to Reid, who handed out papers to everyone.

The paper had a map that marked where the two were located.

"They are being held in a house in Hudson, Wisconsin," Reid explained.

Hudson was just across the St. Croix River that separated Minnesota from Wisconsin. They might be one state over, but it was only about a forty-five minute to an hour drive.

Vaughn jumped up from his seat. "When are we leaving?"

"Half an hour," Vance said.

"We're not waiting for it to get dark?" Saxon was surprised.

He'd figured his alpha would ask for the vampires' help again. After all, Sawyer and Kenzie were the two mistaken for Vaughn and Naya, the vampire's princess. Plus, they were still down three sentinels with Sawyer gone and Tegan and Phoenix protecting their alphena.

"From what we've gathered, the house is on several acres with no close neighbors. Visibility will be better during the day, and we don't need the vampires' help. The new wolf-shifter alpha and his sentinels have agreed to help us."

Murmurs erupted all around the room.

Vance held up his hands, and everyone quieted.

"I have allowed Damien to bring the Minnesota Pack back on a few conditions. I have always had confidence in him, and I believe I am making the right choice. You will trust me on this. The two of us working together will only help bring our pride and their pack closer."

There were a few more mutterings, but deep down, every one of them had faith in their alpha. He had never led them astray before.

After everyone quieted, Vance asked, "Are you ready to go over the plan now?"

It was the moment of truth.

Sawyer and Kenzie were ready to break out.

For the last two days, Kenzie had bled minimally, and it wasn't until this morning after she'd woken up that she felt her period was heavy enough to convince their captors to release them. Trying to go with what a real couple would do in this type of situation, they hadn't taken any actions to get the kidnappers' attention. However, Sawyer would pace like a worried father, and Kenzie would lie in bed as if she were not feeling well.

With their plans for breaking out ready to be set in motion, it wasn't hard for either of them to look worried, Kenzie more than him. But what mother wouldn't worry about the life of her unborn baby?

When she rose from the bed, Sawyer hugged her and whispered, "All right, Kenzie, you can do this."

She stepped back and gave a shaky smile.

Whether it was for show or simply because he wanted to—Sawyer didn't know—he bent down and placed a reassuring kiss on her lips.

She looked startled only for a second before she remembered their roles.

She walked to the bathroom, and Sawyer tapped his foot outside the door.

A few minutes later, Kenzie yanked it open, wearing new jeans, with tears on her face, and she waved her old pants in front of him. "Oh my

God, Vaughn. It hasn't stopped. I'm miscarrying."

Even though no one could hear them, they hoped they were being watched.

In case their captors could read lips, she faced the camera as she spoke, "What are we going to do?"

Sawyer had to hand it to her. She was a decent actress. He dropped to his knees and buried his face against her belly as if he were speaking to his unborn child. With his shifter nose, he had already been able to smell the special female part of her since she started, but he had pushed away any reaction to it with their mission on his mind. Now, he was so very close to that sweet spot between her legs, and he felt his traitorous dick getting stiff.

She ran her fingers through his hair, and he went from semi-hard to full-on erection.

Shit. He was supposed to be distraught, not horny.

He jumped up, snatched the jeans from her hand, and turned toward the camera. At the same time, he adjusted his tactless cock, hoping the other movements would draw everyone's attention. "Let us out!" he shouted. "My wife is miscarrying. She needs to see a doctor." While he showed them the blood on her pants, he spoke the words again, slower this time, "Blood. Miscarry. Doctor."

Kenzie used that moment to moan in pain. Sawyer turned around to see her bent at the waist, clutching her stomach.

She looked up and pleaded, "Please...my baby," as tears streamed down her face.

Damn, she's good. Sawyer was so stunned by her performance that he almost forgot to go and comfort her. At her side, he looked up at the camera and pleaded, *"Please."*

Sawyer pulled her into his arms and held her. She shook from the sobs racking her body. It took him a few minutes to realize the crying was real.

"Maybe we should give up," she whispered against his chest.

"Not yet." He kissed the top of her head. "Let's give them a few minutes."

They waited for what felt like a year, and Sawyer was ready to call it quits when they heard a noise at the door. Kenzie gulped.

"Stand against the wall," a male voice on the other side said. "I'll open the door and take Naya to the doctor, but, Vaughn, you have to stay here."

"No," Sawyer answered.

Kenzie momentarily broke character and shot him an are-you-kidding-me look. But if he'd agreed right away, the human on the other side might think something was up. Any father and husband would want to go with his pregnant wife to the hospital.

"It's the only way. If you don't agree to this, your wife can stay in there, and neither of you will be going to the hospital."

Sawyer cursed. "Fine," he said. "We'll agree to anything, if you'll please get her medical help."

"I don't want to leave you," Kenzie said to him.

"Naya, it's for the baby. You have to."

"No."

"Yes. Please…for me."

She paused. "Okay."

"We agree to your terms," Sawyer told him.

"Stand back."

They stepped farther into the room.

"We're back," Sawyer said.

The male slowly opened the door and threw something in. He was short and scrawny, and Sawyer had to hide his pleasure. This human was no match for him.

"Drink that, Vaughn. I won't open the door again until it's gone," the human said before he closed the door.

It was a bottle with what looked like juice in it. Sawyer picked it up and opened the cap. It smelled like apple juice and something else.

Fuck. It was some sort of drug.

He couldn't be knocked out now. Of course, that was the human's goal. Sawyer had to think fast.

He clutched on to Kenzie with his free hand, and he still held Kenzie's stained pants in his other hand. He used that one to bring the bottle to his mouth, and he drank some of the juice. The rest he let fall onto Kenzie's pants, hoping their bodies blocked any spilling from the camera. He prayed that he hadn't swallowed enough to impact his senses.

When the bottle was empty, he held it up for the cameras to see. A second later, he slumped onto his knees as if the drugs were taking effect.

"Vaughn," Kenzie said and pulled on his hand, "I can't do this by myself."

He knew she meant that for himself, not Vaughn. If he could reassure her, he would, but the door opened again.

"Come with me, Naya," the human said.

Kenzie looked at Sawyer again before she released her hold on him. She looked sincerely worried, but she was still smart enough not to block his path to the door.

Using his shifter speed, Sawyer jumped from the floor, ran to the doorway, and shoved the human. He punched the man in the face, knocking him out.

He whirled around because Kenzie stood frozen in the room. "Come on, let's get out of here. What are you waiting for?"

His words spurred her into action, and she followed after him. He grabbed her hand as they ran up the stairs. He peeked around the corner and didn't see or smell anyone. He pulled Kenzie behind him as they passed by the front door. She tugged on his hand when they didn't stop. He pulled harder to keep her moving. His goal was the garage where he hoped to find a vehicle. He had no idea where they were or how long they would have to travel, and he would rather it not be on foot in winter.

Sawyer went in the direction of the kitchen, keeping an eye and nose out the whole time. They reached the back door where a set of keys sat on the counter.

Jackpot.

Sawyer snatched up the keys and grabbed for the door handle. He missed. He tried again and brushed his fingertips against it.

"What's wrong?" Kenzie asked.

"The drugs." At least that was what he'd tried to say. It came out sounding like, *Blah blugs.*

"Crap," she said behind him. "Give me those." She snatched the keys from his hands without any effort even though he'd tried to keep a hold of them, and she pushed him out of the way.

When she opened the door, he tried to tell her that he needed to be the one in front, but everything out of his mouth sounded like gibberish.

"Come on. There's a car. Hopefully, these are the right keys."

She opened the passenger door of the lone car, a P.O.S. Chevy, sitting in the middle of the double garage, and she shoved him inside. This wasn't right. He was supposed to drive. He planned to tell her that as soon she got in, but he felt himself getting tired, and he closed his eyes. He must have swallowed more of the drugged juice than he'd thought.

He barely heard the driver's side door open and close.

"I can't believe we're getting out of here," she said.

He felt the rumble of the car starting.

Huh? What is going on?

He had almost been asleep when he heard Kenzie's voice. He cracked open an eyelid and looked at her. "Damn, you're beautiful," came out of his mouth surprisingly clear.

She truly was. He wanted to pull her down and kiss her. He wanted to taste her again—everywhere.

"Holy shit, you really are drugged," she said with a slight laugh as she hit the garage door opener.

Drugged? Me? Oh, yeah. It still didn't make her any less attractive.

Kenzie abruptly lost her smile as she looked past him, out his window, with panic. Sawyer turned to see what had caught her attention.

As if in slow motion, either from the drugs or because he knew something bad was about to happen, he saw his door open. Another human male stood there but only for a second. The next second, the human swung his arms toward Sawyer. Sawyer instinctively ducked, but he wasn't fast enough.

The last thing Sawyer remembered was the crack from whatever the human held hitting his skull.

Kenzie screamed the moment Sawyer slumped over onto her lap.

"You'd better get out of the vehicle, bitch. I have backup coming. There's no way you're going anywhere," sneered the man who had just knocked out Sawyer at the same time that the garage door finished opening.

She looked at him. There was no way she was going to be his victim any longer. She threw the car in reverse and hit the gas. She held on to Sawyer with one hand even though she wasn't strong enough to keep him from falling out. The open door knocked the man over, but Kenzie kept going until the car bounced into the street.

She pitched the transmission into drive and shoved her foot down on the accelerator. The forward momentum slammed Sawyer's door shut, so Kenzie could let go of him to put both hands on the wheel. The loud bang of shots being fired and hitting the trunk scared the shit out of her. She crouched down in her seat and prayed she didn't hit anything as she drove faster. She hadn't even realized the guy had a gun. Thank God, or she might not have had the guts to drive off.

After the shooting stopped, she straightened in her seat and quickly glanced in the rearview mirror to make sure she wasn't being followed. The only thing she saw were two big dark SUVs over the horizon, coming from the opposite direction she was heading, pulling up to the house.

She had hoped the man was lying about backup, but apparently, he had not. Afraid they would come after her and Sawyer, she took the nearest turn and then several more. It took about twenty minutes after being the only car on the road for her to feel safe—safer anyway.

Of course, now, the two of them had a whole new problem on their hands.

Kenzie glanced at Sawyer. *What am I going to do?* They didn't have cell phones, and she didn't have anyone's number memorized. She was driving a stolen vehicle with bullet holes, and people were looking for them. This was on top of Sawyer being drugged and unconscious.

They needed to ditch the car in case it had a GPS tracker, and then they'd have to find somewhere to stay out of harm's way. She hoped that Sawyer had someone's number in his head. Knowing him, he had them all memorized, and for once, she was grateful for his uptight attitude.

She looked down at him again.

As long as he wakes up.

Chapter Forty

$\mathcal{P}$ayton flopped back in her chair with a huff. There was no way she was ever going to catch up on all her classes. She had missed a week and a half of classes because of the attempted kidnapping, her mating heat, and being snowed in at the cabin. Today had been her first day back at class, and it was apparent how far behind she had gotten. Her family had told the school that she had been gone for medical reasons, so she wouldn't be penalized and her professors would be understanding and hopefully give her leniency, but she had missed too much. Grad school was hard enough. She seriously considered withdrawing while she still had time before her grades were affected. Then, she could start over next semester.

Her real problem was her lack of concentration. Still at her friend Alaina's townhome since she'd left her parents' house the day before, Payton had thought being away would help clear her head. Hoping to get her mind off of everything, she had spent time with her college friends the afternoon and evening before, and she had gone to class that day, but her thoughts always returned to Damien.

Damien, Damien, Damien—she couldn't expel him from her mind. Maybe it was because she had constant reminders of him.

The big one was, early this morning, Payton had woken up around one o'clock with a discomfort in her pelvis as it contracted to the point of pain. The room had been dark, and she had been half-asleep. For a moment, she'd thought that she was back at the cabin in the middle of her mating heat.

Then, her eyes had adjusted, and she'd recognized the smells were different. She'd moaned in pain as her uterus cramped. This was different, too. Instead of her body needing Damien, it'd wanted to rid her of what he'd placed there.

She'd run to the bathroom, but it was too late. She had already started to bleed. She had known that was what happened before she even removed her pants, but the reality of seeing it had been a shock to her system, and she'd burst into tears.

She had been ninety-nine percent positive that she hadn't gotten pregnant during her heat. Her stomach had slowly flattened in the days since, and he had never sensed her ovulating the whole time. With her father demanding Damien and she not have a relationship and then Damien agreeing, it would be foolish to want a child with him. But it was as if the blood had been the final indication that everything was truly over between the two of them.

There she had sat, sobbing so hard that she had to muffle the sounds so that she wouldn't wake her friend.

It had taken Payton several minutes to clean herself up, rummaging through Alaina's stuff for feminine products, and then she'd crawled back into bed. She'd cried herself to sleep, and she'd woken up at the crack of dawn, feeling like she'd been run over by a truck.

Thankfully, her first class hadn't been until noon, and it was the only one she had that day, so she had an excuse to lie in bed all morning. She'd tried to go back to sleep, but her stupid phone had beeped and continued to do so, reminding her that she had unchecked text and voice messages. Frustrated, she'd picked up her phone and seen the unknown number.

She'd opened the first text. It was Damien, telling her that it was his number, along with four simple yet final words.

We need to talk.

No, they didn't. She'd already known what he was going to say. She had shut off her phone, put it in the drawer next to the bed, and buried herself under the covers without reading the rest of the texts or listening to her voice mail.

When she'd awoken several hours later, she'd convinced herself to shower. She was not going to lie around all day and be depressed over a guy. She was not going to be that type of person.

Of course, one could tell oneself that, but it didn't mean it would work.

When she had finally turned her phone on that afternoon, she'd found several more messages. She'd ignored them all. Despite not bringing herself to erase them, she had felt pretty good for not sitting around all day, wallowing in self-pity. After class, she'd had dinner plans with Alaina and a few other friends.

Then, her mom had called. Just the sound of her mother's voice had broken the dam, and Payton had begun to weep again. Her mother was the best. She'd listened to Payton tell her everything. Her mom never told her that she was being irrational or irresponsible, and near the end of their conversation, she had felt a little better.

She still had her family, and they loved her. Her father was still on her shit list even though he'd exposed how little she meant to Damien. Although it was better to know sooner, she couldn't help but be angry with her father. Her mother, ever so wise, had known this.

"Honey, I know you're upset with your father, but you should really hear him out."

She sighed. "I will, Mom, I just...I just need a few days. Is that okay?"

"Yes. Even if he doesn't understand, I do. Us women have to stick together."

A small smile crossed her face. "I love you, Mom."

"I love you, too. I miss you. I was hoping you'd be home when I got there tomorrow. Will you at least tell me where you are? I know you're mad at your father, but it's not fair for him or me to worry. I promise, I won't tell him where you are, but he'll feel better if he knows that I know."

"I'm at Alaina's."

"Thank you, honey. Please know, things will get better and soon."

Her mother was such an optimist, but Payton wasn't going to argue. "Thanks, Mom. I'll come home soon. I promise."

After all, she couldn't hide forever. Alaina was, however, currently in need of a roommate. Even if she was human instead of shifter, Payton could go to her parents' house every once in a while to shift.

"Please don't worry."

Her mother made a tsk sound. "I'm your mother. I will always worry. You'll understand someday."

Maybe one day. *She closed her eyes and put her hand over her flat belly.* Just not today.

"*I'm sure I will. I'll see you soon, okay?*"

"*Okay, honey. Remember, I love you.*"

"*I love you, too, Mom. Thanks for calling.*"

After they had hung up, she had felt better from just talking to her mom. Even though she had initially cried, their chat had cheered her up some. Payton knew she would be able to pull through this. The tears on the phone with her mother had almost been cleansing tears.

Her phone beeped, and she picked it up to see that it was Damien again. He hadn't sent her a text or called at all for the last few hours, and she had hoped that he'd given up. Yet, at the same time, she'd hoped that he hadn't.

Curiosity got the best of her, and she opened the message.

Last chance. Call me now.

She snorted. *Last chance for what? For him to break up with me?* He'd planned to do that anyway.

She threw her phone down on the desk, leaned forward, and put her head in her hands. If only she could fast-forward her life a couple of months, then all this would be nothing but a memory.

She heard the door slam downstairs. After dinner, Alaina had gone for drinks with one of the neighbor girls. They'd asked Payton to join, but she'd had too much homework. She should have gone because she still had as much homework now as she'd had three hours ago.

"Payton?" Alaina shouted from downstairs.

"I'm up here," she answered.

"Come down here. Look at the dog I found outside. He's huge. He looks like a wolf."

Payton looked up, dropping her arms in panic. *Huge dog that looks like a wolf? Shit. What is he doing here?*

She scrambled out of her chair, almost knocking it over, and marched into the living room. When Payton entered, Alaina's dark blonde head flipped up from where she sat on her knees, petting the wolf-shifter Payton would recognize anywhere.

"Isn't he beautiful?" Alaina asked.

Payton narrowed her eyes at Damien and crossed her arms over her chest. He was not going to charm her friend.

"Alaina, you need to get up and come over here. That isn't a dog."

She paused in her petting. "What?"

"That's a wolf."

Alaina struggled to get to her feet. Payton could smell the alcohol on her, and Alaina tripped in her haste to get away from him. She finally stood and walked over to Payton as if Payton could protect her.

"But he didn't hurt me," she whispered loudly in the way only an intoxicated person could.

"There's no point in being quiet. He can hear you." Payton dropped her arms and waved her hands at Damien. "Shoo, shoo. Get out of here."

She hoped to piss him off, treating him like some stray dog, but his response was to sit on his haunches.

Stupid male. Didn't he understand that she didn't want him here? She didn't want to talk to him.

He gestured with his head toward Alaina. He wanted Payton to get rid of her friend, so he could shift. Payton shook her head, smiling smugly. It wasn't going to happen. Alaina was her safety net, and Payton wasn't going to tell her to go anywhere. She crossed her arms over her chest again and smirked. He was stuck. He either had to leave or sit there as a wolf.

Suddenly, without any warning, he shifted. His limbs turned into human arms and legs. His snout shortened and became his handsome face. His wolf body transformed into his muscular chest and abs. The only thing left of his beautiful wolf coat was now on top of his head. He was six feet three inches of pure male.

Payton's jaw dropped. He had just shifted in front of a human. On the heels of surprise was the pang in her chest. He was beautiful, and she'd missed him with everything inside her. Seeing him as he stood before her, there was no mistaking the fact that she still loved him.

Alaina gasped beside her, and Payton turned to follow Alaina's gaze.

"Oh my God." Alaina's eyes traveled down to Damien's crotch where he was already half-hard. "Holy shit."

He had some nerve, showing up here and ruining her reprieve from everything, from him.

Payton looked at Damien and said in a staged whisper to Alaina, "Yeah, it looks impressive, but it's mostly just for show."

Payton snickered, but it was apparent Alaina hadn't even heard her as she practically drooled over the naked man in her living room.

Damien lowered his head toward his chest. His jaw clenched, his eyes still wolf, and he growled.

Good. Now, he could be pissed off, too.

"You'd better run." The words were spoken ever so quietly to her.

She dropped her arms and shook her hands in mock fear. "What are you going to do? Hurt me?"

Damien would never hurt a female, no matter how angry he was.

"No, I'm just going to fuck you until you can't walk straight for a week."

Alaina sucked in her breath.

Payton rolled her eyes. "You don't have the right to do that anymore."

"The hell I don't."

He barely took one small step toward her, and she spun and sprinted up the stairs. She heard the pounding of his feet behind her. When she reached her bedroom, she quickly swung the door, but he got his arm and leg through before she was able to slam it closed. He pushed the door open all the way and stepped into the room, invading her space. He kicked the door shut behind him.

She raised her chin. "I don't want you here."

"Liar."

Her room smelled thick with arousal—his *and* hers.

Damn it. She didn't want to want him.

"You know you want to lie down and spread your legs for me."

She scoffed. She'd never heard him speak so vulgar before.

She shook her head. "No," she spoke the word, but it didn't sound convincing.

He stalked forward, and she stepped back.

Where was her resolve? Her determination to get him out of her life? It was incredibly hard to concentrate with him in her room.

Her legs hit the bed as he reached her. He tore her shirt in half with his claws as she just stood there. Next, he unbuttoned her jeans and pushed them off her hips.

Why didn't she fight him?

Now both naked, he picked her up, and without any preparation, he pulled her down right on his cock.

It only took five strokes before he pushed her over the edge. He laid her down on the bed with him still inside her and thrust again and again and again. It didn't take her long before she quivered around him once more.

He pulled out of her. He was still hard, and his arousal was slick and shiny from her body. He'd made her come twice, but he still hadn't come himself. He flipped her over and set her on her knees before shoving back inside her. He felt so good, and she had a feeling this was her retribution for her comment about his lack of skills. There really was a possibility that she might not walk straight for a week. Maybe she should insult him more often.

He pounded in and out of her, and she knew he was going to go over the edge with her this time. His breathing sped up, and his tempo increased. He leaned his body over her and grabbed her hair in his hand. He held her head to the side, exposing her neck, and just as she started to tighten around him once more, he bit her neck—marking her—as he let himself go inside her. She felt his dick knot inside her, pushing on her sensitive tissues, and she was overcome with hormones and emotions.

She didn't know whether to burst into tears, shout from the mountaintops, get up and beat Damien over the head, or simply lie there and decide what to do later.

He turned them to their sides, and he held her until his knot receded. He withdrew from her body and rolled her over to face him. He didn't speak, and neither did she. He pulled her head down to settle on his chest.

She wanted to resist. She had a number of things that she needed to ask and say to him, like why he was here. And why had he just marked her?

All she had to do was regain her senses and her bearings, and then she'd talk to him. She would just rest there for a moment. She would ignore how good he smelled and how safe he made her feel.

She closed her eyes. She only needed a minute…

Chapter Forty-One

*P*ayton sat at the counter alone, mindlessly eating her breakfast.

"Holy hickey, Batman."

Payton jumped at the sound of Alaina's voice. Groaning, Payton dropped her spoon and slapped a hand over her neck. "I don't want to talk about it."

Alaina walked past Payton into the kitchen. "Well, I had the craziest dream last night. I found a dog outside, and it turned into a man."

Payton listened to her, acting like this was news, and grabbed her glass to take a sip.

Alaina rummaged for food, taking out cereal, a bowl, and milk. "He was also naked and hung like a horse."

At her friend's last comment, Payton practically choked on her juice.

Alaina brought her breakfast over and stood across from Payton. "You okay?"

Cough. "Yeah"—*cough*—"I'm"—*cough*—"fine."

"Anyway, I thought it was a dream, but now, I'm thinking some of it might be true."

Damien! What an asshat, exposing himself to a human like that.

Payton was worried, but she knew she had to play it cool. She casually pushed her empty bowl away. "What makes you say that?"

"Well, besides the ginormous love bite on your neck…"

Payton was going to kill Damien for biting her.

"There's a half-nude man walking down the stairs."

Payton closed her eyes and groaned.

Damien cupped the back of her neck, rubbing his thumb over his mark, and kissed her on the head. "Morning, baby girl."

He sat down next to her, but she was afraid to look. She'd heard Alaina say *half-naked*, but the last thing that she remembered was Damien sans clothes.

She peeked at him from out of the corner of her eye and breathed a sigh of relief when she saw that he wore a pair of nylon workout shorts. She didn't care where he'd gotten clothes. She was just happy he had. The last thing she needed was to hear Alaina go on about Damien's huge anatomy. She spared a glance at him. Hopefully, he hadn't heard Alaina's remark because he certainly didn't need his ego inflated.

"So, Payton, aren't you going to introduce me?" Alaina asked.

"Alaina, Damien. Damien, Alaina," Payton said unenthusiastically. She still wasn't happy with him.

Alaina leaned over onto the counter, her eyes full of curiosity. "So, Damien, how do you know Payton?"

"I'm her mate."

Payton felt her eyes go round, and her mouth pursed. Not only was she going to kill him, but she would also make sure it hurt.

Where does he get off, making a statement like that and especially in front of my friend?

"Mate?"

"Sorry. Husband." Damien arched his neck and looked around casually as if they had been discussing the weather. "You got any more cereal? I'm starving."

Shocked, Alaina stood up straight. "You got married? And didn't tell anyone? I didn't even know you were in a relationship." She cocked her head to the side. "Were you really on your honeymoon over the last week and a half?" She looked at Damien and pointed her thumb over her shoulder. "Help yourself."

Damien stood and went to Alaina's side of the counter to grab food. When her back was to him, she mouthed, *Oh my God*, to Payton.

"First of all, nothing is official yet," Payton said through clenched teeth, shooting Damien a look, which he conveniently missed. "Second, this"—she gestured back and forth between herself and Damien— "happened really fast."

"Wait until I tell everybody that you're engaged."

Payton put her hand on Alaina's. "Just wait for that, okay? Damien and I still need to work out some details." Like how he'd told her father that he would give her up, and then he'd shown up here a day later, pushing his way into her bed and marking her as his without even talking to her yet. Shifter males still had a few things to learn from human ones.

Alaina wrinkled her nose. "You're no fun."

"I know," she said with a sigh.

She glanced over Alaina's shoulder to see a grinning Damien.

Payton narrowed her eyes. Not only was she going to make his death painful, she was also going to add torture to the list.

Before Damien followed Payton upstairs, he took time to finish his breakfast. Payton had made some flimsy excuse to leave the kitchen while he still ate, and he'd decided to wait to go after her, giving her a minute to process the latest turn of events.

Done with his cereal, he put away his dishes, and then he approached her bedroom and knocked.

The door swung open, and Payton crossed her arms over her chest. "Oh, sure. Now, you take the time to be courteous."

He stepped into the room and shut the door behind him. "Last night, I was kind of on a mission."

"Now that you've accomplished that mission, macho Damien is gone, and civil Damien has returned?"

"Well…" He shrugged. "Yeah."

"*Gah.*" She stood on her tiptoes and clenched her fists. "Do you know what a chauvinistic pig you sound like?"

"Baby girl, that wasn't my intention."

He hadn't meant to sound like an arrogant ass. He also hadn't meant to come into her friend's home and attack Payton. He had only wanted to talk to her. The plan had been to get her friend out of the room before he shifted. But Payton's comment about his lack of skills in the bedroom had kind of put an end to his patience.

She waved a finger in his face. "Uh-uh, you don't get to call me that."

He sighed and dropped down onto the bed. He was going about this all wrong. "Look, Payton, you wouldn't talk to me. You refused to go home. You wouldn't return my texts or answer my phone calls." He grabbed her hand and brought her palm to his mouth to kiss. "Three days ago, when we were lying on your bed, we agreed never to hide anything from each other. I've been trying to keep my part of the promise, but you haven't, and…well, drastic times call for drastic measures."

She yanked her hand out of his grasp. "What are you talking about? What the hell did I hide from you?"

He jumped up and jabbed a finger at her. "*You*, Payton. You hid yourself—the biggest, most important thing you could keep from me." He dragged his fingers through his hair and paced in front of her. "I should be on top of the world, yet I feel like half of me is missing because you're not at my side. Who cares about being alpha and our exile being reversed if the woman I love isn't there to share it with me? I'm sorry I just came here, took you to bed, and marked you without your permission, but I know you love me, too." He stopped to face her. "And I admit I was going a little crazy while waiting for you to come back to me."

She held up her hand. "Back up a second." She pinched the bridge of her nose. "I'm so confused," she said to herself. She dropped her hand and took a deep breath before addressing him, "Okay, I'm sorry I ignored you. I needed space to—"

He raised an eyebrow. *Did she listen to anything I just said?* If she had just talked to him, she wouldn't have needed space.

"Okay. I needed to process things, and *perhaps* I didn't have all the information."

He nodded in agreement.

"I admit I was wrong, and I should've talked to you." She looked down at her hands.

In shame? In sadness?

"I overheard you and Daddy talking. I heard what he demanded of you so that you could bring your pack back, and I knew you couldn't deny them that after everything the pack has been through."

He lifted her chin with his finger. "If you had stuck around, you would've heard my answer."

Her sapphire eyes narrowed. "I did hear your answer. You said, 'Done.'"

He rolled his eyes. "Fine, if you had stuck around longer, you would've heard my whole answer. I told him that I would do the first two things, but there was no way that I would ever give you up. You mean too much to me, and I love you."

Her eyes rounded, and he saw the corners of her mouth twitch.

"But you said the pack has been allowed back?"

"Your father's smart. I'll give him that."

"More like a jerk." She crossed her arms again. "He has to know how I feel about you."

He pulled her arms apart and grabbed her hands. "No, your father's smart. It was a test."

Surprised, her eyes met his. "A test?"

"Yes. He wanted to make sure that you came first, that you were the most important thing to me. After all, it goes…"

"Spouse, family, pack, country," they said together.

"That never even crossed my mind," she said in wonderment.

He chuckled. "Yeah, well, it crossed your father's. You do realize that if I had agreed to never see you again, he probably would've kicked me out for good."

She looked at him, and he laughed.

"That's not why I said it though. I just wanted you to know that he loves you and that he and I never meant to hurt you."

"So, you really love me?"

"Without a doubt."

She cocked her head to the side. "I never said I love you."

"You didn't have to."

She narrowed her eyes, and he pulled her into his arms.

"Baby girl, a woman doesn't give her virginity and her mating heat to just anyone."

She pulled away and gave him a pointed look. "It doesn't mean I love you."

He cupped her head and gave her a hot deep kiss. When they separated, her eyes were half-closed.

"Okay, I love you."

He laughed. "I love you, too."

Payton and Damien had made love, and it had been more intense than any time before. Maybe it was because they'd exchanged *I love you* with one another. Maybe it was because she wore his mark now, and she knew he wasn't going anywhere. Or maybe it was because she was with the male who completed her, made her feel needed, and treated her as his equal. Regardless of the reason, being with Damien was special.

"I have a couple of questions for you," she said.

They were lying on the bed, still tangled up in each other, and she moved away, so she could see his face.

"Shoot."

"How did you find me? And where did you get clothes this morning?"

"Your mother told me," he said with a self-satisfied smirk. "She already calls me son."

"That traitor," she joked. She knew her mother had told him because her mother loved her.

"And after you fell asleep last night, I went to my truck and grabbed my stuff. I thought I should put a T-shirt on in case you drooled on me again."

She groaned. She had thought he was sleeping that morning in her room. "You're such a butthead."

He roared with laughter. "I'm just kidding, baby girl. I love you, spit and all."

"It's still embarrassing, and you're still a butthead."

Damien kissed her on the nose.

"What have I missed the last few days? Have they found Sawyer and Kenzie?"

"Sawyer and Kenzie are still missing. Yesterday, my sentinels and I helped your father and his sentinels find the house where they were being held, but when we arrived, Sawyer and Kenzie were gone. We found two humans in the house, both injured, but they both claimed that they didn't know what happened to them. It took some convincing, but they finally admitted that Sawyer and Kenzie had been there and that they had escaped. Unfortunately, there hasn't been any more news on them, but your father is convinced that Sawyer will get Kenzie somewhere safe, and they will contact us as soon as they can."

"Oh no. Now what?"

"We keep looking."

She really liked it when he said *we*.

"Another reason I am here is because your father needs you to come home. He has something big planned for tonight—a special party that he will tell you about when you get home. You and your family, your pride, and your pack need to be there."

"My pride and my pack?" she asked.

"Yeah, baby girl. You're still the Pride's alpha's daughter, and now, you're the pack's alphena."

"Um…about that. I don't remember you ever asking me to mate with you. What am I supposed to tell my friends? You broke into Alaina's house, bit me, and now, we're an official couple?" she said, trying not to smile.

"You're a minx."

She raised her brow.

"Payton Llewelyn, will you be my mate? I promise to treat you right, love you forever, and give you lots of babies."

She laughed. "We'll see about that."

He brushed his fingers over her flat abdomen. "I'll admit, I'm kind of sad it didn't happen this time."

Oh, Damien. She put her hand over his. "Me, too, even though I know it's for the best right now. Hopefully, it'll happen in the future."

Beaming, he looked up at her. "The future? Is that a yes?"

She grinned back. "Yes."

Damien brushed a finger down her face as his phone rang. He leaned over and snatched it from the nightstand. His smile dropped once he saw the number, his look now serious.

"Who is it?" she asked.

"I'll explain everything later, but right now, I have to take this."

She looked at him, and his eyes filled with sincerity.

She instinctively trusted him to tell her later. "Okay."

He smiled at her trust in him and kissed her. He got up from the bed, whipped on his shorts, and headed out the door with his ringing phone in hand. His body stiff and face somber, he was a man on a mission. Whoever was on the other line, she knew it had to be serious.

Chapter Forty-Two

The cat-shifter arrived home this morning to find a message on his answering machine. It was from his alpha, requesting his presence at a party that he had planned for tonight. Before even returning Vance's call, he grabbed his cell and rang Dwyer.

As the phone rang, his thoughts went back and forth between why Vance would have a party with his children missing to this being his opportunity to get close to Vance and take him out. The plan could finally be finished.

The phone rang six times, and the cat-shifter's heart began to race with panic, but the moment before he was sure voice mail would pick up, Dwyer answered.

"Dwyer here."

"Why the hell is Vance Llewelyn having a get-together tomorrow?"

"How the fuck would I know? I'm not exactly on his list of invitees. Why don't you call him yourself and find out?"

The cat-shifter sputtered. Once he killed Vance, Dwyer would be next on his list. *Who does this wolf think he is, talking to me like that?* "I plan to, but I wanted to be sure I wasn't missing anything. Everything still good with his kids?"

"Yep. They've been taken care of."

He listened to see if he could hear any lies in Dwyer's voice. Everything sounded good. The questioning tone from their last conversation was absent. Tonight, Dwyer almost seemed at peace. This could only be a good sign.

"Excellent." He hit the End button on his phone and sneered.

The end is near.

The first person Payton saw when she walked into her house was her mother. Even though the two had spoken on the phone, she hadn't seen her mom since before her own kidnapping attempt, and the sight of her mom caused her to burst into tears.

Her tears two days before had all been about Damien, but these were for everything else she had endured over the last two weeks. She realized now that she had handled it very well, but there was nothing like seeing her mother to bring out the inner child who wanted her mommy in a time of need.

"There, there, Payton," Lilith said, pulling her into an embrace. Her mother drew away and placed her hands on Payton's shoulders. "I'm sorry that I told Damien where you were, honey. I guess I'm a romantic at heart, and I pictured him sweeping you off your feet."

Payton hiccuped and smiled through her tears. "No, no, Mom. That's not why I'm crying."

Her mother put her hand on her chest as relief washed over her face. "Thank heavens. After your father told me that you and Damien slept together during your mating heat, I was afraid the man wasn't going to do the proper thing and mate you."

"*Mom.*" While she knew that carrying Damien's scent made it obvious that they'd had sex during her heat, she still didn't want her mom to discuss it with her father. *Talk about awkward.*

"Well, Payton, your father and I taught you not to make rash decisions while you're in the heat of the moment. I understand the need to lie with a male when you're in your heat, but—"

Payton slapped her hands over her ears, but it didn't help because her mother raised her voice, and Payton had shifter hearing anyway.

"That doesn't mean you take the first available. You know I can smell him on you. It's not a secret—"

Payton dropped her hands. "I know. I chose Damien because I love him, not because he was the only one there. If it makes you feel any better..." Payton pulled her shirt aside to show her new mating mark.

Beaming, her mother brought her hands to her face. "I'm so happy. Both my babies are mated."

"Oh, Mom." Payton rolled her eyes and looked around. "Where's Daddy? I have a bone to pick with him."

"Now, Payton, everything he did was because he loved you."

"You sound like Damien."

"Then, he sounds like a smart man," her mother said.

The door opened behind them, and they both turned to greet said man.

"You want your stuff in your room?" Damien asked Payton.

"Yes, please."

"Payton," her father boomed from the top of the stairs.

"Hello, Daddy," she said stiffly.

Damien eyed the three of them. Her mother stood on guard, wringing her hands, but her father walked down to them like it was a normal Sunday.

"Damien," her father said when he reached the bottom, "thanks for bringing her home."

Payton glanced in the mirror on the wall of the foyer because she was pretty sure she had steam coming out of her ears.

Damien stepped forward and gave her a kiss on her mouth. "I'll be upstairs."

Slack-mouthed, she watched Damien head upstairs. She'd thought that he would stay there and defend her father or...something. He knew how upset she still was with her father for giving Damien that stipulation. Her father could have warned her before speaking with Damien, but her father had barely talked to her since she came home from the cabin.

"Why don't we go into the sitting room?" Lilith said.

Payton nodded and marched across the threshold. She swung around after her parents entered. "Daddy, how could you? Why didn't you warn me you were testing Damien? I was heartbroken when I heard you say he had to break up with me if he wanted to bring the pack back here."

Her father leaned in. "Why were you eavesdropping on a private conversation?"

He had her there, and she turned red.

"Okay. I guess you're right. But you still shouldn't have asked him. That wasn't fair."

"Payton, if he was going to be the leader and conduct his pack business here, I needed to know if he was as good of a man as I remembered."

She crossed her arms over her chest. "You still could've warned me."

"I didn't want you to give anything away, and quite frankly, my dear, it was between one alpha and another. You aren't allowed to question how I conduct business."

Payton took a step back as if she'd been slapped.

She'd always hoped that, once she was done with school, her father would hire her to work for L & L Construction on the management side. Her father never gave her any indication that he would let her work for him, and his statement was a blatant reminder that he saw her differently.

Her mother placed her hand on her father's arm. "Vance."

He dragged a hand down his face. "This is not going well," he said to himself. "Look, Payton, I love you. You are my only daughter. Not only did I have to make sure Damien would be a good alpha, I also had to make sure he'd make a good mate." He sat down with a thud. "I was pretty confident that he wouldn't let me down, and if you hadn't listened in, you wouldn't have heard me ask him. Or if you hadn't run off, you would've heard what he had to say."

Payton dropped her arms and plopped down onto the love seat across from him. The whole situation was partly her fault. "I'm sorry. You're right." She looked at the floor. "I guess I was too upset to think straight."

"You're young and in love. I understand what that's like. I was young once, and I'm still in love." He grabbed her mother's hand and pulled her onto his lap.

Her mother giggled like a young girl, and Payton wrinkled her nose.

While she didn't feel like everything was completely resolved to her liking, she did feel a little better about the situation. She would always be her daddy's little girl, so he would probably never let her be a part of his business, and she would have to learn to accept it because he did it out of love.

Payton stood. She didn't want to stick around and watch her parents make goo-goo eyes at each other. "Well, I'm going to help Damien unpack."

Her parents didn't even spare her a look, and she took off for the stairs.

"Payton?"

She paused and turned. "Yes, Daddy?"

"Someday, when you have a daughter, you'll understand."

The thought of her and Damien having a baby girl brought a smile to her face, and her father's face suddenly turned to panic.

"Someday. It will be someday in the future, right?"

She laughed. "Yes, Daddy. I'm not pregnant."

The relief on his face was apparent, but he played it cool. "Good, good."

Thinking the conversation was over, she was almost out of the room when she heard her father say, "Because if you're going to work for me, you need to finish that master's degree first."

She froze and slowly pivoted around. "Really? You mean that?"

Her father frowned in confusion. "Payton, you talk about coming to work for me all the time."

"But you've never said yes."

He shrugged. "I didn't know I had to. You're my daughter. Of course you can have a job."

Payton ran forward and gave her parents a hug. "I love you." She kissed each one on the cheek before she released them and stood. "I think I'd better go find Damien."

"Bring him down here in fifteen minutes. We need to fill you both in on what's going to happen at the party tonight."

"Okay, Daddy," she said before she sprinted up the stairs.

The cat-shifter arrived to the party at six on the dot. Vance had told him six thirty, but he didn't like surprises, so he'd made sure to show up early. He exited the car and patted the gun on his hip. Most shifters didn't carry weapons because they had their claws, but he wasn't taking any chances.

He knocked on the door.

Lilith answered. "You made it," she said with a smile.

"Of course."

She was as beautiful as ever, and he couldn't wait to make her his.

She stepped back as he entered. The room smelled like cleaning products, candles, and air fresheners.

"Everyone is downstairs. I'm just in the middle of making supper." She looked at her watch. "You're a little early. I won't be done for another forty-five minutes or so."

He eyed her for any signs of nervousness about his premature arrival. She truly only seemed worried about dinner. It was too bad she wouldn't be serving it once he killed her husband and then claimed her.

"That's fine. This will give Vance and me a chance to catch up."

"What a good idea."

He followed her into the kitchen where the basement stairs were, and he saw Vance's two female sentinels. He was glad to see the women were in the kitchen where they belonged.

The blonde one seemed extra perky, and the redhead wore a scowl. This was nothing new. The blonde, Tegan, wasn't his type, but the redhead, Phoenix, always gave him a woody. The bitch had never given him the time of day though.

He reached the door to the basement and noticed it was closed.

"Oh, go on down. We closed the door because they were getting loud down there," Lilith explained.

The cat-shifter opened the door and slowly descended the stairs after closing the door behind him. When he entered the room, he was surprised to see only Vance. His alpha and cousin gave him a smile, but it didn't quite reach his eyes.

"Hello, Gerald," Vance said.

Gerald swallowed and began to feel uneasy. "Where is everyone?"

"Everyone?" Vance snapped his fingers as if he just remembered. "Oh, you mean, my family."

Gerald smiled nervously. His bad feeling intensified.

Vance lost his fake smile. "The family you tried to have kidnapped and killed."

"I-I don't know what you're talking about." He backed up toward the stairs, but he ran into two of Vance's sentinels, Zane and Saxon, behind him. He hadn't even heard them enter.

"You can't leave, Gerald. After all, you're our guest of honor."

"Wha-what do you mean?"

"Everyone came to see you." Vance opened the door to the training room. "Vaughn and Payton insisted on being here to greet you."

Vance's two devil spawn walked into the room along with two more sentinels, Reid and Camden. They all glared at him, and Gerald felt all the blood leave his face.

"You remember Naya, Vaughn's mate, and her parents," Vance continued.

The three vampires came out next. The king and queen did not look happy.

Is the room getting smaller?

"Oh, and I'd like to introduce you to the newest alpha of the Minnesota Pack, Damien Lowell."

A younger version of Dwyer entered the room, and the anger on the wolf's face made Gerald's knees wobble. The seven wolf sentinels behind him didn't help.

"You know his father, I believe," Vance added.

Unaware that he was even admitting guilt, Gerald said, "I just talked to Dwyer. He said everything was fine."

"I believe his exact words to you were, '*They've been taken care of.*' Or should I say *my* exact words to you?" the younger wolf said.

Those were the words Dwyer had said to him yesterday—or who he had thought was Dwyer. Not only did this punk look like his father, he also sounded like Dwyer.

"By the look on your face, you probably just figured out that you spoke with me. Call forwarding sure comes in handy, don't you think?"

"I don't understand. I didn't sense a lie from you," Gerald stammered.

The wolf smirked. "That's because I didn't lie. You and I just have a different definition of what it means for them to be taken care of."

Gerald looked around. He was in deep shit. What had they done with the former alpha?

"If you're wondering where Dwyer is, he's long gone. If he ever steps in Minnesota again, it will be his death. We're willing to offer you the same deal," Vance said. "As my cousin, I will grant you that leniency—*even though you tried to kill my family.*"

How did this happen? They were never supposed to find out it was him. Had Dwyer given him up? He'd find that wolf-shifter and slit his throat.

"*Gerald,*" Vance said.

First, I have to get out of here alive.

Pretending to surrender, he slowly looked at his cousin and the cause of his hate. "Vance, I just wanted to say…" In a flash, he grabbed his gun, spun, and shot the two sentinels blocking his exit to the stairs. He raced up as chaos erupted behind him. He reached the top, shut the heavy door, and locked it behind him.

If he couldn't kill Vance and his kids or be alpha, he could still have Lilith. But the kitchen was empty. Lilith was nowhere in sight. Of course, Vance would have made sure she was somewhere safe.

He ran for the front door, but the two female sentinels were there to block his way. He raised his gun and shot Tegan. Then, he used the butt of the gun to pistol-whip Phoenix. She fell into his arms, and he scooped her up. If he couldn't have Lilith, the redheaded bitch would do.

He heard the basement door burst open as he flew off the front porch. He threw Phoenix into the back of his SUV and hopped in the driver's seat. As he sped down the driveway, he thought that he might have lost the battle, but he wasn't going to lose the war.

This isn't over, not by a long shot.

Epilogue

Five Days Later

Payton walked in front of Damien with a blindfold over her eyes.

The crunch of snow under their feet gave way to something flat and hard. Next, she heard a door open.

"Take a small step up," Damien told her.

She did as she had been told, and she was engulfed in warmth right away. "Can I open my eyes yet?"

"Just a minute, baby girl."

She heard the door close. Damien grabbed her hand and led her farther into the room before they stopped.

"Okay," he said as he removed her blindfold. "You can open them now."

She took in her surroundings. She was in a big living room with vaulted ceilings. The few items of furniture were beautiful even though they weren't her style, and there were boxes stacked against the wall. The home obviously belonged to humans in the middle of moving, but she didn't recognize the smell of any of them. "What are we doing here?"

"I thought we needed something to smile about."

Sawyer and Kenzie were still out there somewhere, and the Uncle

Gerald and Phoenix situation was complicated. Her father and Damien and all the sentinels were doing everything they could to find them. It didn't help that Zane had just gotten out of the infirmary because of the gunshot wound to his chest. Thankfully, Saxon's injury had only been to his shoulder, and Tegan had jumped out of the way, so she had simply been grazed.

"What do you think of the place?" Damien almost looked nervous.

"From the little I've seen, it's gorgeous. While I do have a smile on my face, I still don't follow."

"I wanted to give this to you as a mating present. Your father has agreed to help us until everything from the Lowell half of L & L Construction can be transferred into my name. Plus, I have quite a bit saved up that I kept hidden from Dwyer over the years."

She was speechless. He had done all this in less than a week.

"It has three bedrooms and four bathrooms. The basement is unfinished, but that can be taken care of. I figured, since we're going to the courthouse tomorrow, we should have our own home away from your parents. Of course, we won't be able to move in right away, but we should be able to soon."

She smiled at her wolf. He was truly wonderful.

Mistaking her silence for rejection, he continued on, "It's close to your parents' house and your brother's. We have a few acres of land so that we can build a bunkhouse for the sentinels—"

She threw her arms around him. "Damien, I'll be happy anywhere if you are there. I don't care where we live as long as we're together." She pulled back to look at him. "I love you."

"I love you, too."

She kissed him, and it didn't take long before it turned heated.

They paused long enough for Damien to say, "Let me show you the master bedroom."

Payton giggled and jumped up to throw her legs around his waist. She buried her nose in his neck, breathing in his cedar scent, as he ran up the stairs with her in his arms. Heading into the empty bedroom, Damien laid her down on the floor. He began tearing at his clothes, and she got rid of her own. He dropped to his knees in front of her. He was beautiful, and his erection stood out, hard and thick, begging for attention.

She reached for him, but he smacked her hand away.

"Not yet, baby girl. I want to play first."

He spread her legs and stared at her. Being open and exposed used to make her nervous, but she loved how Damien looked at her.

He fell to his stomach and put his mouth at her core.

Oh God.

She hadn't expected him to go right for it, and the intense sudden feeling of his mouth on her took her breath away. It felt so good. Damien knew just where to touch her. He flicked her bundle of nerves with his tongue, and despite their lack of foreplay, she knew it'd be over soon.

"I want...you...inside me." She moaned. "Oh, oh..."

"Not yet. I've wanted to do this all week."

It had been hard to find time to have sex while living with her parents. They hadn't wanted to make much noise, and they had often done it when her parents were away, making their time together less like lovemaking and more like stolen quickies. Quickies were great but not all the time. Sometimes, she just needed more.

He sucked her into his mouth and started to hum. That was all she needed. The vibration from his mouth was enough to send her over the edge.

She was still trembling when he mounted her and plunged inside her. He groaned and stilled as her muscles contracted around him. When her orgasm waned, he began to move, ever so slowly.

She watched his face as he rocked inside her. He smiled down and kissed her again.

Will I ever get enough of this man?

He broke their kiss and stared into her eyes. When he got close to his own climax, he rested his forehead on hers. She knew he was waiting for her, and she loved him for it, but she had already gotten hers. She was plenty satisfied.

She eyed Damien's bare and perfect shoulder. She knew just what to do. "Damien."

He lifted his head, and she kissed him.

"I love you," she said when she pulled away right before she bit him where his shoulder met his neck.

"Oh God, Payton," he mumbled right before he exploded.

The force of his orgasm and feeling him grow inside her was enough to set her off for a second time, and she released her teeth from him. She arched her back, and this time, he bit her where he hadn't bit her since the night he tracked her down at Alaina's.

When they both regained their senses, he said, "Sorry about that. I was going to wait until tomorrow when we had the legal papers." He ran his fingers over his mark on her. "Plus, I thought you'd want to wear something strapless to the courthouse."

She kissed his shoulder where her mark was. "I'm still wearing strapless. I will wear your mark with pride."

Groaning, Damien kissed her again, and he grew hard once more.

"Again?" she asked, breathless.

"We can't," he said, pulling out of her. "The realtor is meeting us here in ten minutes."

"What?" She scrambled to get out from underneath him, and she jumped up. She hastily grabbed her clothes and began yanking them on. "Damien, I'm going to beat you."

He just laughed and pulled her into his arms. "I personally like the freshly ravished look."

She scowled at him.

"Okay, I'll let you clean up."

After their hair and clothes were fixed, they spent the next five minutes looking around the home, arm in arm.

"Are you sad that you can't share this with your father or your best friend?"

He snorted. "Dwyer? No way in hell. Sometimes, I wish my mother were still around. She would've loved you." He kissed her forehead. "As for Isabelle, something tells me that she'll come back."

Payton didn't need him to elaborate. The guys had all given Zane crap for sleeping with the female wolf.

They made their way back to the living room. It only took the one tour for her to know that she loved the place.

"You have excellent taste," she told him.

He smiled down at her. "Of course I do. I picked you, didn't I, future Mrs. Lowell?"

"Oh, no, Mr. Lowell. I picked you."

ACKNOWLEDGMENTS

We would like to thank our editor, Jovana Shirley, for all her hard work, and our book cover designer, Viola Estrella, for her stunning cover design.

We would like to thank our beta readers—Heidi Morris, Tera Larsen, and Laura Au. The book wouldn't be the same if we didn't have all your wonderful thoughts and input.

To all the reviewers and bloggers—we couldn't have done it without you. You all are amazing!

Also, we would like to thank our families. We couldn't have done all this without your love and support. You are wonderful.

ABOUT THE AUTHORS

R.L. Kenderson is two best friends writing under one name.

Renae has always loved reading, and in third grade, she wrote her first poem where she learned she might have a knack for this writing thing. Lara remembers sneaking her grandmother's Harlequin novels when she was probably too young to be reading them, and since then, she knew she wanted to write her own.

When they met in college, they bonded over their love of reading and the TV show *Charmed*. What really spiced up their friendship was when Lara introduced Renae to romance novels. When they discovered their first vampire romance, they knew there would always be a special place in their hearts for paranormal romance. After being unable to find certain storylines and characteristics they wanted to read about in the hundreds of books they consumed, they decided to write their own.

One lives in the Minneapolis-St. Paul area and the other in the Kansas City area where they're a sonographer/stay-at-home mom/wife and pharmacist/mother by day, and together they're a sexy author by night. They communicate through phone, email, and whole lot of messaging.

You can find them at http://www.rlkenderson.com, Facebook, Instagram, Tumblr, Twitter, and Goodreads. Or you can email them at rlkenderson@rlkenderson.com, or sign up for their newsletter. They always love hearing from their readers.

Made in the USA
Columbia, SC
29 October 2020